C.

Bread Pudding in BARCELONA

Book One
BLOOMING
The Series

ISBN: 978-1-7365956-7-1 (paperback)
ISBN: 978-1-7365956-8-8 (ebook)

This novel is entirely a work of fiction. The names, characters and incidents portrayed in it are the work of the author's imagination. Any resemblance to actual persons, living or dead, events or localities is entirely coincidental.

Interior design by Corwin Levi, www.gwarlingostudio.com
Cover design by Samantha Sanderson-Marshall, www.smashdesigns.co.uk

Also by Cindy Villanueva

Don't Fight Mad: A Black Belt's Quest to Recapture Joy
(nonfiction)

Dedicated to my mom, Carole Sue Florence Villanueva

1

Azalea walked down the aisle, her fingers lightly tracing the tulle draped between rows. She approached the altar and turned to look back at the empty sanctuary, her face inscrutable. After a few moments reflecting, she sat quietly in the front pew, her elbows resting on her knees, chin in her hands. Glancing around, she admired the huge floral arrangements in front of the pulpit, the sprays of white, purple, and blue flowers elegant and sophisticated. She gazed at the piano and the harp, and once again imagined tomorrow's long walk down the center aisle, her off-white gown, delicately embroidered with lavender and blue flowers, trailing softly behind her.

The walk I'll never take.

Azalea had asked Jeremy to meet her for coffee earlier that afternoon, hours before the rehearsal. She'd sat in her car for a long moment, doing the box breathing that calmed her. Breathe in for the count of four, hold for four, exhale for four, hold four more. After three rounds, she was ready. *At least I hope so.*

Jeremy had arrived at Starbucks before she did, already dressed for the evening festivities, looking handsome and confident. He stood and kissed her cheek as she approached.

"Got your chai, babe," he said, offering her favorite drink. Ever the gentleman, he pulled out her chair for her. Azalea thanked him and sat. He looked at her expectantly. "So…? I thought we weren't seeing each other until the rehearsal."

Azalea looked at the man she had loved for two years. "I cannot begin to tell you how sorry I am," she began. She brought her clasped hands to her mouth, then looked directly into his eyes. "I'm calling off the wedding." She'd thought long over the exact words she'd use, knowing she would not say, *I can't marry you,* since he'd just attempt to talk her out of it. "Can't" wasn't a Jeremy word.

Jeremy stared at her, his smile vanishing. "What are you talking about, Azi?" he asked tightly.

"I am truly sorry, Jeremy, but I…I'm not marrying you." She took a deep breath. "I can go to the church and tell everyone—you don't have to be there if you'd rather not. I know it'll be awkward." She took a sip of her chai and noticed her hands were steady. One more confirmation she was doing the right thing.

"Oh, no." He shook his finger at her like he was scolding a child. "You're not cutting me out like that. You can't just do this, Azalea!" His voice notched up and he glanced around. Lowering his voice he said, "You don't just walk out on a marriage like this. We love each other!"

"I'm not actually walking out on a marriage," she pointed out. "I'm leaving before the marriage, saving us the heartache of another divorce." Both Jeremy and Azalea had suffered through previous breakups—five years earlier for him, seven for her. He never spoke about his ex-wife, but Azalea still hurt from her ex-husband's infidelity. "And I do love you, Jeremy. But we aren't right for each other, as much as we might want to be."

Jeremy leaned forward and reached for her hand. "I'm not David, Azi," he said. "It makes sense you're scared, but I'm not going to betray you."

Azalea was shaking her head even as he spoke. "I know that, Jeremy. I *believe* that." She gently pulled her hand away. "But you need something more than I can give you." She looked away, considering her next words. "I've lost myself in this relationship. I don't even know who I am any—"

"I know who you are," he interrupted, back in control. "You're my wife. We've planned this for months and now you're just scared." He paused and softened his expression, but Azalea saw the steel in his eyes. "You'll feel different once the wedding is over and we can get on with our lives."

She looked back at him and nearly broke. *Is he right? Am I just afraid?* She thought back over their years together. Jeremy was complex—a charming entrepreneur who'd been orphaned as a child and turned his father's Florida business into a multinational success. Fluent in Spanish and English, he'd expanded Fowler Enterprises into most of Latin America. Then he'd turned that charm and ambition toward Azalea and she fell in love—but his deep-seated need to be in control had finally proven too much. Even the wedding had been a Jeremy Fowler production. He planned everything, telling her to *Relax and enjoy the day, darling.* She refused to let him select her dress, but everything else was his decision, albeit couched as a gift to her.

No. She'd made the right decision and she would stick with it. She saw the moment he understood.

"I'll see you at the church. We keep this short and sweet and say it's a joint decision." His face was hard and his tone brooked no disagreement. "You don't answer any personal questions, and you're going to manage giving gifts back. Call the restaurant and let them know we won't be needing our reservation."

She nodded. It had gone better than expected.

Three hours later, Azalea walked into the sanctuary. The pastor stood at the altar, thumbing through his Bible. He glanced up when he heard her footsteps and smiled. "Welcome to the lovely bride!" he called cheerfully.

Azalea slowly approached the front of the church. "Hi, Pastor." Her face betrayed her mood and Steve frowned.

"Oh, dear," he answered. "What's wrong?" His eyes flicked up as Jeremy strode up the aisle. "Hi, Jeremy," he said warmly.

Jeremy looked from Azalea to her pastor. "You couldn't wait for me? I said we'd do this together."

Azalea held his gaze. "I just got here, Jeremy. I haven't said or done anything." She turned to Pastor Steve. "Jeremy and I have decided to cancel the wedding."

Azalea's pastor looked long at both of them, his kind face showing concern and love. "I see," he said thoughtfully. "Do you need more time? Is this something you can work through?" He reached out to place a hand on each of their shoulders. "You know I'm here for you both."

Azalea shook her head as Jeremy brushed off the pastor's hand. "It's over, Steve," Jeremy said abruptly. "We're just here to let people know."

Pastor Steve nodded slowly. "How would you like to handle this? I want to support you in any way—"

Jeremy broke in. "When everyone gets here, I'll let them know we've changed our minds and there won't be a rehearsal tonight or a wedding tomorrow."

Azalea patted her pastor's hand. "Thank you," she said quietly. She continued speaking to him but looked at Jeremy. "*We* will let everyone know, and it would be great to have you stand with us. I'm sure there'll be questions and it would be nice to have you help everyone process the news."

Pastor Steve nodded, frowning slightly. "Of course, of course. As I said, I am here for—"

Jeremy turned away from them and walked toward his best man. Tim had just entered the church, followed by Sara and Lauren, Azalea's bridesmaids and long-time friends. Her sons, Tomás and Landon, also in the wedding party, were close behind the women. Azalea glanced at Pastor Steve, then back at her children.

"Hey, Mom!" called Landon. Her young men, tall and athletic, walked easily up the aisle. *They're old enough to get married themselves*, she thought.

"Hi, Pastor," said Tomás, offering his hand, which Pastor Steve took warmly. Landon looked over at Jeremy and Tim, huddled in the back of the church, obviously in serious conversation. Tim looked up with a frown, then returned his attention to Jeremy.

"What's up with them?"

"Just hang on a minute, guys," said Azalea, scanning the church for her matron of honor. Susana was never on time. *I live on Latin*

Eastern Time, hermana, she always said. They'd been best friends for decades, and Susana had never let her down. Azalea knew she'd roll in at the last possible moment.

As expected, at five minutes past six, Susana rushed through the door, walking hurriedly up to Azalea, with a breezy wave at Sara and Lauren as she passed them in one of the pews. "Girl, the traffic was horrible tonight and—" She stopped suddenly, looking around. "What's going on?"

"Just sit down, Suze," suggested Azalea. She turned to her sons. "Guys, would you sit in the front pew?"

Tomás and Landon nodded and sat. Susana slid into the seat just behind them.

Azalea looked around at the small gathering. Jeremy and Tim rose and moved toward the front of the church, Tim taking a pew away from her family and friends. Jeremy stood next to Pastor Steve, his gray eyes flicking to her, then looking away.

"Thanks for coming," he began. "Unfortunately, this evening isn't going to be what you expected." He continued without looking at Azalea, without seeking her involvement. *And that's why we're in this situation,* she thought. "We've decided to call off the wedding. Sorry to have ruined your weekend, and I ask that you respect our privacy. Azalea will take care of getting your gifts back to you. Thank you for wanting to be a part of our event."

His coldness cut through her, and she looked out at the shocked faces. *I need to say something,* she thought. *I know he's hurt, but it's coming out so harsh.*

"We're very grateful for each of you," she started.

"There's lots to do to communicate with all the guests tonight," Jeremy interrupted, "so that's about it."

Azalea looked at her pastor, then at her former fiancé. *Is this pain or anger?* she wondered. She may have broken off their engagement but she still cared about his feelings. Pastor Steve nodded at her, his encouragement nearly imperceptible.

"Each of you is very important to us," she continued, as though Jeremy hadn't just tried to cut her message short, "and we're grateful you were willing to be a part of our wedding. I can only imagine how confused you are by this, and I join Jeremy in asking that you respect our decision and just continue to love us. I'm sure we'll both be in touch in the coming days. For tonight, I think that's probably enough."

Pastor Steve smiled at her and then nodded at Jeremy. Without asking, he took each of their hands and bowed his head. "Father, be with these precious children. Be glorified in this decision and give them peace. Amen."

Azalea murmured, "Amen." She looked up to see Jeremy beckoning Tim and striding out of the church. She mouthed *One minute* to the boys and went to hug her friends.

"I know you guys have questions—I promise we can catch up next week," she said, squeezing Sara and Lauren's hands. She glanced at Susana, who wore a slightly smug smile. "Come over to the house on Wednesday night for a glass of wine—I'll make dinner for us, okay?"

The women hugged, murmured love and concern, and gathered their belongings. Sara kissed Azalea's cheek lightly; Lauren squeezed her arm. Susana hugged her again and whispered, "You did the right thing, '*mana*." The three women said their goodbyes to Pastor Steve, Tomás, and Landon, and left the sanctuary together.

Pastor Steve was talking to her sons but broke off as she returned. "Okay, guys. Looks like you can return the tuxes tonight instead of Sunday. And you get your Saturday back," she said with a weak attempt at a grin.

Tomás began to speak, but Landon grabbed his arm. "Leave her alone, bro," he said. "Let's go."

"I'll walk you out," the pastor told them. "Stay as long as you need to, Azalea. I'll lock up later tonight." Her sons hugged her without a word, then the three young men left. Azalea watched them go, relief washing over her. She clasped her hands and then bent her head, the strength leaving her as she sagged into a pew.

"Hey, Mom," came a quiet voice behind her. "It's been a couple of hours. You okay?"

"Oh, Tomás…I'm fine, honey. Really." She patted the pew. "Come sit with me."

Her sons slid in on either side of her. Landon leaned against her, his tall frame bending so he could rest his head on her shoulder. She reached up with her right hand to tousle his curls. Even as a grown man, he was still her baby. Tomás took her left hand and kissed it lightly. "I know that wasn't easy. I'm proud of you."

Azalea closed her eyes. "Easier than going through with it," she murmured.

She arched her back and sighed. The boys moved, giving her space. She looked back and forth at each of them, grateful for their presence, though she could barely smile.

"Mom?" asked Landon, always ready to jump in and take care of her.

"I'm good, honey," she said, patting his knee. "I'm ready to go home." Azalea took one last look at the beautifully decorated church and sighed. "It really is lovely, isn't it?" she asked. Tomás put his arm around her shoulders and squeezed. No one felt like talking anymore.

The three eased out of the pew and walked to the parking lot. Azalea hugged them once more and fished for her keys. "Do you need us to come over?" asked Landon.

"No, thanks," she answered, then grimaced. "I'm just gonna knock out this super fun email and then pass out in the tub."

"Call if you need anything," said Tomás.

Azalea smiled wanly and climbed into her car, waving and blowing kisses to her sons.

An hour later, it was finished. Her short email to her guests stated the facts and asked for privacy. Within minutes, her inbox was flooded with mail she had no intention of opening, at least for a day. She stretched and walked to the bathroom, turned on the bath, and dropped her favorite bath bomb into the water. The warm citrus fragrance immediately began to fill the room. She lit two candles, turned out the light, and went to the kitchen to pour a glass of wine while the water ran.

Back in the bathroom, she stripped, turned off the faucet, and slid into the scented, almost too hot water. She sipped her wine, then slid farther into the tub, the water at her jawline. Slowly, she began to relax.

Only then did she allow herself to cry.

2

Wednesday came and Azalea was determined to face the world. She'd cocooned at home all weekend, responding only to the *Are you OK, Mom?* texts from her sons. On Monday, she'd steeled herself to address the voluminous inbox. By and large, the notes were kind and concerned. She noted how many had added Jeremy's email address to their replies. She didn't know if he'd answered any of them; he hadn't included her if he had. No matter. She wrote one or two sentence replies, thanking her guests for their love and concern.

Susana, Sara, and Lauren had all texted but otherwise gave her the privacy and quiet she needed. They knew she'd tell all on Wednesday—but Azalea was certain they were dying for details while they waited.

Jeremy's sister had written one note that she still bristled over. "Seriously? How bourgeois of you, Azalea. You couldn't do this in a less public way? My God, I can only imagine how much money Jeremy spent on this thing." Azalea hadn't answered her. Sophia hadn't bothered to come to Florida for the wedding—she was far too busy with her new husband in Milan. Azalea rolled her eyes, remembering the first time they'd met. She loved nice clothes, but Sophia was a walking magazine spread. Jeremy's sister was dressed head to toe in St. John, with a gigantic diamond engagement ring and what was easily a $10,000 handbag. Sophia had looked at her as if she were a bug under glass. Interesting, but beneath her. Azalea hadn't been the least upset when she learned her sister-in-law-to-be wouldn't make the trip for the wedding.

Azalea's parents were both gone. She was glad they weren't around to see what had happened, although she'd have given just about anything to have her mom with her now. Jeremy's father, Leonard Jeremy Fowler, was an entrepreneur—Jeremy never really explained what he had done for a living. He was known as Len to his friends and Mr. Fowler to everyone else, while Jeremy's mother, the former Miss Florida Pearl Tennyson, was simply Mrs. Fowler or Miss Pearl. Jeremy had no photos of them in his home or wallet. It was as if they'd never existed. Azalea only knew they had died when he was young, leaving him a modest fortune and a distant aunt and uncle who had promptly sent him and Sophia off to boarding school.

Azalea went to the beach, walking in the surf down to her favorite café. She sat on the sand to sip her coffee, watching the birds and the people—so many people now that it was summer. She preferred the off-season when it wasn't as crowded but didn't hold it against the tourists. The beach was her favorite place, too.

Jeremy had tried to get her to sell her little cottage. When she protested, he pointed out that he not only owned the big house in Orlando, he had a place in the Keys. They didn't need "her little bungalow," as he put it with a laugh. But it was hers—the first thing she bought that was all hers two years after her divorce. It was all she could afford at the time and she loved it. A stone's throw from the beach, it was perfect for her, and she made it even cozier with the lanai she added on once her marketing consulting practice took off. She dug in her heels—so unlike her—and Jeremy had given in. "All right, all right," he chuckled. "We'll keep it. It'll be nice for little weekend getaways." He looked fondly at her, as if pampering a spoiled child. She wondered why she'd needed his permission to keep her house.

Coffee finished, Azalea walked home, the warm sun making her feel lazy and lethargic. But she forced herself to open her laptop and check her email when she got in, hoping to kickstart her energy. She knew she'd have to spend time rebuilding client relationships if she wanted to keep her business afloat. Since their engagement, she'd only kept a few clients, again at Jeremy's insistence that she didn't need to work. She had told them all she'd be off for a couple of weeks for her honeymoon, however, so there wasn't much to read. She washed her dishes from the previous night, swept the never-ending sand from the kitchen floor, and tried to figure out what to do for the rest of the day until her friends came over.

At seven o'clock, Lauren and Sara knocked on the door. They were roommates, so they usually traveled together. Azalea hugged each of them as they came in and Lauren handed her a box of expensive chocolates.

"It just seemed like the right choice," she said, shrugging. Lauren could always be counted on to bring decadent food.

"Is it ever not the right choice?"

The women followed her through the French doors and out to the lanai. The sun was still out—this time of year, it went down late. The evening air was warm and humid but the tiled floor was cool and kept the room from sweltering in the Florida summer heat. The coffee table was laid out with chips, salsa, and homemade guacamole, and Azalea's favorite pitcher was filled with sangria.

Lauren started in on the appetizers right away and poured glasses of sangria for each of them. "Where's Susana?" she asked. Sara laughed and Azalea rolled her eyes.

At that moment, the front door opened and Susana strode in. "Knock, knock! The party can start now!" She walked quickly through the living room, tossing her purse on the sofa, and passed through the kitchen and out to the lanai in seconds. "Oh, girl—this looks so pretty!" she exclaimed, looking around. Susana kicked off her high heels and flopped onto one of the chairs. "What a day…is that your guacamole? I'm starving!" Susana reached for a plate and began piling chips onto it. "Sara—be a love and pour me a glass, will you? *Muchisimas gracias!*"

Azalea smiled fondly at her best friend. Susana was a whirlwind wherever she went and Azalea was out of breath just listening to her rapid-fire entrance.

The four women made small talk, nibbling the appetizers and chocolates and finishing the entire pitcher of sangria in short order. Azalea looked at her friends and smiled. "Okay. I guess we've gotten the niceties out of the way. But before we have 'the talk,' let me serve dinner." She nodded toward the small dining room.

The four went inside, carrying their dishes to the counter. They all got to work setting the table and Azalea dished up the gigantic salad she'd made. Sara groaned. "You always do this! You make a salad so you can pretend we're eating healthy but then you give us enough to feed fifteen people."

Azalea laughed—her friend was right. "But you always eat it, don't you?"

Susana opened a bottle of champagne and winked at Azalea. "Bit of a celebration, huh?" She poured each of them a glass and raised hers in a toast. "To Azalea," she said, her face serious. Then she grinned and shouted, "Now tell us *everything*!"

When they stopped laughing, Azalea began, her tone hesitant. "I just couldn't do it. I had to finally admit I wasn't happy. I wasn't even sure what happy was. I wasn't sure who *I* was.

"Jeremy has such a strong personality...." Her friends snickered. "And it's not like the things he wanted were bad or wrong. It's just they weren't *me*. He decided for us about almost everything." She looked at her friends, eyes pleading for understanding. "How do you complain when someone wants to give you the world?

"And then a couple of weeks ago I went shopping. I wanted to buy something special for our wedding night." Azalea's three friends alone knew she and Jeremy hadn't yet slept together. They knew how important the wedding night was to her.

"I went to just about every store in the mall," she continued. "I tried on elegant nightgowns and sexy teddies. I must have tried on a dozen different things but I couldn't decide. And it wasn't like I couldn't decide what *I* wanted. I couldn't decide what *he'd* want. And it got to the point where I made myself sick trying to figure it out." She frowned. "What was supposed to be this fun, sexy outing turned out to be so stressful I didn't buy anything. I was worried I wouldn't get it right." She shook her head, as if trying to dislodge the memory, then sighed. "I spent a lot of time trying to *get it right*—about everything."

Susana's face darkened as she reached for her best friend's hand. "I'm sorry, *hermana*. That's terrible and I hate that you went through that alone." She paused, glancing around the table. "I think we all had some *feelings* about you and Jeremy. And you know me—I don't usually hold back." The other three women chuckled. Susana was opinionated and rarely hesitated to share how she felt. "But you haven't been…I don't know…*accessible* lately. You seemed like you just wanted to spend your time with him and not us."

"He wanted us to spend all our free time together," Azalea answered, frowning. "He said it was important for us that we not repeat mistakes from our previous marriages. I guess for him that meant being together all the time. Said we needed to concentrate on our relationship—that he was my best friend now and it was," she dropped her voice to a manly tone, "'unnecessary to spend so much time with my friends.'" She sipped her champagne, gazing out the window to the moonlit backyard. "I think I felt guilty about not sleeping with him so I just sort of gave in to everything else."

"Can I ask you a personal question?" Sara spoke hesitantly.

Azalea knew what was coming. "You want to know why no sex."

"Well…yeah. It's not like you were giving away your virginity."

Azalea took a moment before answering. Thoughts swirled in her head but finally resolved enough to answer.

"You know David cheated on me, right?" Her friends all nodded, well aware of her ex-husband's numerous infidelities. "I believed him when he said he was sorry—when he swore it would never happen again. He'd cry and beg me to forgive him." She scowled, then pressed on. "And then we'd make love and he'd swear his undying commitment to me and I'd fall for everything he said."

"*Mana*," began Susana.

"No, Suze," Azalea broke in firmly. "Don't try to let me off the hook. I was an idiot and I stayed with a man who betrayed me over and over, because I couldn't think straight and I wanted to believe him." Her chin came up in defiance. "I didn't trust myself to be that vulnerable with Jeremy when we were dating. And once we got engaged, I figured it wouldn't be a big deal to just wait until the wedding." She softened. "He may be a lot of things, but I did trust him to be faithful.

"The truth is, I can't seem to pick the right man. It's pretty obvious love isn't for me."

Sara shook her head. "No," she said slowly. "I don't believe that. You're so full of love, you'll find the right one." Her eyes shone. "Some day, someone will deserve you."

After dinner, they moved back into the lanai where Azalea served them coffee and *pan dulce*. She asked Susana, "How's Kique? It's so nice that he doesn't fuss at you for hanging out all night with your girlfriends." Enrique was Susana's husband of over 20 years and all the friends loved him.

"Oh, you know Kique," shrugged Susana. "He'll just laugh at me tomorrow morning when I'm all bleary-eyed and exhausted when the alarm goes off."

The women laughed but Azalea frowned. "If only Jeremy had been like that," she mused. "I do believe he loved me. He just didn't have any experience with putting someone else first. I was so—"

"Stop it," commanded Susana. "We were all suckered by him." Lauren and Sara nodded as they munched the pumpkin-filled *empanadas*. "'*Mana*, if he'd started out like that, you'd never have dated him. It was more like that frog in the hot water kinda thing. He just slowly broke you down. Give yourself a break—and give yourself some credit for snapping out of it and dumping that jackass before you married him!" Susana got worked up as she spoke, nearly knocking over her coffee mug.

"You know that whole frog in the water thing isn't true, right, Suze?" asked Azalea with a smile. "Real frogs jump out when the water is uncomfortable. It's just an old wives' tale."

Susana rolled her eyes. "Whatever." She reached for a pink *concha*. "I'm going to regret this tomorrow."

"I feel like I owe you an apology," began Lauren, her eyes sorrowful. "The truth is, I never liked Jeremy. And when we met Sophia, it was obvious there was something very wrong with their family."

She looked up at Azalea, tears pooling in her eyes. "I should have said something, but you seemed to really love him. I'm so sorry."

Azalea reached across the coffee table to take Lauren's hand. "Please don't cry, Lauren. And you don't owe me an apology. I don't know that I would have listened even if you'd told me." She looked at her three best friends. "I owe you all an apology—for being stupid and headstrong and putting myself and all of you in such a crappy situation. I'm so sorry."

It was midnight before they finally left Azalea's house.

They said their farewells, hugging Azalea and thanking her for the lovely evening. "I'm proud of you, Azalea," said Sara, holding her friend's hands. "What you did took courage."

Lauren and Susana nodded, smiling. "Love you, *hermana*," said Susana, kissing her cheek. Lauren just hugged her hard, and the three friends left.

Azalea stood at the door, waving as they drove away. She returned to the lanai, picked up the dishes, and fought the urge to grab one more treat. She cleaned up quickly and readied for bed.

Tomorrow is a new day, she thought. *Tomorrow, my life starts*. She had no idea what that meant, but for tonight, the thought was enough.

3

Azalea finished wiping down the fourth and last small table, looking around at the tiny, spotless café. She was tired but content. She had tried a new recipe today, treating her regulars to a bread pudding she found in an old cookbook. The thick slices were redolent with cinnamon and sticky with raisins and apples. Esteban agreed: the ingredients were perfect. It would be a recipe she'd return to again very soon.

Esteban shook the last bit of crumbs off the broom at the front door, looking back at her with a wink. "Was there any left?" he asked.

"I saved just enough for us," she responded, smiling. He locked the door, turned the Cerrado sign facing out the window, and joined her at one of the tables. "Cafecito?" she asked.

"Si, con leche, por favor."

Azalea brought the steaming cups to the table where she set the plates of warm bread pudding. They sighed in unison, then laughed at their shared exhaustion. He reached for her hand and held it to his lips. "It was a good day, querida."

She smiled and squeezed his hand. It had been a good day.

Azalea woke with a start. Fully awake, she looked at her phone—only four in the morning. Even after the late night with her friends, she'd set her alarm for six forty-five hoping to get an early start on her day. But not this early. She rolled over, firmly grasping her pillow under her arm. Determined to go back to sleep, she tried breathing deeply, refusing to open her eyes.

But that little café.

It was adorable. Cozy and warm, clearly European. Nothing like the homey, beachy place she favored in her Florida village. She knew somehow that she lived there, above the café. All she had to do was walk upstairs to her flat—*their flat?*—each night, returning before daylight to bake the day's delicacies. The dream lingered in her mind, with tendrils of longing and contentment woven lightly, teasingly together.

She didn't know who the man was, but he certainly wasn't Jeremy. *He called me 'Querida'....*

Azalea woke with the alarm, cross and unrested. All she wanted was to put the pillow over her head and sleep the day away. But no—there was too much to be done and not sleeping well and drinking too much the night before didn't absolve her of any of her responsibilities. If she were going to make a go of restarting her business, she needed to get up and get after it.

After one more minute of feeling sorry for herself, Azalea got out of bed. She made the bed neatly, making sure the shams were arranged just so, angling the throw blanket on the corner. Since her divorce, not a day went by that she didn't make her bed. While they were married, David had arisen after her and never made the bed, comfortable climbing into the messy sheets each night. It was a metaphor for their life together, she supposed. Always unkempt, never cared for. Jeremy, on the other hand, left his bed for the maid. *Typical,* she thought. *Let someone else clean up the mess.*

"Ay, *gruñosa*," she mumbled. She didn't know a lot of Spanish, but she knew the word for *grouch*. She was rapidly getting annoyed with her self-pity.

She dressed quickly, brushed her hair, and applied her make-up. She didn't have any meetings today, but who knew? Maybe something would come up. She couldn't let herself sink into melancholy. Today was supposed to be the first day of her new life.

Azalea sat at her computer, just staring. She was restless but without direction. One minute she'd scour her email, then click over to an open browser to look something up, only to forget what she was seeking. She was a bundle of energy but had no idea where to direct it.

What's wrong with me?

Over time, the days stabilized, with Azalea waking at dawn to walk her beloved beach. She spent time collecting her thoughts, ruminating on regrets, and finding the twinkling of hopes and new dreams.

In those early mornings, she still found herself thinking of Jeremy—wondering what he was doing and how he'd adapted to life without her. It wouldn't have surprised her if he'd been able to jump right back to focusing on his business and forgetting her. He wasn't the type of man to let his emotions take over. He was always in control—especially of himself.

I wish it were that easy.

Some mornings, she simply breathed and walked. On Sundays, she walked nearly eight miles to the jetty and back to her cottage. For Azalea, it was sacred: the beauty of the ocean, the powerful connection with nature as her bare feet gripped the sand. The sunlight sparkled across the waves and she was sure it was the same pelican every Sunday who greeted her at the rocky barricade and flew nearby.

One Sunday two months after their breakup, Azalea got a text on her walk home. It was Jeremy.

I know you're on your walk, so no need to respond right away, the words appeared in their onscreen bubble. *Just wanted to say hello.*

Azalea's stomach tightened. She hadn't spoken to Jeremy since the night at the church. He'd written a terse email letting her know that he canceled their honeymoon reservations and there was no need to concern herself with the money—he'd handle it. She was prepared to reimburse him for the lost deposits and the airfare to Nice where they planned to spend the first week at a beachside estate. She knew it would make a sizable dent in her savings account to make things financially right with him—they had a lavish trip planned and it had been an unwelcome, but necessary consideration in her decision to cancel the wedding. She was relieved not to spend the money, but felt a lingering remorse and, truthfully, a bit of offended pride at not paying her share.

She resolved not to be petty. It was done and over, and she needed to move on. She put her phone in her pocket and didn't respond.

Azalea woke slowly in the dark. She was on one side of the bed, and her pillow was wet. *Why am I crying?* she thought, feeling sad and listless. After her divorce, she decided to sleep in the middle of the bed, refusing to mimic any remnant of her married life. Yet now she was curled up on the left side with a wet pillow, her face and hair still damp from tears. David had always slept on the right, and she wondered which side Jeremy would have chosen.

She reached for her phone and groaned. It was only three o'clock. Azalea had a busy day ahead—she had a project due in two days for a client and wanted to complete it early enough for a thorough review. She briefly considered just getting up and working but knew she'd regret it by lunchtime. She kicked off the comforter and stretched, closing her eyes, trying to fall back asleep. Curling around her pillow, her tears threatened once more.

The next morning, Azalea faced the truth. She missed Jeremy. She missed being a couple, the knowledge that someone loved her enough to marry her. Her head told her she'd made the right decision in breaking off the wedding. Her heart wasn't so sure. She'd been David's wife, then Tomás and Landon's mother, then Jeremy's fiancée. *Who am I now?*

And so she dove into her work. *This is who I am*. She was a businesswoman—an entrepreneur—and she was determined to make her consulting business a success. She finished the project for her client, answered emails, and sent out a new proposal. The hours flew by as she ferociously tamped down personal emotion for professional output.

This is who I am.

One day, Azalea's phone screen lit up with a text from her client Denice. Was it really six o'clock already? Where had the day gone?

Hey, Azalea, big changes and a significant new project. I need your brain—can we talk tomorrow?

Sure, she texted back. *I'm open all morning.*

Denice was her favorite client, the vice president of marketing for Seaside Technologies. Azalea was curious about the project but satisfied herself with the knowledge that she'd learn more in the morning. She closed her laptop and realized she hadn't eaten all day. She made herself a cup of coffee and poured a bowl of granola, too tired to cook.

She curled up on the couch in the lanai to read and enjoy a typical Florida rainstorm. She especially loved the nighttime storms—the crackle of the lightning and the explosions of thunder thrilled her and she often turned off the lights to experience them at their rawest. Tonight, after her tears and long day, there was nowhere she'd rather be, soaking up the sounds, smells, and comfort of her coastal home.

At last the storm moved on and Azalea stretched and went to bed. For the first time in weeks, she slept soundly.

She woke early and refreshed, got in her sunrise beach walk, showered, and prepared to tackle her day. *No more tears,* she thought. *It's time to move on.*

She sat at the kitchen table sipping her coffee and booted up her laptop. She glanced at her phone, remembering Jeremy's text from the day before, and turned it face down on the table. *Not now,* she decided. She'd found a place of equanimity and wasn't about to squander her fragile peace. *I'll think about Jeremy later.* For right now, she needed to make a living.

An email popped up on her screen. Denice sent a meeting request for ten o'clock. Two hours to prepare…for what? She quickly accepted the meeting and began thinking through everything she'd done for Seaside Technologies. It had started small: Two years ago she helped their marketing team with a regional campaign which had been so successful they rolled it out globally. She had quickly become a trusted resource, a strategic partner who understood the company's product mix and value proposition. When they acquired Banner and Hill, a small software outfit in London, they brought

Azalea in to help guide the rebranding efforts. Denice tried to hire her permanently but Azalea made it clear she wasn't interested in joining the team. She welcomed the work and loved the people, but was determined to build her own consulting company.

And then Jeremy had gently but persistently suggested that she give them up. He insisted he was simply looking out for her time and energy, that she didn't need to work so many hours. In fact, he laughed, she didn't need to work at all.

Azalea had pushed back. "I'm not ready to retire, Jeremy. I need purpose."

"You have purpose," he said, wrapping her in his arms and kissing her forehead. "You have me. You have us. Isn't that enough?"

No, Azalea whispered in her mind. But she simply hugged him back and pared down her engagement with Seaside Tech.

Yet now there was a "significant new project." Azalea wracked her mind for what it could be and scoured her laptop for clues that could be hidden in the projects she'd already completed. Azalea went quickly through her files, reviewing the work she'd done over the past two years. The acquisition had been positive and the newly combined executive team hadn't been stingy with bonuses for the employees. Yet there would always be grumblers, those who bemoaned the loss of their previous culture, manager, projects, parking spots…whatever. Azalea had put her natural storytelling gifts to work, crafting the messages the executive team delivered to the market and their employees.

Seaside Technologies was ambitious. Headquartered in Orlando, they had offices across Latin America. Once, when she briefly considered accepting Denice's job offer, Azalea thought about taking Spanish classes to improve her nominally conversational skills, making her more valuable to the company. But she worried that Jeremy would treat it as just a little hobby and she'd be mortified that his command of the language was so far beyond her own. Jeremy's ability to speak perfect Spanish had given him opportunities in Mexico, Central America, and South America where he did a sizable amount of business, despite his pale skin and English heritage.

And so she'd neglected her formal Spanish lessons, consoling herself with random Spanish chitchat with Susana.

Azalea glanced at the clock on her laptop. Five minutes until ten—time to shut down her exploration, pull out her notebook, and sign on to the video call. She hadn't found anything that gave her a clue as to the new project, but she was excited to speak with Denice and learn more.

The screen opened and Denice's smiling face appeared. "Good morning!" she exclaimed. "How are you?"

"I'm well," said Azalea. "Super intrigued to hear about this big project." She shifted her laptop and pulled her notebook closer. Twirling her pencil in her fingers, she smiled. "So? What's up?"

"Ah…no small talk today, huh?" grinned Denice. "Okay, here's the deal. You know we've been working across LatAm and we have the old Banner and Hill office in London." Azalea nodded. "Anyway, with Brexit and the expense of being in London, we're looking at opening a new western European headquarters. We've decided on Spain."

"Spain? Why?"

"The economics are great. They're actively recruiting tech companies and with our current presence in Latin America, we felt it was a natural extension for us. We already have several executives who speak fluent Spanish, and Barcelona is rapidly becoming a tech hub in Europe."

"Barcelona?" asked Azalea, a flutter of excitement in her stomach.

"Yep," answered Denice. "We've been confidentially researching locations for months and it seems to be the best place for an office. Small at first, but it will definitely grow. Have you ever been there?"

Azalea couldn't keep the smile from her face. "It's one of my favorite places on the planet."

"Good! We need help," said Denice, ticking off the items on her fingers. "Setting up the office. Hiring some staff, communicating to the new team, hiring a PR agency." The Seaside Tech vice president continued her staccato enumeration. "Managing the grand opening…the whole shebang. How's your Spanish?"

Azalea's thoughts spun. *Barcelona? Spanish? New office?*

Denice finally slowed her recitation. "Interested? It's a six-month gig, all expenses paid. We have executive apartments where you can stay." Azalea nodded, her face thoughtful.

"So when can you leave?"

Denice laughed at Azalea's stunned look. "I'm just kidding," she said, grinning. "We're finalizing the office lease and finishing up some legal stuff. We're thinking it would be good to have you start after the first of the year. No one here wants to go to Spain during the holidays."

Azalea looked out her window, thinking rapidly. "Can I think about it for a couple of days?" she asked. "It sounds exciting, but it's a big commitment. I'd like to think it through."

Denice made a face. "I was hoping you'd just jump at the idea," she said laughing. "But yeah, take a few days—can you get back to me by Friday?"

"Of course." Azalea's mind was racing. Was this the new beginning she was hoping for?

The women exchanged goodbyes and hung up. Azalea leaned back in her chair, pensive. She loved Barcelona and the thought of working there for six months intrigued her. She thought back to her first trip to the city. There on business for a week, she extended her stay for a few days to lounge on the beach and stroll along Las Ramblas, stopping to sit at sidewalk cafés, drinking *café con leche y azucar*. She remembered giggling at the English and Irish tourists—they were the ones whose breasts turned hot shades of red on the topless beach as they soaked up every bit of sunshine on their continental vacations. Azalea hadn't taken off her top—she was far too modest—but wondered what it would be like to have grown up in a culture that had fewer restrictions and hang-ups about women's bodies.

She had strolled along the stalls of the open-air market, admiring trinkets—meticulously crafted silver, leather, and wood items. And she had wandered the strange and sacred beauty of Gaudi's cathedral, La Sagrada Familia, looking out over the captivating city as she reached the roof.

On her second trip to Spain, Azalea had been in Madrid, again for work, again staying over for a long weekend to experience the city without the pressures of a business schedule. On her first night there, after a very late dinner of the best *paella* she'd ever tasted, she and her colleagues wandered cobblestone streets until they found a charming café. They ordered churros and European chocolate—a hot, rich, almost pudding-like drink that quickly became a habit.

Her next trip was back to Barcelona, hitching a ride with Susana who was there for a conference. Thanks to her best friend's generous expense account, Azalea got the benefit of staying at the swanky Hotel Arts, just yards from the beach. She wouldn't have stayed somewhere so expensive on her own and was grateful for her friend's invitation. They hung out every evening, eating tapas and drinking sangria, laughing over their good fortune. Susana attended her conference during the day and Azalea would jog or lie out at the beach, reading a book. It was a glorious four days in paradise.

She thought back to her last trip to Spain. She spent eight days in Lanzarote, geographically closer to Africa than mainland Spain, but Spanish territory nevertheless. It had been less than a week after her mom died—a birthday trip her mother made her promise to take *no matter what happens.*

Azalea closed her laptop. She missed her mother every day. She sighed and sat with the memories. Her mother was so proud of her, always bragging to friends about her daughter's great life, her beautiful boys, her business travels around the world. She missed her father, too, but in a different way. His quiet strength had been a constant in her life. It had made her the responsible woman she was.

But being responsible only went so far. The truth was, Azalea was sick of her life. She was tired of all the have-to's and the obligations and the duty. She was weary of the regrets. *I probably have fewer days in front of me than behind*, she thought ruefully. What would she do with what was left? Could half a year in Barcelona be the answer?

She and Susana talked late that night. After listening to Azalea's tentative thoughts, Susana encouraged her: "*Mana*, why would you even wonder about this? What an incredible opportunity!" Her friend chuckled. "Just gives me a good reason to visit. *Pero no hables con ese acento catalán!*" Like Azalea's family, Susana's family came from Mexico, and the accent used in Barcelona was odd to their ears.

"Bar-the-lona," responded Azalea, exaggerating the accent.

"Aaarrggh!" shouted Susana. "You almost made me spit out my wine!" The two friends laughed, and she continued. "But seriously, *chica*. When do you leave? Because you know you can't turn this down."

"They want me there in January. Seems like a long time from now, but I'm sure it will fly by." Azalea smiled, her mind made up. "Thanks, Suze. You're right. I'm going to Barcelona!" The friends air-kissed the phone and hung up, promising to talk the following week. Azalea sat back, allowing the excitement to take her.

It was only October and she had plans to celebrate the holidays with the boys. It would take her a few weeks to figure out what to do with her home—she was sure Tomás and Landon would come by and check on things, but she didn't want to make any assumptions without talking to them first. They were coming over for dinner on Sunday—she'd talk to them then.

New beginning, indeed.

4

The alarm on Azalea's phone rang just loudly enough to wake her from a light doze. She rolled over on one arm, reached into her beach bag, and lightly tapped the repeat button. She opened her book and propped herself up on her elbows to read. Sara had loaned her *How Not to Die*, a book about the benefits of a plant-based diet. Azalea was skeptical, but Sara had followed the program for six weeks and raved about her results.

Children shrieked and giggled up and down the shore as they built sandcastles or jumped nimbly over the rippling waves. It was a Sunday afternoon, and the beach was packed with families. The sun glistened on the water and caressed her bronzed back. Azalea sipped her water and gave up trying to read. She lay her chin on her hands, glanced fondly around, and then packed up her things to leave.

Even a hundred yards from the ocean changed the temperature. The light breeze by the water vanished as she walked across the street to her home. In the two minutes it took to get to her front door, Azalea was already sweating. She unlocked the door and stepped into the coolness of the air-conditioned cottage.

Azalea set down her bag and stretched, yawning broadly. She could feel the prickle of sweat along her hairline and scratched absently at her neck. Shower first or get started on Sunday dinner? She washed her hands in the sink—she'd get the potatoes started at least.

Azalea mused on her good fortune. How many parents would love to have their adult children come over for Sunday dinners? Of course, for the boys it meant one less day they had to buy groceries or fend for themselves, but whatever their motivation, she treasured their weekly gatherings. As she walked to her bathroom, she wondered yet again how they'd take her news.

After a quick shower, she went back to the kitchen to check on the potatoes. The bottoms were browning with just enough crispiness. Dessert was already baked and sitting on the table. She knew the boys would eat it all before they left. It was their cheat day, after all.

Her sons came in, calling out "Hey, Mom!" in unison, breaking into her reverie. Azalea wiped her hands on a dishtowel and walked to meet them. The three hugged, and Landon pulled away, sniffing the air. "What smells so good?"

"Swordfish, Brussels sprouts, and fingerling potatoes," she said, knowing what was coming.

"That sounds way too healthy for a cheat day," groused Tomás. "We didn't work hard all week for fish and vegetables."

Azalea grinned at her predictable eldest. He worked out daily, meticulously watched his eating during the week, and took full advantage of the Sunday cheat days. She was quite sure he'd made a trip to Dunkin' Donuts that morning for breakfast.

"Don't get so snippy," she chided. "The s'mores bars are on the table, just waiting for you."

Landon laughed and Tomás answered, "That's more like it. I hope you know those aren't just dessert—they're appetizers!" He went straight for the silverware drawer and pulled out a spoon, diving into the rich sweets without hesitation.

Azalea sent her sons off to wash up as she brought the food to the table. The three chatted amiably, the food disappearing in no time. When they finished, she brought out small plates and served more of the gooey dessert to each of them, doubling the amount for the boys when they looked askance at her serving size. For a long moment, they sat quietly, savoring the rich dessert and coffee. Then Landon looked at his brother, raising his eyebrows, and Tomás set down his fork, nodding at his brother to continue.

"So, Mom…we need to tell you something," began her youngest. Azalea looked from one to the other. They were suddenly awkward. She willed her mind to stop leaping to catastrophe.

"Okay. What's wrong?" she asked.

Tomás frowned. "Why does it have to be something wrong? We just need to tell you about a decision we made. We're actually pretty excited about it."

Azalea relaxed and smiled. "Tell me."

"We've decided we're moving to Colorado. Probably after the first of the year."

She steeled her features to belie her surprise. "Colorado? Really? What's in Colorado?"

Landon, ever sensitive to his mother's emotions, put his hand on hers. "It's a great place for us, Mom. You know we both love the mountains and—"

Tomás broke in. "I found a great philosophy program and you know I don't want to be in Florida. Landon can get a job and I'm sure I can get a teaching assistant gig."

She looked at her boys—no, her young men. She knew they had never planned to stay at the beach. Tomás the adventurer had planned to live in Europe ever since he was in high school and had surprised her when he decided to come back to the States after two years abroad. Landon the outdoorsman had talked about North Carolina, Utah, and Oregon. But Colorado?

Azalea hated the cold.

And the thought of being so far from her family struck her forcefully. Somehow Barcelona hadn't seemed so…separate. Knowing they would be home in Florida while she was away meant things hadn't really changed. She could come home any time and Tomás and Landon would be there. She'd known they'd get married and have families of their own, of course. But halfway across the country?

"You okay, Mom?" asked Landon.

Azalea looked across the table at her sons. Her heart swelled with pride and love—*Oh, how precious these boys are!* Tears pricked at her eyes, and Tomás frowned worriedly. "Mom?"

"It's okay. I'm really proud of you. And excited for you!" She grinned, feeling suddenly nervous. "I actually have something to tell you guys." Azalea looked back and forth between her sons. "I'm going to Barcelona for six months for work. I'm leaving in January, too."

Landon burst out laughing. Tomás just gawked at his mother. "Um…when did you make this decision?" he asked stiffly.

Now it was Azalea's turn to laugh. "I just found out Thursday," she said. "Seaside Technologies is opening a new European headquarters and they've asked me to lead the effort. They have an apartment for me just a couple of blocks from the office. It's an incredible opportunity," she finished with a smile. "And you know how much I love Barcelona."

Tomás began, "So what will you do—" but Landon broke in.

"That's awesome, Mom. Really, really great. I'm happy for you." His smile was genuine and love shone from his eyes.

Her eldest looked sideways at his younger brother. "Kiss up," he muttered and then shook his head. "I'm super happy for you, Mom. But seriously—what are you going to do about the house?"

Azalea shook her head. "I have no idea," she admitted. "I had planned to ask you guys to take care of it while I'm gone. I guess I need to figure something else out. Maybe I'll rent it out for six months. I could always just put my special stuff in storage and make it a half-year rental."

The remainder of the afternoon passed leisurely as they talked about their respective moves. The boys planned to rent an apartment for a few months while they found work and narrowed down the areas where they wanted to live. Tomás animatedly described the graduate program; clearly, he'd been thinking about this for a while. Landon talked about being near the mountains and indulging his bouldering hobby. Until now, he'd only been able to climb at indoor climbing facilities and longed to test his skills on the real thing.

By the time they left, Azalea felt far more at peace. No matter where they lived, her little family was intact. Her heart was full. As she loaded the dishwasher, she started daydreaming about Christmases in Colorado. Surely, she could manage a couple of weeks in the snow every year.

Azalea took off her sunglasses as she walked into the restaurant. She looked around and saw Sara and Lauren at the bar, waving.

"Cute place," she said as she hugged her friends. "What are you having?"

"This gorgeous Prosecco," said Lauren, holding out her glass. "Even Miss Plant-Based Diet over here is indulging in some bubbly calories." Sara laughed at her roommate and best friend. She climbed down from her barstool and spun around, arms akimbo.

"So? What do you think? Six weeks and I've lost ten pounds," she said proudly. "And I feel amazing. I'm never eating meat again." Sara had always been the curvy one of the friends, struggling with her weight and self-image since she was a child.

Azalea smiled. "You look wonderful," she said. "But you don't have to be thinner to look fantastic. I'm just glad you've found something that makes you feel good."

The three women turned as Susana approached. "Hey, girlies!" she called breezily. "Please tell me we're ready to eat. I'm starving!"

"Hey, Suze," said Azalea. "We were just talking about Sara's new diet."

"Oh, Lord…" groaned Susana. "Not still the plant thing? I'm sorry, *chica*, but this *mujer* needs meat." She stopped suddenly and stared at Sara. "But you do look pretty amazing. Really great. Your skin is glowing." She looked at Lauren and Azalea. "Are you guys trying this, too?"

Lauren rolled her eyes. "Are you kidding? No way." The lithe Lauren was an avowed carnivore and rarely touched vegetables unless they were smothered in melted cheese.

"I'm not sure," said Azalea. "I'm reading the book right now. It's pretty compelling."

"Hmmph," responded Susana, wrinkling her nose. "Maybe I'll read it when you're done. Stranger things have happened."

Sara gave Lauren a satisfied smile as the hostess came to take them to their table.

"…and then he stops and stares at me like I grew horns or something," continued Lauren. "Like, 'Who do you think you are not letting me take credit for your work…*again*?'" The four friends laughed, dinner long finished, a second bottle of Prosecco emptied.

"I don't know how you stand it there, *chica*," said Susana. "I'm happy for you that you finally stood up to that *pendejo*, but damn— this has been going on for a year." Sara and Azalea nodded in agreement.

Lauren grimaced. "I know, I know. I have to get better about sticking up for myself." She offered a bemused smile. "We aren't all as courageous as Azalea."

"I'm not really that courageous," she said quietly. The women looked at her, their eyes questioning. "Jeremy texted me last week out of the blue."

Susana sat up straight, her brows furrowed. "I hope you haven't answered him."

"I kept it very impersonal. But today he asked if we could get together for dinner. I don't think it's a good idea, but I feel bad about just saying no."

Lauren gaped at her friend. "Seriously? You earn a badge of courage for bailing the night before your wedding and *now* you're worried about hurting his feelings? Not trying to be mean, but that's some kind of bullshit." Azalea's friend grew heated. "You pulled out of the wedding for a reason. Don't forget that." Sara was quiet but nodded her agreement.

Azalea looked at her friends, then shook her head. "You're right. I don't know what I was thinking. It's not like we're getting back together. We aren't even gonna be friends." They sat quietly, no one quite sure what to say in the face of Azalea's discomfort.

She cleared her throat. "I'm sorry—that's not what I wanted to talk about tonight. I actually have some really exciting news." She looked around the table, hoping the mood would lighten. "If I haven't completely ruined the evening."

"Of course not," said Sara, clearly happy for the change in subject.

"Tell us!" She leaned forward and patted her friend's hand. "It's okay, Azalea. You know we just love you. C'mon—what's the news?"

Azalea smiled crookedly and then blurted, "I'm leaving in January for six months in Barcelona. Seaside Tech is opening a new office there and they've hired me to lead the project. I'm so excited!"

Susana, already in on the secret, sat back with a smile. Sara and Lauren squealed with delight and talked over each other. "That's amazing!" "I'm so excited for you!"

"The only downside is figuring out what to do with the house. This weekend the boys told me they're moving to Colorado. I had planned for them to take care of the place but it looks like they'll be leaving about the same time I am. I guess I'll try to rent it out for six months."

Lauren glanced at Sara, then said, "If you just want someone to look after it, Sara and I could do it." She grinned, an impish look on her face. "Gives us a chance to hang out at the beach on the weekends."

"You'd do that? For six months?"

Sara burst out laughing. "Are you kidding? Make sure the plants are watered and the mail gets picked up and we get six months of weekends at the beach? Um, yeah. That sounds miserable."

"You guys are the best. I'd much rather not have the hassle of renting it out."

After another half hour of conversation, the restaurant was closing and the women rose to leave. They hugged each other outside and Azalea stopped them before they went to their cars.

"I'm sorry if I overreacted about the Jeremy thing...."

Her three friends exchanged concerned glances. "*Mana*, we weren't trying to upset you..." began Susana.

"I'm not upset, Suze. At least not with you guys. I just feel stupid—*again*—for even considering seeing him. It's like I can't trust myself. I know I did the right thing breaking off the engagement. And I'm proud of myself for doing it." Azalea looked out into the night. "I want to be strong and courageous and...and...." She looked back at her friends and tears gleamed on her lashes. "I just want this to be done. I never wanted to hear from him again. I want to prove to myself that I can make good choices and be a woman I can be proud of." The tears slid down her cheeks. "Why does this have to be so hard? Why can't he just let go?"

Susana opened her mouth, but Sara shook her head at her fiery friend. She gently wiped a tear off Azalea's cheek. "Don't beat yourself up. You're grieving—and that's okay. It's only been four months! No, Jeremy wasn't the right one. And you *are* strong and courageous. You did something unbelievably difficult and you did it with grace and class. We're all so proud you! And you know Tomás and Landon are, too." Azalea gazed at her friend with tear-filled eyes.

"But you were about to get married. You were about to start a new life and that's not a small thing to get over. It's a death, my friend. You're allowed to grieve that loss. No one's looking down on you for that. And you shouldn't either."

Lauren looked at Azalea, tears in her own eyes. "You're the bravest woman I know, Azalea Mora," she said quietly. "I can only hope to have your strength one day."

5

The next two months flew by as Azalea planned for her half-year away. She and the boys celebrated Thanksgiving with Susana and Enrique, enjoying the warmth of a Florida November along with their turkey and pies. Christmas was just the three of them at Azalea's house, the boys spending the night on Christmas Eve and waking early to presents, hot cocoa, and a huge breakfast.

Azalea bought them gifts she feared they might find dull: kitchenware for their new home in Colorado. She splurged and bought them a fancy coffee maker with a month's worth of pods, knowing how much they liked having coffee at her house. She filled their stockings with gift cards and each got a new watch.

"Mom," said Tomás, admiring his wrist, "this is too much! You always spoil us." He smiled at his mother and shook his head. "One gift would have been plenty. This is like Christmas, birthdays, and who knows what all rolled into one."

Landon playfully punched his brother's arm. "Shut up, bro. This is awesome." He grinned at Azalea. "I don't mind being spoiled at all, Mom."

They spent the day laughing, watching movies, and eating tamales and *pan dulce*. The boys left late, promising to stop by before they left the following week to drive to their new home.

And then, faster than she imagined, it was January.

Azalea settled her backpack onto the handle of her suitcase, wearily pulling it into place. She sighed and brushed a stray hair out of her eyes. Opening her purse, she found her glasses and slipped them on. Customs hadn't taken too long, and she was thankful the company was sending a driver. No worries about finding transportation to the apartment. She smoothed lip balm on her airplane-dried lips and began walking.

She hadn't slept nearly as much as she'd hoped to. The seat next to her had been empty so she stretched out a bit, hoping to fall asleep after dinner and a glass of wine. She figured she got three or four hours total and knew her only hope to avoid lingering jet lag was to power through the day, however much she wanted to nap.

Azalea scanned the area, quickly reading the cards held by drivers. After a quick back and forth she saw her name emblazoned in all capitals: AZALEA MORA, SEASIDE TECHNOLOGIES. She picked up her stride when suddenly she noticed a woman running up and embracing a man. The man, however, clearly did not welcome her affection.

"Gloria!" he said, putting his hands on her shoulders to stop her and then stepping away. "*Te dije que no vinieras al aeropuerto. No necesito que me lleven.*" I told you not to come to the airport. I don't need a ride.

Gloria's loving embrace turned to hands on her hips, her chin jutting out, lips pouting. Azalea didn't mean to stare, but she was exhausted and found herself engrossed by the scene. The young man, his dark eyes glancing around, his handsome face sorrowful yet stern, pleaded more quietly with the woman. "Gloria, *por favor no hagas esto tan difícil.*" Please don't make this so hard.

Azalea tripped over the arm of her jacket. She'd wound it around the handle of her suitcase but failed to notice when it began to drag as she walked slowly past the couple. *For crying out loud*, she thought, *stop staring and leave those poor people alone.* She re-wrapped her jacket around the handle and took two more steps toward her driver, meeting his eyes and waving.

"*Señorita!*" said the driver. "*Bienvenidos a Barcelona!*"

"*Muchísimas gracias,*" she replied wearily. The driver reached out for her suitcase and Azalea gratefully handed it over. Just then, she heard the woman again.

"*No mas, Esteban! No mas. Adiós. Ve a tu estúpido bistró y haz café todo el día. No me importa.*" Go to your stupid bistro and make coffee all day. I don't care.

Gloria spun on her heel, her long hair flung behind her. Azalea barely heard Esteban whisper, "*Finalmente.*"

Esteban? Café?

Azalea walked into her new apartment and tiredly looked around. She hadn't known what to expect from a corporate apartment but was pleasantly surprised. The kitchen was spacious and bright, with a small dining table across from the open counter. She hoped to cook at home most days—she knew how eating out became less a novelty and more an annoyance for business travelers. The next room was a small but beautifully decorated living area, with a large sofa and two sitting chairs. She could imagine lying on the couch with a book....

Thirty minutes later, she was out the door and ready to explore. The air was crisp, just cool enough to wake her up, and she was thankful she brought plenty of sweaters. She waved off the taxi that appeared at the front door of the apartment building and set off for Las Ramblas.

The streets were full of people and Azalea listened avidly to snippets of conversation as she walked. *It's not eavesdropping if I can't understand, right?* She giggled at the thought. She was eager to improve her limited Spanish and was thankful this assignment would give her the opportunity.

She looked again at her phone to ensure she was going the right way to the office. Better to make sure she knew where it was before her first day, she thought. The ten-minute walk invigorated her and she found the building easily. She decided to meander around the quarter, watching people and acquainting herself with her new short-term home city.

After an hour of wandering, she began to tire again. She passed a café door just as someone walked out, and the rich scent of strong coffee convinced her it was time for a break. The filigreed etching on the window proclaimed *La Rosa de Barcelona.*

The small room was filled with people, a low hum of conversation enveloping her. There were mothers with young children and old couples sitting at rustic wooden tables, all sipping the aromatic brew. Azalea reached the front of the line and met a handsome young man. *"Hola, señorita,"* he said, smiling. *"Que quieres comer?"*

She looked at him, wondering. He looked familiar, but she didn't know anyone in Barcelona. *It's just the jet lag,* she thought. She hadn't considered eating but suddenly realized she was hungry. *"Lo siento mucho,"* she said. *"Mi español es muy pobre."*

The young man smiled and laughed. "No problem. My English is not so good either."

Azalea grinned. *"Un cafecito con leche y azúcar, por favor. Y un... um, bocadillo?* That's a sandwich, right?"

"Si, perfecto! Que tipo quieres?" The young man seemed to enjoy her attempt and she was thankful she wasn't holding up a line of people trying to order.

*"Cual...*um, oh goodness." She shook her head, frowning. "Which do you suggest?"

"Ah," smiled the young man. *"'Recomendar' es el verbo. Digame 'Cual recomendas?'"* He paused. *"Entiendes?"*

Azalea's sluggish mind took a moment, but she brightened and answered, *"Si! Entiendo."* She straightened and smiled. *"Señor, quiero comer un bocadillo. Cual recomendas?"*

His smiled broadly. *"Perfecto, señorita!"* He pointed at a tray in the case. *"Recomendo el bocadillo con jamón y queso. Es brillante."* He tilted his head flirtatiously. *"Y me llamo Esteban."*

Her laugh burst out before she could hold it back. "Ah...Esteban. *Soy mas mayor que tu madre.*" I'm older than your mother. She hoped she said that right.

A flicker of sadness passed over his face, so quickly she thought she imagined it.

Then he shook his head. *"Lo dudo!"* He pointed at the menu. "So...*quieres esto?*"

"*Si, gracias.*"

As she paid for her sandwich and coffee, he winked at her. "*Hasta luego, viejita.*"

"*Me llamo Azalea,*" she replied laughing, as she walked out with her takeaways.

And then it hit her: *Esteban.* The young man from the airport. *What a small world*, she marveled.

As she approached the door, a man rose from a table. Their eyes met and he bowed slightly, then reached for the handle. "Allow me, *señorita*," he said, his voice deep and resonant.

With her hands full, she appreciated the offer and smile. "*Muchas gracias,*" she replied as he held the door for her.

"Enjoy your lunch," he said. "*Que tengas un buen día.*"

She smiled, taking in his handsome face, then looking at the sunlit courtyard. "I will," she answered. "It's a very good day."

After her long stroll through the shops of Las Ramblas, Azalea walked back to her apartment, feeling tired but happy. She kept half of her sandwich—no, *bocadillo*, she reminded herself—in the bag and bought some orange juice and a fruit-filled *empanada* at a small grocer in the square. She planned to shop for groceries once she got her bearings, but this was enough for breakfast in the morning. The day had warmed slightly, and she was ready to head back to what would be home for the next six months. She daydreamed as she walked the cobblestone streets, laughing again about Esteban. It was nice to be flirted with, even if it were a young man no older than her sons.

She wondered what Jeremy was doing now. Had he gotten over her? She thought again about his texts before she'd left. They hadn't met and she found herself glad that she was thousands of miles away. Surely this job would occupy her and she'd stop thinking about what she'd given up.

About being loved.

6

The next six weeks were a flurry of activity as Azalea settled into her new job. She was on the phone with Denice nearly daily and worked hard to temper her American impatience with the Spanish pace—quite a bit slower than she was used to. She supervised the office setup, working with designers to furnish, paint, and outfit the meeting rooms and was pleased with the results. Her basic Spanish slowly improved as she talked with contractors, PR agencies, and temp firms. She hired a receptionist and looked forward to having him start the next week. And now, Denice had arrived in Barcelona and Azalea was eager to show off what she'd accomplished.

Azalea looked up from her desk as Denice walked in. "*Bienvenidos*! How was your flight?"

Denice scowled. "Long. Tiring. And a fussy baby the entire time from JFK. I feel like I got hit by a bus."

Azalea grinned. "Oh, what glamorous lives we have!" she joked. "Why don't you put your stuff down and let me show you around? Then we can walk to Las Ramblas and have something to eat. You know you have to get through today to get rid of the jet lag." Denice nodded; they were both experienced international travelers and she knew the drill. She rolled her suitcase into the corner and set her backpack down on a chair. She cocked her head toward Azalea's door. "All right," she sighed heavily. "Let's see the place."

Azalea smiled, sympathizing with Denice's mood. She took Seaside's vice president through the entire office, pointing out the décor—paintings she'd found from local artists exhibiting on Las Ramblas, making the environment warm and inviting. They looked through the various meeting rooms, with Azalea describing the audio-visual setup in each. Denice smiled and nodded, stifling yawns.

Azalea realized she wouldn't get the woman's full attention until they had gotten outdoors and had some food and coffee. "C'mon," she said, reaching for Denice's arm with a laugh. "Let's do this after lunch. It's a beautiful day and you'll feel better once we're outside."

Denice shook her head ruefully. "I'm sorry—" Azalea held up her hands to forestall any more apologies, and they walked back to her office.

The two women grabbed their purses and walked two blocks to Las Ramblas where they found a small bistro. They sat at a mosaic-covered table and ordered Azalea's new favorite, *bocadillos con jamon y queso* and steaming *cafecitos con leche*. They nibbled companionably for several minutes, and then Denice wiped her mouth to talk.

"I'm sorry for being such a grouch," she began. Azalea started to protest, but Denice held up a hand. "No, it's true. That screaming kid meant I didn't sleep a wink on the way here. Normally I can get a couple of hours, but I'm just beat. No excuses." She took a long drink of her coffee. "This is delicious and I'm feeling a lot better." Denice raised an eyebrow and smiled. "And I have something interesting to tell you now that I've somewhat recovered."

Azalea knew there was nothing like a bit of fresh air and strong Spanish coffee to perk up her friend after a long, napless flight. "Do tell!"

"So there's been a new development with Seaside Technologies," she began. "We've been bought."

Azalea set her sandwich down. "Bought? As in we don't have jobs or as in we have new leadership?"

Denice smiled crookedly. "We definitely have jobs. Evidently our new CEO is mad for Barcelona and keen to open the office. He'll be here in a couple of weeks to check things out himself. It sounds like our little Spanish outfit might become the jewel in the crown of the new company. I don't have a lot of details, but the buzz is really positive, especially with the sales team. They're already looking for a Spanish sales exec." She took a bite of her sandwich and closed her eyes appreciatively. "Does anyone do ham better than Spain?" she asked. "Anyway, they're also sending over his personal assistant from Florida. Cuban-American, I think. She's fluent in Spanish and has been with the company forever. She'll be here with the CEO."

Azalea's mind raced. *What's one more new thing to juggle?* she thought. "I'll let Ambos know he's coming," said Azalea. She signed the new Spanish public relations agency only two weeks before. "They'll want to work with the US agency to get the announcement out." She sipped her coffee, gazing thoughtfully toward the bustling plaza. "Did you have any inkling Seaside Tech was looking to sell? I mean the Banner and Hill acquisition just barely finalized last year."

Denice shook her head. "It came as a surprise to everyone," she responded. "I hadn't even heard of Fowler Enterprises before. I guess they're big in Latin America, but mostly Central and South America. This opens up Spain and Europe for them."

Azalea almost dropped her coffee cup. *Fowler Enterprises? Jeremy purchased Seaside Tech?*

No longer hungry, she pushed her plate away. "So what's your role now?" she asked. "Does it change? Are you still my contact with Seaside?" Azalea tried to remain nonchalant, but her insides roiled.

Denice didn't seem to notice. Stifling a yawn, she answered, "I am, but I guess the new CEO wants to meet with you when he gets here. He's apparently pretty picky about the company's offices—sort of a micromanager is the buzz. I heard he got hyper-involved with details in their Mexico office, even picking paint and artwork. And he spends a lot of time in Buenos Aires. I heard he even overruled his marketing team down there on a font they wanted to use." She laughed. "Lots of rumors, but I haven't met the guy yet. He may be a pain, but it still sounds like it's good for the company and great visibility for you. I know you love running your own consulting gigs, but are you sure you don't want a permanent job?"

Azalea frowned, staring at nothing. She remembered the Argentine office opening and how particular Jeremy had been about every detail. She'd tried to laugh off his obsession with the opening, especially something as minute as the font choice, but he was adamant. It was the first time his perfectionism made her question their relationship.

"Azalea?" Denice touched her hand. "Hello? I thought I was the one with jet lag."

Azalea shook her head, looking back at her friend. "Sorry, just thinking."

Denice laughed. "You were somewhere else. Anyway—what do you think? Do you want to make this permanent? Maybe move here and set up shop?"

Azalea looked at the mosaic tiles on the tabletop. The glorious mixture of colors—that quintessential Spanish beauty—called to her. After her short time there, she'd come to love Barcelona in a new way and had flirted with the idea of staying after the Seaside Tech engagement was complete. Taking a permanent job would make it easier to get a long-term visa, maybe even buy a house. She looked up at Denice, suddenly sorrowful.

"No, I think I'll just finish this up and head home," she said. "It's great here, but I miss my family and friends. And I'm not ready to settle down just yet," she finished with a rueful grin.

"I understand," said Denice. "You know I had to try." She sat back, looking around the plaza. "It really is a beautiful city," she murmured.

Azalea nodded in agreement. But there was now a shadow darkening her experience.

And it was heading to Barcelona.

Why would he do this? she thought that night sitting in her living room. Azalea sipped a glass of wine and considered the situation. Nothing Jeremy did was coincidental. Her emotions bounced from anger to confusion. Should she acknowledge they knew each other?

Tell Denice before he arrived? Or act as if they were strangers, meeting for the first time?

Will this man ever be out of my life? she wondered. Just when she was building a new life without him, now she would have to see him every day. She wondered if she could do it and considered resigning. She opened her laptop and began searching for flights back to the States. Her fingers flew over the keyboard, her eyes darting across the screen. She could be home in no time and put all this behind her. Would Denice require a two-week notice to abandon the account? What about all the work she'd done? Could she just walk away?

Azalea slammed her laptop closed and began pacing. *Slow down,* she urged herself. *Take a breath and make a rational decision.* There were flights as soon as tomorrow—if she didn't mind completely burning a bridge with an important client and ruining any chance of a decent referral from Denice. There were flights in two weeks, if she could manage to stay that long.

Azalea picked up her phone. It was lunchtime in Florida and she hoped to catch Susana—who picked up on the second ring.

"*Mana! Como estás?*"

"Hey, Suze," she answered. "Do you have a minute?"

Susana voice was serious. "Azalea, what's wrong?" Her friend knew her better than anyone in the world and instantly picked up on her tone. "What happened, honey?"

Azalea blurted, "Jeremy bought Seaside Tech. He's on his way to Barcelona."

"Ay, *Dios mío,*" muttered Susana. "What is wrong with that *cabrón?*"

"I don't know," admitted Azalea. "I'm trying to decide what to do. Part of me wants to pack up and come home, but I know that's not smart. I've invested so much in this project and I'm doing great. I don't want to abandon what I've accomplished."

"*Mana,* watch out," Susana warned. "I didn't say a lot when you were together, and I probably should have. But I don't trust him. He's not used to not getting his way. Girl, you know no way was this just a business decision. He's after you—either to get you back or to get revenge." She sighed. "I don't trust him," she repeated firmly. "But you're right. This is your business and your decision."

Azalea nodded. "I think I'm gonna tackle this head on and just text him. I don't want anyone to know we have a history. We can keep this completely professional and maybe I can come home a little early."

"Just be careful, '*mana*."

Azalea promised to be on her guard and the two friends ended with commitments to talk more frequently, especially once Jeremy arrived in Barcelona.

She knew it would be difficult—*damn difficult*—but she could do it. For her own pride and sense of self, she had to do it. There was no longer love between them, but she believed she could move beyond their personal history and was determined to finish this dream project. She squared her shoulders and texted Jeremy.

Just heard that you purchased Seaside Tech. I guess congratulations? I'm sure you know I'm setting up the Barcelona office and will be here for another few months. I would appreciate it if we didn't share our history with anyone. Let's keep it professional, please.

Jeremy's response was quick.

No problem—was going to ask what you'd prefer. Thanks for being great about it. See you in a couple of weeks.

7

For two weeks, Azalea and Denice worked twelve-hour days. Staying at the same executive apartments meant they walked together to and from the office each day, planning the grand opening event. They were a good pair, each bringing passion to her work and the project. More than once, Azalea was tempted to tell Denice about her relationship with Jeremy, but each time she held back. *That's in the past*, she scolded herself. *Now it's all about the job.*

Azalea worked with Ambos, the Spanish PR agency, to craft the event day agenda, identify industry analysts and journalists to invite, and prepare briefing documents for the Fowler Enterprises executives.

For Jeremy.

It wasn't just Jeremy, though. *Get your head in the game*, she thought crossly one afternoon. Ricardo García, Fowler's executive vice president of sales, would want details on every single person he'd meet. Fastidious, charming, and determined, Ricardo had flown in just days after Denice. He interviewed salespeople daily, scoring a major coup when Javier Mendiola, the top sales guy from competitor Terrazos joined the company. Ricardo and Javier were closeted in the sales conference room but came out occasionally to refill coffee cups or walk outside for a cigarette. They were friendly with the staff, but clearly focused on their desire to make a big splash in the market.

Ambos turned out to be an excellent choice. With deep relationships in the European tech industry, they had a ready list of contacts and the RSVPs were already coming in. Denice and Guillermo, the new receptionist, worked together on the catering and gifts they'd give to attendees. The entire office was abuzz with energy and excitement, and Azalea tried to match their enthusiasm. It was a fantastic career opportunity, she continually reminded herself. She knew she was doing great work—the office was beautiful, the staff was in place, and the event was well in hand. She hired two interns to help execute the marketing plan that would debut Fowler Enterprises in Spain. Monday would kick off the campaign leading up to the launch event and Azalea checked the schedule, yet again, determined not to overlook any details.

Denice strode into her office. "Okay, Azalea—it's Friday. We've been busting our butts for two weeks and it's time for a break. We're all heading for Las Ramblas and Ricardo is buying. Grab your *bolsa, amiga!*" Azalea looked up from her screen and laughed. Denice had picked up a few words of Spanish over the past fortnight and loved to sprinkle them into conversation.

"Listen to you, Ms. Bilingual," she answered with a smile. "You guys go ahead. It's only six o'clock and it's gonna be dead everywhere for another few hours." She gestured at the calendar on her desk. "Monday they'll be here and I'm not ready."

If you only knew how unready I am.

Monday arrived and Azalea watched Denice walk to the small, well-appointed lobby to greet their guests. Azalea couldn't hear anything they said, but she watched them carefully. Next to Jeremy and Ricardo stood a tall, striking woman. Long dark hair cascaded across her shoulders and her fuchsia dress hugged her curves. Poor Guillermo was obvious in his admiration, clearly trying not to gape at the beauty. As they spoke, the woman turned to look and met Azalea's eyes across the lobby. She was dark skinned with a perfectly outlined mouth—her lipstick the same fuchsia as her elegant dress. She stared frankly, knowingly at Azalea, who stood rigid behind her desk.

Eyes not leaving Azalea's, the tall woman spoke to Guillermo. He nodded and beckoned her toward Azalea's office. Azalea took a deep breath, stood, and walked around her desk, smoothing her skirt.

"Azalea, this is Maricela," began Guillermo. Long, shapely legs moved the woman to Azalea's side in a second. Maricela grasped Azalea's hands, leaned forward, air-kissed both her cheeks, and then stepped back to look directly into her eyes. Maricela was easily three inches taller, with espresso eyes flecked with amber. Incredibly long lashes smudged with brown liner stared back at Azalea. *She looks like she just stepped off a Vogue cover.* The woman was stunning.

"*Gracias*, Guillermo," she said, feeling awkward. "Hello, Maricela."

Guillermo glanced at Azalea, then to Maricela. "Uh…I'll leave you to it," he said, then returned to the lobby.

Maricela cocked her head, still holding Azalea's hands. "And so we finally meet," she said with a rich accent. "*La Azalea famosa.* Zheremy"—Maricela stroked his name languidly—"has told me so much about you. I've been very eager to meet you."

Azalea pulled her hands away, willing herself to remain calm in the face of such intent, almost brazen regard. "It's a pleasure to meet you, Maricela. Welcome to Barcelona. I hope you had a good flight." She took a step back—Maricela was far too much in her personal space—and gestured at a chair. "Won't you sit down?" Azalea stepped back around her desk and sat, keen to put more than physical space between her and the elegant woman. *Jeremy told her about me?* Azalea struggled to keep the anger from her face.

Maricela sat, effortlessly crossing her long legs. Azalea noted the pristine red soles of the Louboutin stilettos. Azalea smiled tightly. *Get it together!* she thought. *Now you're comparing shoes?*

She started to speak, but then Ricardo entered her office, Jeremy right behind him. "Azalea!" boomed the sales executive. "This is Jeremy Fowler, our new CEO. Jeremy, this is Azalea, the wonder woman behind the Barcelona office." His admiration for Azalea was clear, and she felt her face grow hot.

She stepped out from her desk and shook Jeremy's hand. "How do you do?" she asked, her best professional voice covering her nerves.

"I'm well, thank you," he answered. "I'm told you're the one to see about this new office and the big launch party. I'm completely booked today, but I'd like to schedule time to meet tomorrow. Would nine o'clock work for you?"

"Of course," she replied. "I'll clear my calendar."

Jeremy nodded, smiling. "Excellent. Well, then, I'll see you in the morning. Mari, shall we go find our apartments and get some lunch? Ricardo and I have a lot to discuss and I can't do it on an empty stomach." He turned back to Azalea: "*Adios*, Señorita Mora."

Azalea nodded. "*Adios.*"

Maricela glided past her with a wink. "*Hasta mañana*, Azahhlea."

Azalea tossed and turned all night, finally dragging herself out of bed at six. She stared at her bleary eyes in the mirror and sighed. It was going to be a difficult day.

She stood in front of her closet. What to wear? She tried to shake the nagging discomfort. *It's just a client meeting*, she told herself, knowing all the while it was something more. She decided on simplicity, slipping on well-tailored black slacks and a white silk blouse. She added tasteful gold jewelry, putting on the beaten gold hoops Tomás had given her for Christmas. Remembering Maricela's sky-high Louboutins, she slipped on elegant black patent slingbacks, knowing she could walk the cobblestone blocks in them without danger of breaking an ankle.

She wondered again why Jeremy had told Maricela about her. She hadn't told anyone that she knew him—and it appeared he had done the same, except with his assistant. Why would he tell her? He had agreed to keep their history private, and she tamped down a flicker of anger that he had already broken their agreement.

He called her *Mari*. Was that just her nickname or a special name between them?

It's been eight months, she chided herself. Azalea hadn't dated since the breakup, hadn't even been tempted. But who knew what

Jeremy had done? *None of my business*, she told herself firmly as she pulled her long dark hair into a French twist. It was in stark contrast to Maricela's tresses that fell in perfect waves halfway down her back.

Azalea looked questioningly at her reflection. Her green eyes were wreathed in fine lines but were still bright. She knew she was attractive, although not a walking Vogue model. She reviewed the lipsticks arrayed on her counter. The classic Dior red to make a statement? Or stick with the understated look and wear the Yves Saint Laurent nude?

The fact that she gave Maricela a moment's thought irritated her. *YSL it is.*

Azalea walked into her office at eight o'clock, coffee in hand. Since her first day in Barcelona, she'd visited La Rosa de Barcelona where she could grab a takeaway cup on her walk to the office. There was a Starbucks around the corner from the apartment, but she always favored local spots when she traveled. She found it far more interesting to explore and taste local brews away from tourists. As usual, Esteban greeted her with a cheerful *hola* and strong Spanish coffee. Some mornings, Azalea would sit at one of the outdoor tables and visit with Denice while they people watched. Today, she headed straight for the office.

Azalea assumed she'd be the only one in so early, so she was surprised to see Jeremy and Maricela already in one of the small glass-walled conference rooms, deep in conversation. They turned as she walked by, Jeremy smiling broadly while Maricela simply lifted one perfect eyebrow. Azalea felt awkward, worried she'd trip or spill her coffee. She smiled, nodded, and tried not to run to her desk. She set her coffee down and opened her laptop bag.

As soon as she booted up, a message appeared from Jeremy: *9:00 still OK?*

Perfect, she replied.

Great. See you then.

Right, she thought. *See you then.*

Azalea stared at her monitor, unable to concentrate. She pulled out her phone and sent a quick message to Susana. It was the middle of the night in Florida, but she knew her best friend would see it first thing in the morning.

Today's the day. He's here and we're meeting in half an hour. Say a prayer for me. It's weird.

She put her phone back down on the desk and opened Jeremy's briefing book. *Concentrate on the event,* she told herself. *Do your job.*

Azalea was deep into the binder of information the PR agency had compiled when Jeremy knocked on her open door. "Nine o'clock, on the dot," he said. "Are you ready for me?"

Azalea brushed aside the double entendre and smiled. "Of course," she said, keeping a professional tone to her voice. "Won't you sit?" She gestured to the small table across from her desk and walked to one of the chairs. "I have your briefing book all ready." She sat down across from Jeremy and opened the book. "I think you'll be very pleased with Ambos—they're your Spanish PR agency and they've done a great job with the prep work." Azalea felt a flicker of pride, pleased that her voice didn't betray her discomfort.

Jeremy hadn't taken his eyes off her. At last, he looked down at the book, a faint smile at the corner of his mouth. "That's great, Azi. Let's see what they've done."

She spent the next thirty minutes going from page to page, describing the schedule of interviews for the following week's launch event. Ambos had been thorough—the day was completely booked, with top European tech journalists and analysts eager to speak to the Fowler Enterprises CEO. Jeremy knew several of them from his years in tech but was eager to make more connections to build his new Spanish business.

"So Timothy Reynolds is coming over from London, huh?" he noted, stopping her from turning a page. His fingers lightly brushed hers, and she willed herself not to jerk her hand away.

"Yes, he's quite keen to meet you. You can see here he's written extensively on American companies coming over to Europe. He'll want to know about the technology, but he'll likely grill you on your hiring practices and what development you'll promote in Spain." Azalea moved her hand to turn the page and pointed at the copy of Reynolds' latest article. "Here's the most recent thing he's written. He's a big fan of the true multinational companies and not so much of anyone he considers an…" she hesitated. "An opportunist," she finished, with a wry smile.

Jeremy sat back in his chair, steepling well-manicured fingers and tilting his head. His grey eyes looked directly at her. "And is that how you see me?" he asked quietly. "As an opportunist?"

Azalea flushed. "Of course not. I know you're always looking for ways to grow your business and I'm sure Seaside Tech meets some long-term strategic objective." Even to her own ears, she sounded stilted and false.

Jeremy leaned forward and she could just catch a faint tendril of the cologne she'd bought him a year ago. "You're right. I'm going to take advantage of every opportunity to achieve my strategic objectives." After a long moment, he sat back and laughed. "I mean, isn't that what a CEO does?" He patted her hand. "C'mon, Azi, don't look so worried. We don't want the rest of the office to think I'm a lousy boss. What else do you have in that magic binder of yours?"

8

Azalea left the office at seven, declining to join the team for dinner again. They went out to eat several nights a week and always asked her to join. She went a few times but relished her evenings alone. She didn't mind working long hours and she enjoyed everyone in the office. But twelve- and fourteen-hour days for weeks on end were enough. Her evenings were the only times she could catch Tomás and Landon, even for a quick chat. She occasionally enjoyed a brief video call with her friends—Lauren and Sara loved spending their weekends at her house and were always quick to show her how well they were keeping up the place, walking around with a phone or laptop to capture the plants flourishing in the lanai.

And since Jeremy had arrived, she was even less likely to go out after work.

Thankfully, he didn't push—he left with the sales team, Denice, Guillermo, and Maricela, offering a simple "See you in the morning." She was grateful not to have to keep up pretenses for another moment.

Tonight she longed to change into workout clothes and hit the beach while the sun was still up, hoping to grab some takeaway for dinner after her run. She planned to spend time on the phone and then take a nice long bath.

After their meeting earlier in the week over the briefing book, Jeremy spent the remainder of the day huddled with various sales team members. There was a palpable urgency to their conversations, obvious even through the glass-walled conference rooms. They stood, gestured, scribbled on the whiteboards, or connected to others via the new video conferencing systems. At one point, as everyone stepped out for a break, Javier popped his head into Azalea's office. "*Dios mio*," he said, shaking his head and widening his eyes. "This guy wants details on *everything*. Whenever I think I have all the data he could possibly ask for, he comes up with *mas preguntas*."

Azalea bit back her reply—very familiar with Jeremy's proclivity for asking tough questions, she was nearly ready to commiserate when she realized it would be a mistake. Instead, she asked, "So is it going all right?"

Javier grinned. "*Si, si, por seguro*. We are going to own this market in a year."

Jeremy and Ricardo walked past her door and noticed Javier smiling at her. "*Deja a la bella en paz*," said Ricardo with a wink. Leave the beauty in peace. Javier smiled at Azalea, shrugged, and followed the men to the conference room.

She was acutely aware of Jeremy's gaze throughout the interaction, although she didn't look directly at him.

The rest of the week went as smoothly as could be expected. Her interactions with Jeremy were professional and he didn't make any more comments that caused her anxiety. He was a seasoned executive and, despite the weight of their past that seemed to hang over every meeting, they worked well together. She knew she was doing a good job preparing him and felt confident the next week would prove her value and confirm the company's decision to engage her.

She realized with a start that she was actually enjoying their time together.

The one person she didn't enjoy was Maricela. At every opportunity, the woman found a way to get under her skin. Her sly looks and snide comments when they were alone never seemed bad enough for Azalea to confront. "What a cute little dress, Azahhhlea," she cooed one day, overdoing the accent when pronouncing Azalea's name in Spanish. "You aren't going to wear that to the launch, are you?" Her overblown politeness and backhanded praise when they were around others made them think she was truly complimentary. "Azahhhlea is such a, how should I say it? A *workhorse*," she said to the table one day at a team lunch. "Thank God she's alone here in Spain and can spend all her time and energy making sure we look good at the launch." It was maddening, and Azalea felt constantly outgunned. Maricela was gorgeous, smart, fluent in Spanish, and had everyone eating out of her hand. And the way she fawned over Jeremy.…

Once everyone had left for dinner, Azalea packed up her laptop bag and reached under her desk for her purse. As she sat up, she saw Maricela walking back into the lobby. Their eyes met as Jeremy's assistant strode into her office. Even at the end of the day, the woman was immaculate. Today she wore yet another perfectly fitted sheath, this one in a deep wine color. She placed her hands on Azalea's desk, leaning down as her gold bangles clanked lightly. Maricela looked directly at Azalea as she spoke.

"You don't have to keep avoiding him, you know," she said. "I don't have any problem with you being around him. And it starts to look strange if you won't join the group after hours."

You don't have any problem? thought Azalea. She stood, eyes narrowed. *That's it. I am done with this.*

"Maricela," she began in a conversational tone, proud that her voice didn't quaver, "Let me be very clear: I'm not avoiding anyone. I don't have any idea why you are somehow privy to anything about my personal life, but I don't intend to have this conversation with you again. I keep my personal and professional lives separate, both here and in the States. I will join the group when and if I decide to and that does not happen to be today." She stepped around her desk, settling her bag over her shoulder and looking directly at the taller woman. "And now, if you'll excuse me, I'm leaving."

Maricela lifted a perfectly arched eyebrow and gazed at Azalea as if seeing her for the first time. "But of course," she said, stepping aside and sweeping her arm toward the door. "*Que tengas un buen noche.*"

She spun and flounced out, not looking back as Azalea locked the door to her office.

Azalea closed her eyes briefly, then turned to leave. *Damn right I'll have a good night.*

It was beach time.

After a good hard run on the beach, she took her shoes off and walked in the surf until the sun went down. She treated herself to an Uber ride back to the apartment and had a long talk with Susana. Her best friend was furious over Maricela's behavior.

"What a bitch," she snapped. "They deserve each other."

Azalea laughed but grew serious. "It's weird, Suze," she said. "Now that we're not together, he's so much better. It's like there's a level of respect he didn't have before."

"So respectful he *buys* you and then flaunts his hootchie in front of you every day?" asked Susana, scorn dripping from her voice.

"Yeah, you're right." She laughed. "And he still calls me 'Azi.'"

Susana snorted. "That will never stop bugging me."

Azalea showered and dressed, pulling her hair into a rough bun. She replayed her conversation with Susana and felt sure of herself, confident she could maintain a professional relationship with Jeremy. It did rankle that he called her Azi, though. Azalea never went by anything other than her full name. Her parents named both of their children after plants they loved. Her father told stories of the huge azalea bushes in Mexico where he grew up. Her mother, with her Celtic heritage, loved the symbolism of the rowan, known as the tree of life. Azalea and her brother Rowan never shortened their names.

But Jeremy insisted on calling her Azi. He explained that it was a term of endearment and she gave in, rationalizing that he loved her and it was special to him. But it never stopped bothering her. She shook her head, dismissing the thought. *It doesn't matter. It's just work with us now.*

Azalea picked up her book but after reading the same paragraph three times, she realized she wasn't in the mood for reading. As she sipped her wine, Azalea thought again about Jeremy. Clearly, he'd moved on and found someone else.

But why did it have to be her? she thought, surprised to care. Maricela was completely different from her. Azalea knew she was attractive, but Maricela was stunning. While Azalea relied on brains and hard work, Maricela didn't hesitate to use her physical attributes—the woman exuded sensuality. Every day she came to work in a dress that seemed to have been molded to her curves, never wobbling on the sky-high heels that were a part of her daily outfit. Her hair was luxurious and deep brown, nearly black, hanging in gorgeous waves down her back. Her makeup was perfect, her lipstick never escaping the neatly drawn lines around her Cupid's bow.

Azalea set down her wine glass, hard enough that the wine sloshed onto the table.

It's all business from here on out. I'm not wasting another thought on her.

Azalea awoke the next morning determined to put Maricela out of her mind.

She was walking to the office when someone touched her elbow. She spun quickly, ready to respond to the ever-present pickpocket threat. Jeremy threw up his hands—"Whoa, tiger!" he laughed. "It's just me."

Azalea flushed. "Sorry," she muttered. "I just thought—"

"I know, I know," he responded, looking around. "It's gotten bad around here. I'm glad you're cautious. I'd hate to be the idiot who tried to steal *your* purse," he laughed. They resumed walking, and Azalea gradually relaxed over the ten-minute stroll.

"Azi," he began, "I know it probably looked weird, even bad, when I bought the company. I won't lie to you: I knew you were managing the Barcelona office opening. But that's not the reason Fowler acquired Seaside Technologies. We'd been looking into a Spanish expansion for over a year—you probably remember that."

Azalea nodded. Jeremy had been obsessed for months over talks with a company in Madrid that had ultimately fallen apart.

Jeremy continued, glancing at her as they maneuvered their way across the plaza. "I can imagine it must be awkward, but I appreciate how professional you've been. I wish you'd consider staying on permanently."

She stopped and looked at her former fiancé, the man she once thought she'd love forever. "You know I can't do that, Jeremy," she said. "It's not good for either of us." She looked back the way they'd come and saw Maricela turn the corner, coming their way. "And I'm pretty sure it's not good for your girlfriend."

Jeremy looked back and saw Maricela. He turned to Azalea, "It's nothing like what we had, Azi. *Nothing*. No one can ever replace you." Azalea stared at him, unsure how to respond. Just then, Maricela joined them and slipped her arm through Jeremy's, kissing him on the cheek. "You left early, *querido*. I didn't realize you needed to be in the office so soon." She looked sideways at Azalea through her long lashes, still speaking to Jeremy, but clearly intending the message for Azalea. "I thought we could sleep in a bit today."

"You know," said Azalea with a tight smile, "I think I'll grab a quick coffee before I get to my desk. Either of you want anything? I'll be back shortly." She took a step in the direction of La Rosa de Barcelona as she finished talking, looking over her shoulder, eager to get away from the palpable discomfort. Jeremy shook his head, but Maricela answered. "I don't need anything, Azaaahlea." As usual, she drawled out Azalea's name in languid diphthongs. "I have what I need."

Azalea turned away, rolling her eyes and taking a deep breath as she willed herself not to run.

Susana is right: What a bitch.

Azalea sat at a table outside the café, not ready to go to the office after her run-in with Maricela and her confusing conversation with Jeremy. She set her bag on the chair next to her, pulling it close enough for safety. Frazzled, she had walked into the café and ordered her typical *cafecito con leche y azucar* and then decided to add some *pan dulce*. Esteban smiled as he rang up her purchase, calling out, "*Señorita?*" when, distracted, she walked off without her pastry. She walked back to the counter with a rueful smile and noticed a stack of Catalonia Today, an English-language paper on the counter. "*Cuánto cuesta?*" she asked him.

"For you, Azalea? Nothing today. You look like you're having a hard morning," he answered with a kind smile. She closed her eyes briefly and nodded.

"You know me too well, Esteban," she said, smiling slightly. "*Muchisimas gracias*." She took the paper and went outside.

Once settled, she opened the paper, dipped her *concha* into the steaming mug, and finally felt her heart rate slow. She scanned the front page of the paper, determined to put everything in her mind on hold, if only for a few minutes.

The headline at the top of the page read, "Talks Falter as Pro-Separatists Plan for Midday Protest." Barcelona had seen its share of usually peaceful protests over the years, with the pro-separatists gaining in popularity in the region. While many in Catalonia remained loyal to the crown, there were enough who yearned for a separate nation, apart from Spain. And now it appeared they were going to protest in the square outside her office.

On the same day as her big event.

9

Azalea continued reading, her mind racing. There was no way to hold a launch event with a protest going on outside. Even if it didn't get messy, the noise would carry to the office and the attendees would have an uncomfortable walk through the plaza, whichever way they came. She was sipping the last of her coffee when her phone rang. It was Lorena from Ambos.

"Lorena," she began, "Did you see the news about the demonstration?"

Lorena sighed. "*Sí*, Azalea. Such terrible timing! I can't believe they couldn't wait until next week!" Her rich accent was melodious and beautiful even when she was clearly upset. "We have analysts coming from all over but some of them called already this morning—they don't want to be here during a protest."

"I'm not sure I do either," confessed Azalea. "So what do we do?"

Azalea's phone buzzed and she looked at the screen. *When are you coming to the office?* read the text from Jeremy. *We have a problem.*

"Hang on one second, Lorena," said Azalea. She typed quickly into her phone: *Already on it. Be there soon.*

"Okay," she told Lorena. "I'm guessing we will try to reschedule, but what's the downside of that?"

Azalea and Lorena talked for thirty minutes, half of Azalea's pastry lying untouched as they strategized. They knew Fowler Enterprises was counting on this event making headlines across the European tech press and giving the company a jumpstart with customers. They worked hard to cover every eventuality—but they hadn't planned for this. Azalea wondered why Ambos hadn't considered the possibility when Lorena suddenly apologized.

"I know we haven't worked together long, Azalea, but it is important that you and Fowler Enterprises can trust our recommendations. When we are in Barcelona, we always take into account the possibility of demonstrations. But things have been relatively quiet lately and the talks have been positive." She paused, considering. "My brother is part of the pro-separatist movement," she said finally. "Please don't share that with anyone. I usually know what's happening through him, but even he said this is a last-minute thing."

Azalea was glad she hadn't lambasted the account executive. "It's okay," she said. "We'll just have to figure it out. How many journalists and analysts will we lose if we postpone the event by a week?"

Lorena laughed. "You know these tech guys. We're offering a chance to spend the day in Barcelona with food, gifts, and access to the new CEO and the sales VP. They'll grumble about their schedules and their valuable time, but I'm pretty sure none of them is going to miss out on this opportunity."

Azalea picked up her bag and began walking to the office, still talking to Lorena. The situation wasn't dire—it just wasn't optimal. She went into problem-solving mode and soon hung up with a solid plan. Yet even in the midst of it all, her mind flitted back to that morning's conversation with Jeremy: *No one can ever replace you.*

Not now, she told herself sternly. *Solve the problem, fix the mess, concentrate on what's important.*

But she wondered what that truly was.

Azalea strode into the office with a brief nod and smile at Guillermo. She tossed her bag on the chair and opened her laptop, mentally reviewing the list of items to handle first. She needed to talk with Denice and Guillermo to reschedule the catering, and work with Ricardo to rebook the potential clients anticipating customized demos.

She looked up as Jeremy walked in, frowning. "So you heard," he said.

"Yes," she answered, her voice authoritative. "Lorena and Ambos are all over it. We've had several analysts and reporters calling this morning to cancel. We'll retrench and hold the event in a week. It won't be great, but it will be fine."

Jeremy grimaced as he sat down across from her. *He hates anything that takes him off stride*, thought Azalea. She reached across the desk to touch his hand. "It'll be okay, babe," she started, then jerked her hand back, eyes wide. "I mean…I…Jeremy—"

His eyes narrowed and he leaned forward. "You mean what, Azi?" he asked quietly.

Azalea briefly closed her eyes to gather herself. What had she been thinking?

"I'm so sorry," she answered. "I don't know where that came from. Please forgive me. Let's just get to work—"

"I hope I know where that came from," Jeremy interrupted. He rubbed his hand along his jaw. "Can we go for a walk? Just for a bit?"

Azalea cursed herself for a fool. Seeing him nonplussed seemed to stir compassion in her, but why the sudden intimacy? She was about to respond when Maricela entered.

"Zheremy, we need you in the conference room. Ricardo is losing his mind over this—" she glanced sideways at Azalea, "this *fiasco*. It looks really bad to the customers." Her tone made it clear she was eager to place the blame squarely on Azalea. "*Ven conmigo, querido.* Let's fix this."

Jeremy looked at Maricela, expressionless. He looked back at Azalea and stood. "Let me know what you think," he said, clearly referring to more than the protest. "I'll be in with Ricardo." He stood and followed Maricela but stopped at the door to Azalea's office. He turned and said, "I trust you, Azi. This will all work out, I'm certain."

Azalea nodded as two thoughts struck her.

What just happened?
Susana is going to kill me.

The day flew by as Azalea and Lorena worked the phones calling all the invitees to the launch event. Thankfully, most were able to reschedule to ensure they could attend and were understanding about the circumstances. Azalea spoke to Timothy Reynolds personally to assuage any bad feelings about the delay.

"Not brilliant to launch in Barcelona, eh?" he asked Azalea. "You'll want a proper opening without those beastly terrorists around. Why couldn't you have chosen Madrid or Seville?" Azalea declined to let the conversation devolve into a political debate over the Spanish monarchy and the separatist movement. She assured Timothy that Fowler Enterprises believed Barcelona was the best choice, with access to talented software developers, a strong economy, and an excellent standard of living. "I do realize this is inconvenient, Timothy," she soothed. "I'll be certain to carve out extra time for your one-on-one interview with our new CEO. I know he's keen to meet you and discuss his plans for the European market in general and the Spanish market in particular."

The British journalist sighed and responded halfheartedly. "It's all a bit rubbish, but I'll be there." Azalea thanked him and hung up, rolling her eyes at Reynolds's ego and put upon airs. It was the last phone call of the morning and she was looking forward to getting outdoors for a walk along Las Ramblas. She wasn't hungry and decided she'd grab a coffee and just wander for a bit to clear her head. Closing her eyes, she kneaded her temples, slumping slightly in her chair.

"Hard day?" asked Jeremy gently, leaning against her door.

Azalea opened her eyes and folded her hands in front of her, tapping the backs of her thumbs against her lips. Jeremy sat in the chair across the desk and said, "I know that gesture. Someone giving you a hard time?" He started as if to reach for her hand, but stopped, rubbing his palms together and looking out the glass wall of her office. Azalea sat still, unsure of her response.

"This is much harder than I imagined," he said quietly.

"It doesn't have to be. Yes, we have a history. But we're working together now and we can be, I don't know…friends sounds kind of stupid, I guess. And colleagues sounds far too cold. Maybe we just need to make up something ourselves—something that works for us."

"You called me 'Babe,' Azi."

"I know, I know…. I'm sorry for that. I saw that you were upset and it just sort of popped out. I didn't mean to cause you pain or confusion—please believe me."

He looked at her for a long moment. "I believe you. I just want to believe there was more to it." Jeremy stood. "I think you do, too."

Azalea frowned and briefly closed her eyes. "Jeremy, we aren't good for each other. You need someone who is one hundred percent behind you, whatever you want, and doesn't feel like she's losing herself in the process." She sighed. "That's not me."

"I can be different, Azi. I don't need you to give up your dreams or your personality or anything to be with me. I see you here and I recognize how strong you are—how phenomenal a partner you are. I don't know how I missed it before, but I see it now." He ran a hand through his hair. "I know we're swamped with the launch and I'm buried with trying to make this acquisition successful. But we can take some time to talk, can't we? Why don't you have dinner with me tonight?"

Azalea looked down, folded her hands, then resumed the tapping on her lips. One part of her wanted to believe him—that he had truly changed, that he saw her differently and would be a different partner. As much as she was forging a successful life alone, she missed being a couple. In the space of seconds, her emotions oscillated between annoyance—*How did he miss it before?*—and longing.

It would be so easy to let him love me.

She thought again about Susana's warning and she wondered how her sons would take it if she reignited her relationship with Jeremy. And what about Maricela? She and Jeremy were living together in the corporate apartment—she'd made that abundantly clear to Azalea only that morning. Azalea's ex-husband had cheated on her and the thought of doing that—even to someone she detested as much as Maricela—was loathsome.

Her mind made up, Azalea looked up at Jeremy and shook her head. "No, Jeremy. Go home to Maricela and let's keep working on getting this company launched."

His face tightened and he nodded once. He looked as if he were about to say something, but instead turned abruptly and walked out of her office.

Azalea managed to avoid Jeremy for the remainder of the day, closeting herself with Denice and Guillermo as they finalized the details of the rescheduled event. While she was disappointed to wait a week, she was pleased with the work everyone had done. Lorena joined the three of them on a conference call and assured them Ambos was on top of all the communications with journalists. Short of a catastrophe at the protest, they should be ready for a great launch the following week.

"I was pretty excited about tomorrow," said Guillermo. "We've been gearing up for this for so long, it feels weird to be just another Friday."

Denice and Azalea nodded as the two interns knocked on the door. Azalea waved them in, and the team sat around the conference table to discuss the social media posts they'd prepared. She approved the week's posts just as Maricela walked into the conference room.

"Jeremy has an announcement for the staff," she said, her eyes taking in each of them. *Funny how she says his name without her accent when she's not taunting me*, thought Azalea. "Come out to the lobby," finished Maricela, and left the conference room without waiting for a response.

Denice looked at Azalea with raised eyebrows as they stood and left the conference room. Ricardo and Javier sat in the lobby chairs while Maricela stood at Jeremy's side. The two interns walked behind Azalea, clearly uncomfortable at being called into a meeting with *el jefe*. Denice and Guillermo took the remaining chairs, but Azalea remained standing.

"Don't look so worried," started Jeremy with a smile. "I know we were all looking forward to tomorrow's launch, but waiting a week isn't going to kill us. In fact, I've decided to give everyone the day off. It's gonna be crazy here tomorrow. There won't just be protesters. The press will be here, the police will be here, and plenty of people will just come to watch." He looked around the room, noting the surprised smiles all around. "We've all been working crazy hours preparing and I appreciate the incredible work each of you has done." He looked directly at Azalea. "You all deserve a day off." He looked at his watch. "And since it's already almost six o'clock, let's just pretend we're in the States and get out of here. I'll see you all bright and early on Monday."

Azalea turned to the interns, both of whom were grinning. "You heard him," she said. "Go enjoy a long weekend!"

The two mumbled a brief *Gracias* and quickly went to retrieve their things. Azalea turned to walk toward Denice but was intercepted by Maricela. "Enjoy your weekend, Azahhhlea," she purred. "I'm sure you can find something interesting to do. We'll be in Madrid—the jet leaves in an hour."

Azalea stared at the woman for a long moment and then couldn't restrain herself. She burst out laughing. "That's great," she said, covering her mouth to suppress her giggles. Azalea shook her head and walked away. *What on earth does he see in that woman?* she marveled.

As she packed her things, Denice came into her office to say goodbye. "Doing anything fun with your day off?"

"I've been trying to get to La Sagrada Familia for months," Azalea answered. "Looks like tomorrow's the day. I'm hoping the crowd won't be too bad and I can get in without waiting in line for hours."

"You can buy those 'skip-the-line' tours online," said Denice.

Azalea frowned. "Yeah, but I don't want to do a tour. I just want to wander around on my own. Maybe I'll get there before all the Spaniards get out of bed and get my ticket early enough to beat the crowd," she laughed. "I'll take a book and a cup of coffee and I'll be fine." She finished collecting her things and walked out the door with Denice. "I haven't been there in a decade and I'm eager to see the progress." Denice smiled, looking aside as Jeremy approached them. She looked back at Azalea. "Have a good time," she said, then nodded at Jeremy. "Thanks again for the day off, *jefe*," she joked.

"Have a good one, Denice. Thanks for everything." She waved at them and headed for the door.

Jeremy asked Azalea, "Do you have a minute?"

"I do," she answered. "But it doesn't sound like you do. Don't you need to get to your plane?"

He looked down then back to Azalea. "We talked about a trip to Madrid quite a while ago," he started. "Now that the launch is postponed—"

"Jeremy," she broke in. "Go enjoy your weekend." She took a deep breath. "You have your life. Bring me back a bottle of wine and have a good time. We'll get through this and all will be well."

They stood awkwardly, unsure how to end the conversation. *It feels like we should be hugging it out*, she thought.

"When will this get easier?" asked Jeremy. "I feel like I should be hugging you." They stared at each other.

"Have a good time," repeated Azalea roughly, surprised to find tears pricking her eyes. *Why am I crying?* Confused, she turned away, determined not to let him see.

She saw Maricela out of the corner of her eye as she walked back to her office. She slumped in her chair and dabbed at her eyes. *I'm just tired*, she lied. *I need a nice weekend to decompress.*

There's nothing else going on.

10

Azalea slept fitfully and rose early. She showered, made her coffee, and curled up in her favorite chair. As she sipped her morning brew, Azalea reflected on her emotional reaction of the previous evening.

Jeremy clearly was conflicted over his relationship with Maricela…and with her. *Or maybe not so conflicted*, she thought. He was making it more and more apparent that he wanted more from her. *But what do I want?* Azalea was uncompromising when it came to cheating: If Jeremy were involved with Maricela, she would never cross that line. But if he were free?

Everything always had to be his way, she remembered. He was never rude, just insistent. They didn't argue. Jeremy had a way of subtly yet firmly directing them to his way of thinking. She thought again about his relationship with Maricela. Did the fact that they had a sexual relationship change things? Did he listen to her in ways he hadn't listened to Azalea?

She knew she'd given in too many times, rationalizing that his decisions were minor, that Jeremy was the one sacrificing because of her insistence on celibacy. She wondered, not for the first time, what their life would have been like had she gone to his bed the first time he'd asked.

She wondered if Maricela ever had a second thought before agreeing.

What had he said? *It's nothing like what we had, Azi. Nothing. No one can ever replace you.*

Azalea stepped out of the taxi and approached the Nativity façade. It was nine-thirty, later than she planned to arrive, but still early enough that the line wasn't terribly long. She dressed for a cool day—the forecast said no rain, but the morning would be chilly enough for jeans and a light sweater. As she waited in line to go through security, she checked her phone for messages she'd received while she slept.

Tomás had sent a photo of his new girlfriend's puppy, a little ball of fluff they rescued from the shelter, only three months old. Landon texted to tell her the new Denver account was *Blowing up, Mom—I'm killing it here!* There were messages from Lauren and Sara telling her that her favorite next door neighbor was moving and they found a new restaurant on Canal Street they knew she'd love. Azalea smiled, glad to connect, albeit hours later and only onscreen, with her loved ones.

The Basilica had changed dramatically in the ten years since she last visited. The soaring ceilings and intricate details took her breath away. She wandered throughout the sanctuary, content to be one of the crowd, lingering whenever something struck her curiosity. She loved listening to the various languages—thousands of tourists from all over the world visited the magnificent cathedral every year. Azalea had been a tourist herself on two previous occasions, but the massive amount of work done between each of her trips to Barcelona made it feel brand new each time. At one point, she stood for what seemed hours, mesmerized by the otherworldly sunlight streaming through the stained glass. She marveled at the work required to sculpt the Passion façade with its intricate figures. The day passed slowly and serenely, the peace of the church soothing her.

Azalea decided to take the elevator to the bell tower on the Nativity façade. The only tower built by Gaudí, it had been closed to the public on her last visit. She knew she'd have to take the narrow, winding stairs back down, but it was worth it to see the breathtaking view of Barcelona, a city she'd come to love.

As she rode the cramped elevator, Azalea glanced at a young couple wedged closely next to her, clearly oblivious to anyone else around. The man's arms were around the woman's waist and his hands were in her back pockets. She looked up at him and whispered in Spanish, too quietly for Azalea to catch the words. The young man laughed, pulling her closer. She turned her head so her cheek rested on his chest and her eyes met Azalea's.

Azalea smiled, inclining her head at the young couple. Then she looked away, unwilling to further intrude on their private moment. The elevator doors opened, and she hurried out, suddenly and keenly aware of her aloneness. She hurried up the narrow staircase to reach the observation area. As she gazed out over the beautiful city, she thought how much Tomás and Landon would enjoy seeing it. Before she left Florida, they had talked about coming to visit her. But then Tomás met a girl and Landon started his new job. *They have their own lives*, she thought. *I have to make a life of my own.*

She glanced at the young couple from the elevator as they likewise looked out over the city. The woman leaned her head on his shoulder, her arm wrapped around his waist. He draped his arm around her and leaned down to gently kiss the top of her head. The tenderness of his kiss struck Azalea and she felt a profound sadness. *What would it be like to share this moment with someone special?* she wondered. The beauty of the city, the bright blue sky, the kaleidoscope of the stained glass…. Experiences so deep were meant to be shared, weren't they?

Azalea thought about Jeremy and Maricela. Were they somewhere sharing a magical moment like this? She remembered the last time she'd been in Madrid—the palpable energy on the streets, the incredible food and music. What would it be like to walk those vibrant streets hand in hand with someone she loved?

Love is not for me.

Steeling herself, she turned and made her way back to the narrow staircase, its walls uncomfortably close. *How many damn stairs are there?* she thought crossly as she hurried to leave the young couple behind. She'd seen enough for one day.

Azalea made it back to the apartment, feeling empty. She dropped her purse on the counter, walked into her bedroom and flung herself on the bed. Her heart was heavy and she hated the feeling of weakness.

She tapped the speed dial for Susana.

"'*Mana!*" Susana's voice nearly shouted in her ear. "Why are you calling me so early? *Como estas?* I miss you so much."

Azalea crawled backward on her bed, plumped up the pillows behind her head, leaned back, and answered. "I'm okay, I guess," she said.

"Girl, who do you think you're lying to?" answered Susana. "What happened? What's wrong now?"

Azalea thought a moment before answering. "Nothing's really happened," she answered finally. "And nothing's really wrong. I think I'm just homesick. Jeremy gave everyone the day off because of the protest today and I went to La Sagrada Familia."

Susana's *mmhmm* made it clear she was waiting for something more.

"Anyway, it was beautiful, as usual. But it struck me that it would have been so much more meaningful if I were sharing the day with someone special." Azalea took a deep breath. "And Jeremy is in Madrid for the weekend with Maricela—"

"You have got to be kidding me, Azalea," broke in Susana. "You have some epiphany about not being alone and your very next sentence is about that jackass?" Azalea sat up at her best friend's caustic tone. "Look, I get that you were engaged to the guy, but you broke it off for a reason." Susana was clearly upset. "I warned you,'*mana*. I warned you to stay clear of him. He's a snake and a charmer and a manipulative jerk. Dammit, Azalea! Are you seriously thinking about him again?"

Tears began to run down her cheeks as Azalea answered. "I know he's not right for me, Suze. I do. I know it was the right thing to break it off. And he has a new relationship—it's not even a possibility on so many levels." She reached for a tissue on the nightstand. "I'm sorry. I don't want to disappoint you—"

"Forget about disappointing *me*," responded Susana with a quiet laugh. "Worry about disappointing yourself. You deserve someone who treats you like a queen, who respects everything from your intelligence to your kindness, and who doesn't think it's his job to program every detail of your life!" Susana's tone grew more animated as she spoke. "So what if he's handsome? So what if he's rich? He is not a good man, Azalea." Susana finished her last sentence slowly, punctuating each word.

"Do you think people can change, Suze?"

Susana hesitated. "I do, but it's hard for me to imagine him being any different."

"I know—I'm not naive. But he genuinely is acting differently toward me." She sighed. "It doesn't matter. He's in a relationship and I'm just being stupid."

"You're not stupid, Azalea. I think you're just lonely." Susana chuckled. "I think you need to go find some hot Spaniard and fall crazy in love."

Azalea opened her mouth to respond when she heard Susana speaking to Enrique. "Sorry, honey—I have to go. We need to drop Kique's car at the shop and we're already late."

Azalea chuckled, well used to her friend's casual relationship with time. "It's okay, thanks for listening to me. Give your man a hug for me."

Susana parted with, "You know I love you like a sister, Azalea. I don't mean to hurt you. Go buy a new bikini and hit the beach. Find that hot Spaniard!" The two friends promised to talk again in a few days, and Azalea lay back against the pillows, her thoughts swirling.

She awoke to a dark room, still dressed in her clothes. She'd fallen asleep for several hours—it was midnight and she was disoriented. She undressed and put on pajama shorts and a tank top, brushed her teeth, and climbed under the covers. She felt certain she'd struggle to go back to sleep but soon was in deep, dreamless slumber.

11

Azalea woke early. It was the day after the protest, and she hoped the shops were open with no problems. It was her usual day to buy food for the week. She loved the energy of the market, the richness of the Catalan language, the vivid colors of the booths. Hundreds of people crowded the *Boqueria*, stopping to look at the beautiful displays of vegetables, fruits, cheeses, and meats, or just to visit with friends they might encounter. It was her favorite way to spend a Saturday morning and she hoped it would refresh her spirit.

Azalea washed her face, pulled her hair back into a ponytail, and put on casual clothes. She grabbed a shopping bag and headed for the market.

After an hour of lingering among the stalls, she finished her shopping and put everything away in her kitchen. She put the *gambas* in the refrigerator, planning to sauté them that evening in white wine. The shrimp in Barcelona were so fresh, far tastier than anything she'd ever eaten, even living at the beach in the States. She toyed with making paella, but realized she could never eat the whole thing, even in a week, and it wasn't worth the trouble to make a small batch. Shrimp and vegetables it was, then. She decided to head back to the plaza for a late breakfast of coffee and some *pan dulce*.

The café was busy but she found an empty table outside. She dipped her *marranito* into her coffee and took a satisfied bite. The little pig-shaped pastry had been her favorite as a child, and she was delighted to find them in Barcelona. Azalea giggled as a drip of coffee ran down her chin, and she hastened to dab it with a napkin. *Servilleta*, she corrected herself, determined to practice her Spanish. She looked around the broad street, content to relax and observe. There was no indication there had been a political rally the day before. Shops were open and people bustled everywhere. *The worst day in Barcelona still beats the best day just about anywhere else*, she mused.

She finished eating and headed back to the apartment. It was after one o'clock already—*Where did the morning go?* she thought in surprise. She decided to head to the beach for a quick power walk. She didn't feel like running after eating her sweets, but she thought a brisk walk in the surf would do her good.

As she rounded the corner toward the corporate apartment complex, she saw a tall woman walk out of the lobby and climb into a waiting taxi. It was too quick to be sure, but Azalea thought she looked like Maricela. *Don't be ridiculous*, she chided herself. *Maricela is in Madrid with Jeremy.* Surely she was mistaken.

Azalea changed quickly and walked the fifteen minutes to the beach. She slipped off her running shoes and stepped into the surf, feeling the warmth of the water even in the springtime. She began her walk, looking around at hundreds of people enjoying the unseasonably warm weather.

She walked nearly three miles up and down the beach and wished she'd worn her swimsuit. The afternoon sun was warm and she was sure she was getting tan lines from her shorts and tank top. She decided to go back to the apartment, change into a bikini, and come back to lie out in the sun. It would stay light for several hours and she had nothing else to do. *This is when it's not so bad to be alone*, she thought. *No one else to consider—just me.* She determined to put a good spin on her situation and hailed a taxi to take her quickly back to the apartment.

Once in her room, the thought of a nap lured her, but she decided she could always sleep on the beach. Spritzing sunscreen on her chest, she looked at herself in the mirror. Tired eyes looked back—her fitful night's rest wasn't enough to overcome her weariness and sadness. *A beach nap is just the thing*, she decided and headed back to the taxi stand.

The sun had begun its downward arc when she got back to the beach but was still warm. She spread her towel on the sand and was asleep before she knew it.

She walked downstairs, yawning. It was dark outside, but she knew the sun would rise soon and she needed to get the baking done in time for her early customers. She turned on the lights in the kitchen and started the coffee first so she'd have the chance to wake up a bit. Today would be hearty brunch casseroles, cranberry scones, and the new bread pudding recipe she'd found. As she set up her ingredients and tools, she smiled, knowing her customers would purchase every single thing she made this morning, despite everything being foreign and unusual to their Spanish palates. Being American and baking different foods had meant a slow start to her shop but she had relentlessly won over her little village. Esteban had been a huge help, cajoling the viejas, *flirting shamelessly with the venerable white-haired neighborhood matriarchs. She didn't know what she'd have done if she hadn't met him shortly after moving into the combination flat and café, naively determined to build a small business. Her family had thought she was crazy, but it had become her passion and after a year, she'd completely woven her life into her new community.*

Esteban joined her in the kitchen, kissing her lightly on the cheek then sliding the apron over his head. "Demasiado temprano," he said, stifling a yawn.

"You shouldn't have kept us up so late," she replied, ruffling his hair and pulling him in for a passionate kiss.

Azalea jerked awake. That was the same café she dreamed about before she came to Barcelona—and the same Esteban. She wished she could keep his face in her memory, but both times it seemed to disappear. He was tall and dark, she knew. But beyond that? Azalea blew out a long breath and took a drink of water. *Dios mio…I need a swim after that*, she thought with a laugh.

Looking about her, Azalea noticed fewer people on the beach than when she arrived. The air was beginning to cool, although the sand still felt warm beneath her and she decided to get in the ocean before it grew too cold. A woman stood in the shallows nearby, wearing only a fuchsia Brazilian-cut bikini bottom. Her hair was piled on top of her head, and she walked slowly into the water. Azalea wondered if she'd ever have the courage to go topless on a Barcelona beach—or to wear the thong so many of the Spanish women wore. She watched as the woman dove into the waves, only to surface a few yards farther. She stood and decided to follow her example.

As Azalea walked to the water, the woman turned and began walking back to the sand. Her hair had come undone and hung in loose curls across her shoulders. Her perfect breasts were as bronzed as the rest of her, and her long legs covered the distance between them slowly. It was like watching a Sports Illustrated cover shoot and Azalea suddenly felt ugly and out of place.

Maricela.

Azalea forced herself to continue walking to the water, keenly aware of her thudding heartbeat. *What was Maricela doing in Barcelona—especially at my beach?* she thought. *And why do I let her fluster me like this?*

The two women stopped a few feet from each other. Maricela made a show of looking up and down at Azalea, clearly contemptuous. "I didn't want to disturb your beauty rest," she said at last. "I'm sure you need every minute."

Azalea frowned, exasperated. "Maricela, what precisely have I ever done to you? You've been rude and condescending since the day we met." She squared her shoulders. "And frankly, it's getting old."

Maricela looked coolly at Azalea. "Don't play games, Azalea," she said, without the usual taunting drawl. "Thanks to you, Jeremy and I are through and I'm sure you aren't surprised. I should be marrying him but instead I'm out here at this godforsaken beach by myself." Even in her fury, Maricela stood proudly, looking as if she'd materialized from the sea, a mermaid transformed into earthly perfection.

She should be marrying him?

Azalea felt a pang of jealousy but pushed the thought aside. "I *am* surprised, Maricela. And I have nothing to do with your relationship. Jeremy and I have been apart for nearly a year. If your... marriage—" she nearly gagged on the word—"isn't happening, it has nothing to do with me."

Maricela looked skeptical. "You can't possibly be serious. You knew we were back together. Why couldn't you just leave us alone?"

Were those tears on her lashes or water from the ocean?

It was hard to feel anything but anger toward Maricela. A small part of her wanted to feel pity or compassion, but Maricela's petty bullying over the past weeks made it nearly impossible.

Back together?

Azalea stood, puzzled. "What do you mean, 'back together'?"

Maricela shook her head. "Don't play games, Azalea. You know we were together years ago. I helped him build this company—we were together for two years before he met you at that conference." Her composure slipped. "He wasn't the same when he came back and it was clear we were through."

What?

"Maricela," she began, "I had no idea—"

"Spare me," snapped the nearly naked woman, once again in command of her features. "What you knew or didn't know then has nothing to do with now. *We were happy...* and then you have to show up and be the perfect business partner—all smart and ambitious—"

Azalea's patience was exhausted. "I didn't 'show up' anywhere," she retorted. "Your boyfriend bought the company I worked for—I had nothing to do with it. Perhaps you should spend your time talking to him instead of stalking me at the beach.

"I'm going back to my apartment and I'm going to forget about this conversation. We have a lot of work to do this week and I'm going to make sure the launch Friday is perfect. After that, I'm going to spend a month tying up loose ends and then I'm going home." She lifted her chin and repeated, "I'm going home, Maricela."

Azalea turned and walked back to pack her things and head for the apartment. She was far too unsettled to take a cab—she needed the walk.

Jeremy broke up with her? For a second time?
Because of me?

The air was cooling by the time Azalea reached the apartment. She walked into the lobby without sparing a glance at the doorman. She didn't notice his surprised look as she strode past him without her typical smile and wave. As she stood at the elevator door, she shifted her bag to her other shoulder and prayed she wouldn't run into Jeremy.

The almighty must have had other ideas because the elevator door opened and Jeremy stood in front of her, looking at his phone. Azalea took a step back as he looked up, unsure if she should casually enter the lift or run away. His smile lit his face and he was by her in one long stride. "Azi!" he said. "I was just texting you—"

She backed away—*Why is he standing so close?*—and said quietly, "Well, now you don't have to." His smile turned to a puzzled look at her pensive demeanor and she added, "I ran into Maricela at the beach."

He focused long on her before he finally spoke. "I would rather have told you myself." He looked around the lobby, then asked, "Could we go sit somewhere quieter? Or I can come to your apartment, if that's all right with you." Azalea was shaking her head before he finished the sentence.

"I'm exhausted. It's been a very long week and I just want a shower and some sleep." Jeremy reached up and touched her cheek, brushing it lightly with his finger. "You got a little too much sun," he offered. "That always takes something out of you."

Azalea wasn't sure if she were touched or repelled by his intimate comment. He knew her well and how her body reacted to a long day in the sun. She turned her face just enough to move from his hand. "Jeremy," she began.

"Azi, it's okay. We can talk tomorrow. We both have a lot to think about and I won't rush you." He stepped aside and pushed the elevator button, taking her arm to usher her in when the doors opened. "*Señorita*," he intoned with a bow. Azalea stepped into the elevator and turned to look at her former love. "Tomorrow," he said, as if it were a guarantee.

The doors closed and she didn't respond.

12

Azalea walked into her apartment, drained. She tossed her bag on the bed and kicked off her flip-flops, uncaring where they landed. She went straight to the bathroom and started the shower but, before stepping in, turned to look at herself in the full-length mirror on the back of the door. Jeremy was right. She got too much sun. She noticed the fine tan line across her thighs from her shorts, and the pink on her stomach and shoulders. She looked long at her body. Her breasts, never large, seemed smaller now that they were less firm. Middle age hadn't destroyed her looks, but bearing and nursing two babies hadn't done her any favors. Her legs were strong from all her running, but there were faint stretch marks on her hips and thighs. *Thanks, boys*, she thought wryly.

She quickly washed off the sunscreen and sand, then stepped out of the shower, looking again at the mirror.

What does he see in me?

Azalea noted how different she looked from a dripping Maricela. Where Maricela was sexy and curvaceous, Azalea was no nonsense and muscular. Maricela was bronze, while Azalea was more light tan…*and now pink*, she thought humorlessly. Maricela looked like she was born to wear a hot pink thong, while Azalea wondered if she were too old for a two-piece swimsuit every time she put one on.

Once dressed, she was surprised to find she was hungry, but when she opened the refrigerator, she forgot why she was there. Azalea stood staring, vaguely taking in the contents of her morning purchases. Had it really only been this morning that she'd gone to the *mercado*? Nothing sounded good. Instead, she poured a glass of wine and wandered back to the bedroom. For the first time in ages, she thought about her mother. They'd been close until her death from cancer. Azalea called her mom every day the final year, visiting as often as she could, and sharing her life with the woman who always understood her, cheered her on, and loved her without reservation. She missed her mom—how odd that she thought of her now. *I just need someone to talk to*, she realized. She briefly considered calling Susana but dismissed the thought almost immediately. As much as she loved her friend, she wasn't in the mood to be scolded. She wasn't sure what she was in the mood for, but it wasn't that. She thought about calling Sara and Lauren, but they were likely enjoying their weekend on the coast. She didn't want to disrupt them.

Azalea drained her glass and thought about her life. She was content for the most part. She had great friends and an amazing family. She was successful in her career and owned a beautiful cottage at the beach.

But she was lonely. Susana was right: For maybe the first time in her life, she was lonely.

She thought back to the café from her dreams. *If only*, she thought. *If only there really were an Esteban.* She rubbed her hands over her face and sighed.

Jeremy had said they'd talk tomorrow. As always, he sounded very sure of himself, but she felt certain she wasn't ready for that conversation. There were far too many things she needed to process. Maricela's revelation that she and Jeremy had been together previously—and that they'd broken up after Jeremy met Azalea—troubled her. She hadn't known he was involved with anyone when they met.

I didn't exactly ask, she thought.

She frowned at her discomfiture. *I was so peaceful yesterday morning.* Azalea thought again about how she'd felt at the cathedral, standing in the dappled light of the stained glass window. She hadn't been to an actual Sunday morning service since she arrived in Spain. And while she wasn't a particularly regular attender in Florida, she had enjoyed Pastor Steve's sermons once or twice a month. Maybe going to church in the morning would clear her head, give her some perspective.

Her damp hair, partially escaped from her bun, stuck to the back of her neck. She absently brushed at it while she pulled out her laptop and walked back to the kitchen.

Azalea poured another glass of wine and ripped a hunk of bread off the loaf she bought that morning. She booted up her machine and typed *chapels in Las Ramblas* in the Google search bar. La Sagrada Familia was first on the list, but that wasn't in Las Ramblas and she didn't want to go to the massive cathedral.

There. That was it. The International Church of Barcelona, a short walk from her apartment, with English services at nine-thirty. She could sleep in and still be at church on time. *I just need a minute to breathe. It's too much.* Azalea finished her bread and wine and prepared for bed, tired but with a glimmer of optimism.

As she pulled the comforter around her, she resolved to put Jeremy out of her mind for the rest of the night.

She awoke earlier than she hoped but felt rested for the first time in days. She reached for her phone and saw a text from the boys. April in Colorado was still cold, and it snowed the previous day. She laughed as she looked at the photos they sent, all bundled up, standing beside a pathetic-looking snowman.

She winced at the burn on her shoulders as she rolled over, but then laughed again at the juxtaposition with her boys in the snow. How different their lives were! Azalea was grateful for the close relationship with her sons—she marveled at the notion that two grown men still thought enough about their mama to reach out like this. It made her day…and it was only seven o'clock in the morning.

I love this! she typed. *I guess I won't tell you about my sunburn from falling asleep at the beach yesterday.* She finished with a smiley face and a heart, along with *xoxoxo*. A minute later, she received another message from Tomás on their family chat. *Hey, old lady—be careful in the sun! I thought you were there for work, not vacation haha!*

Azalea sat up in bed, smiling broadly. *What are you doing up??? It's 1 am, isn't it?*

Landon chimed in. *We're not in Florida, Mom. It's only 11 in Colorado. We're just hanging out talking and before we knew it, you were texting us. Not that it's any of your business when we go to bed =) And besides, why are you up so early on a Sunday morning?*

Azalea sighed. She missed her sons—their Sunday afternoon dinners had been a highlight of her week. It was the one day she could cook to her heart's content, knowing every bit of the meal would be devoured—or taken to their house as leftovers.

Gonna try an English-language church, she wrote. *I'll let you know how it is.*

Don't text for a few hours, warned Tomás. *I don't want the phone to wake me up!*

Azalea heart swelled. *I love you both to the moon and back.*

Landon responded with *Love you, Mom* while Tomás wrote *Have a great day!*

Azalea walked out of the elevator in the apartment lobby and looked around. She was grateful not to see either Jeremy or Maricela, and she smiled and waved at the doorman as she left the building. The morning air was crisp and she was glad she'd grabbed a scarf to add to her spring coat. She'd changed her mind several times about what to wear, but finally opted for slacks, a light pullover, and flats, knowing she'd be walking for several blocks. She thought briefly about putting in her earbuds and listening to music but decided instead to enjoy the sounds of the city.

She left with plenty of time before the service started and decided to stop for coffee on the way. She stepped into the familiar café and breathed the rich scent of dark roast along with the sweetness of *pan dulce*. Standing behind an elderly couple, she glanced around the room. The low buzz of conversation was soothing, its warm and caressing susurration like a blanket around her.

"*Señorita?*" A voice brought her out of her reverie and she looked up at the man behind the counter. Azalea frowned, suddenly disoriented. How did she know him? He wasn't Esteban. She approached the counter and spoke hesitantly, still unsure. "*Ah...cafecito con leche y azucar, por favor.*" She looked at the man again, her mind running through her months in Barcelona. "*Takeaway,*" she added.

She paid the handsome man and stepped aside to await her order. She didn't mean to stare but kept glancing up as he waited on the people in line. When her drink was ready, he looked over at her and smiled. "*Que tengas un buen dia,*" he said, holding out her cup.

"*Muchas gracias,*" replied Azalea. And in a flash, she remembered. He'd held the door open for her on her first day in Barcelona. Did he work here?

She walked back to the main thoroughfare, thinking back to her first day in Spain. She wondered what had happened between Esteban and the woman. *What was her name? Gloria?* Azalea thought about the argument she'd witnessed at the airport. Esteban had clearly been embarrassed while Gloria was fiery and angry. Azalea had never had a relationship where she'd flown off the handle like that. She couldn't even imagine raising her voice, especially not in such a public place. She was too self-controlled for that.

Or maybe she had just never cared enough.

What must it be like to be so passionate about someone that you'd come unglued like that, even in public? Azalea wasn't cold or reserved. She could be warm and loving with friends and family. She'd even been that way with Jeremy. But she'd never just let go, whether in anger or love or any passionate expression. As she finished her coffee, she wondered why. *Am I unable to feel that deeply? Is there something wrong with me?* Or had she not found the right relationship?

It doesn't matter, she reminded herself firmly. *Love is not for me.*

She frowned at her inner turmoil. Between her exhaustion and her roller coaster emotions, she was a mess. She turned onto the street where the church stood and saw dozens of people entering, mostly young adults, although there were families, too. Azalea wondered if she should walk back to the apartment or go for a long walk on the beach to clear her head. Once again, she felt the powerful pang of being alone, wishing she were walking into the sanctuary with someone. She thought about the couple at La Sagrada Familia and wondered if they attended church together. Or maybe they were still sound asleep, taking advantage of a lazy Sunday morning.

Azalea realized she was just standing in front of the church—how long had she been there nursing these idle thoughts? She straightened her shoulders and climbed the steps.

The worship band had begun playing and the music was contemporary and familiar. The greeter at the door shook her hand with a hearty "Good morning!" and a smile. Azalea noted the woman's name tag—the shiny metal rectangle read *Leticia Duran* in dark letters. "Thank you, Leticia," she answered and walked into the sanctuary.

She found a seat toward the back, sitting along the aisle. As she removed her coat, she had a sudden and unexpected memory of the aisle of her Florida church, bedecked with tulle and flowers in preparation for her wedding nearly a year ago. Tears pricked her eyes and Azalea looked in her purse for a tissue. She pressed it to the corners of her eyes, dabbing to keep her mascara from running. She bowed her head and prayed silently.

This was a mistake, she thought.

The worship band moved into a familiar song, this time a hymn.

When peace like a river attendeth my way
When sorrows like sea billows roll.
Whatever my lot, Thou hast taught me to say
It is well, it is well with my soul.

The congregation sang and the words pierced her. It was suddenly, painfully too much and Azalea choked back a sob. It seemed that everything—*everything!*—hit her at once. The unexpressed grief from losing what she thought was going to be a lifetime relationship with her ex-husband buffeted her heart. The guilt she felt at the pain the divorce caused her sons hammered her. The loss of her relationship with Jeremy, the recognition that she'd wasted two years of her life on someone who wasn't right for her, felt raw—as if it were brand new. The emotions crashed into her, one after another, leaving her breathless and bereft.

She was soul-weary and sorrowful. She felt terribly and profoundly alone.

The service ended and Azalea slowly rose from her seat. The sermon had been warm and comforting as Pastor Janelle spoke from the gospel of Mark, the story of the paralytic and the friends who brought him to Jesus for healing. They'd ripped the roof off a house just to get him in front of the rabbi. The pastor stressed the need for faithful friends who would do everything to bring someone to a place of healing when they were unable to find it themselves. Azalea thought about her special friends and how they'd played such a pivotal role in her own healing—not spiritual, exactly, but emotional. Once again, she thanked God for Susana, Lauren, and Sara. She knew they'd rip a roof off for her any day.

She managed to exit the church without being addressed by anyone. She wasn't in the mood to stay and visit, especially with strangers. As she began her walk back to the apartment, she thought about the sermon and wondered if she'd accomplished anything by going to church that morning. She walked slowly behind a young family, mom pushing a stroller and dad carrying a toddler on his hip. She remembered those days. With two little ones only two years apart, she was constantly exhausted—yet filled with love and contentment at the sheer joy of being a mother. Smiling at the memories, Azalea stepped off the curb into the street to pass the family.

The day was cool and clear, the early chill replaced with a warm spring breeze. The trees along the street, beloved for their purple blossoms, flowered cheerfully along her path. The air was clean and fragrant, and she noted the vibrantly colored bougainvillea crawling up the sides of the buildings. She passed one home with huge pots in front of the wrought iron gates, the pots full of flowers.

Azaleas.

She smiled to herself, wiping away unexpected tears. Her father had loved the white and pink blooms that reminded him of growing up in Mexico.

Her phone vibrated and she saw Jeremy's text. *When can we meet? I'm free all day and really want us to talk.*

Not today, she thought. *I can't do this right now.*

I need some time, she wrote back.

His answer was immediate. *How much time?*

She drew a shaky breath. *Why does he have to be so persistent?*

Before she could respond, he wrote again. *Take all the time you need, Azi. It's hard, but I'll wait. We're worth it.*

She stared long at the screen before putting it in her purse.

13

Azalea was deep in thought and two blocks from her apartment when she passed a Catholic church. She noted a woman hurrying down the steps, her head covered in a lace veil. Azalea slowed as she recognized the woman.

"Lorena?" she called out.

Lorena turned and looked at Azalea. The woman was clearly in distress, and Azalea reached out her hand without thinking. "Are you okay?"

Lorena took Azalea's hand and squeezed. She let go and reached up to remove her veil, putting it in her purse before looking back at her friend. "I'm fine," she said, sighing. "You're out early."

"I went to church," answered Azalea. "I went to the International service so I could understand the sermon. I keep thinking my Spanish is going to improve, but…." She trailed off and looked up at the Catholic church Lorena had just left. "Your church is beautiful," she finished.

Lorena looked back at the church with reddened eyes. "*Si*," she responded at last. "It's lovely. I don't go often enough." She looked back at Azalea absently. "So what are you doing today? More sightseeing?"

Azalea stood awkwardly. She and Lorena had struck up a work friendship over the past few months, but they'd never had a genuinely personal conversation. She didn't want to pry, but the woman was obviously upset. "I think I'll probably just head back to the apartment. Maybe go out for lunch." She knew she didn't want to run into Jeremy or Maricela whatever she decided to do.

"Would you like to join me?" The words were out before she considered them but as soon as they were uttered, she realized she didn't want to be alone all day. And yet Lorena didn't look like she was up for company. "I mean, only if you're free, please don't feel like you have to—" Azalea grimaced inwardly for putting herself and Lorena in such an awkward position. Would the woman feel obligated to have lunch with her because Azalea had hired Ambos? *Why can't anything be easy today?*

"I'd like that," said Lorena simply. "I don't really want to go home right now." She didn't explain, but instead turned to walk. "There's a great little tapas place a couple of blocks from here. It's not very touristy—they won't speak English, but I think you'll like it."

Azalea smiled and nodded. "That sounds great."

The walk took no time and the women found the restaurant only half full. They took a table at the front window and looked over the menu. "What's your favorite?" asked Azalea. She tried to decipher the Spanish words. "I'm better with the wines," she laughed.

Lorena smiled. "I think coffee is better for me this morning." Azalea looked at the circles under Lorena's eyes, darker now that she viewed them indoors. The waiter approached and Lorena ordered a *cafecito negro*, Azalea her usual *café con leche y azucar*. The young man returned quickly with steaming cups and asked to take their order. She looked at Lorena and asked, "Would you just order for the two of us? I'm sure I'll like anything you choose."

Lorena nodded. "*Claro, claro….*" She picked up the menu again and spoke rapidly to the waiter. "*Patatas bravas, por favor.*" The waiter wrote in his notebook as Lorena scanned the menu further. "*Un poco de jamón ibérico de bellota y pan con tomate.*" She looked up and smiled wanly. "*Y dos tasos de agua, tambien.*" The waiter took their menus and Lorena looked at Azalea. "I hope you'll like what I ordered, but we can always add something else if you prefer." She stifled a yawn and apologized, "I'm sorry. I—I didn't sleep last night."

Azalea took in Lorena's weary visage, her red-rimmed eyes. She pushed aside her own worries as she considered Lorena. "Are you sure you're all right?" she asked softly. She held up a hand. "I don't mean to pry. Forgive me if I'm overstepping."

Lorena shook her head. "Don't apologize—it's fine. I'm fine. I'm...." She took a long breath and looked out the window, the tears pooling at her lower lashes. She dabbed at them with her napkin and looked at Azalea, embarrassment written on her face. Briefly closing her eyes, Lorena gathered herself.

"You remember what I told you about my brother and the separatists?" she asked, looking around to ensure no one was within earshot. Azalea nodded. *I guess we did have one personal conversation*, she thought. Lorena continued. "He was arrested last night. Evidently there was a plan to create some sort of violent disturbance at the rally on Friday. The *policia* stopped it before it happened, but they believe Eduardo was responsible for it." She took a shuddering breath. "They found a gun in his apartment," she whispered. She closed her eyes briefly, tears shining when she reopened them. "He's just a boy, Azalea. He's only nineteen."

Azalea frowned, her heart going out to Lorena. Eduardo was younger than Tomás and Landon—she couldn't imagine what Lorena was feeling. "Have you seen him?" she asked.

Lorena shook her head, a rueful look on her face. "I tried. He called me when he was arrested but when I got to the station, they wouldn't let me see him. Instead, they took me to a room to question *me!*" She picked up her cup with shaking hands and sipped slowly. "I was there all night long. They finally let me go this morning and I went straight to church from the police station." She looked again out the window. "I didn't know anything about this," she whispered. She looked back at Azalea, eyes bright with unshed tears. "I promise you, Azalea. I had nothing to do with this."

Azalea looked at Lorena. "Of course you didn't!" she responded. "I can't believe they kept you all night. You must be exhausted."

She reached out a hand to touch Lorena's arm. "I'm so sorry you're going through this." She hadn't met Eduardo but thought about how she'd react if something happened to Rowan. "Don't they have to let you see him?"

Just then, the waiter returned with their order, spreading the dishes between them. The women set aside their conversation and, to her surprise, Azalea was soon in love with fried potatoes and *aliloli*— she never used mayonnaise at home. But this was different—warm, creamy, with a rich but not overpowering garlic flavor. They savored the warm food for long minutes before Lorena spoke.

"Things are…different here than in the States," she continued. "I'm not allowed in to visit because he's considered a possible terrorist. They have to let his public defender in, but they haven't let me see him yet." Azalea frowned, unsure how to respond. "The Spanish penal system is one of the best in Europe," said Lorena. "I'm not complaining, but they aren't being very cooperative right now. I'm sure they'll let me visit him soon." She set down her fork as a tear rolled down her cheek. "I know he must be so afraid," she said, her lips trembling. "I wish he had never gotten mixed up with those people!" She covered her face with her napkin. "I'm sorry," she whispered.

Azalea squeezed her arm. "Oh, Lorena," she began, suddenly at a loss for words.

Lorena shook her head, wiped her eyes, and lifted her chin, looking directly at Azalea. "I don't want this to affect our relationship or Ambos' business with Fowler Enterprises," she said, her voice growing stronger, yet no louder. "I will deal with my brother's situation, but I couldn't stand it if I lost your friendship or your business."

Azalea was shaking her head even before Lorena finished. "This has nothing to do with us," she said. She debated whether to tell Jeremy and decided it was unnecessary. What did Eduardo have to do with Fowler Enterprises?

"The Ambos-Fowler partnership is solid—you've done so much to get us this far. And Friday will be a great success in large part due to your work." She reached across the table and took Lorena's hand. "We're good. You have my word." She nodded her head at the lace peeking out from Lorena's handbag. "And I'll pray for your brother."

The two women finished their lunch, both tacitly deciding it was time to change the subject. Lorena reminded Azalea that Timothy Reynolds would be prickly since they'd inconvenienced him by postponing the event. Azalea rolled her eyes. "The ego on that guy," she marveled. "He acts like he writes for the New York Times and not just a networking magazine."

"Yes, but he's hugely influential in the European tech market," warned Lorena. "You'll need to persuade him that it was worth the wait."

"Well, Jeremy can charm just about anyone," responded Azalea. "I'm pretty sure Mr. Reynolds will be quite convinced that Fowler Enterprises is not only worth covering, they're worth a cover story."

"He is charming…" began Lorena.

Azalea steeled her features against a sudden rush of emotion. She pushed away her empty plate and looked at her watch. "Anyway, I should probably go."

Lorena looked quizzically at her but raised a hand for the waiter. "*La cuenta, por favor.*" When the waiter arrived, Lorena paid over Azalea's objection. "You're the client, Azalea. This was…a business lunch."

They walked outside and Lorena said, "We're heading in opposite directions now. I'll see you tomorrow?"

Azalea nodded. "It's going to be a crazy busy week to get ready for Friday." She wanted to say more, but Lorena smiled and kissed both of her cheeks in the traditional *dos besos* manner.

"*Muchísimas gracias*, Azalea," she said, then turned and walked away.

14

Monday morning dawned and Azalea prepared for a busy week. As she dressed and put on her makeup, she resolved to put Jeremy and Maricela out of her mind. Their relationship was none of her business, she thought. She looked in the mirror and was thankful for the Latin skin that no longer bore the pink tinge from her burn on Saturday. As she slicked on her favorite lip gloss, she decided the most important thing this week was making the launch a success. When it was over, she had only six weeks left on her contract—so after this Friday, she'd need to start seriously considering her next gig. The money she earned and saved while her housing and expenses were paid was a nice cushion. But Azalea knew that she needed to secure more clients once she was done with Fowler Enterprises. She'd head back to Florida, maybe take a month off to get resettled, but then she needed to work. She thought longingly of her own beach and home. Barcelona was beautiful, but she missed her little cottage.

A knock on the door startled her. No one ever came to her apartment, and she was puzzled as to who it could be. Looking out the peephole, she saw Jeremy standing in front of her door.

She opened the door and looked at him. "Um…hi. What's up?"

He looked back at her and held out a small bouquet of mixed flowers. "May I come in?" he asked.

Azalea hesitated—she hadn't been alone with Jeremy in months. They'd talked in her office or outside the building, sure… but there were always people around. Jeremy saw the indecision on her face and laughed mirthlessly. "I'm not going to ravish you, Azi," he said. "I just brought some flowers to say thank you for everything you've done and to start off our big week with something…I don't know," he looked around, trying to find the word. "Friendly? Hopeful?"

Azalea felt a rush of emotions. She stood back, holding the door open. "Of course, I'm sorry," she said. "Come in. I'm sure there's a vase in the kitchen somewhere." She began opening cabinets and soon found a small glass vase. "Here we go. And thank you. This is really lovely of you." Her hands shook slightly as she took the flowers from him, their fingers brushing. Azalea turned quickly to the sink to fill the vase and trim the stems.

"So, are you ready for this week?" he asked.

"I am," she replied, as she set the vase down on the counter. Azalea arranged the stems as she talked. The fragrance was light…teasing at first, but soon filled the small kitchen. "We're prepared—now we just need to execute. I ran into Lorena yesterday and she reminded me that Timothy Reynolds might be a bit of a problem. He's got a pretty big ego and he likes to remind people how influential he is." She finished moving the flowers around. "In a very British way, of course," she added with a smile. "I'm sure you'll charm the stiff upper lip right off him."

"I wish I could charm someone else right now," answered Jeremy, looking pointedly at her.

Azalea returned his gaze, her cheeks warming. "Jeremy," she began, "I—"

"It's okay, Azi," he said, stepping toward her. "I told you I'd wait, and I will. Now, let's go out there and be amazing…the way we always are when we're together." He reached up as if to touch her cheek but dropped his hand. "Do you mind walking over with me?" he asked.

Azalea turned to walk to her bedroom. "I'll just grab my things," she said over her shoulder, unwilling to let him see her face. The conflict she felt was all too apparent, she feared. One side of her knew there was nothing that had changed between them. He was still supremely confident and unwilling to lose. That knowledge warred, however, with the other side of her, the Azalea who longed for love and companionship, who genuinely missed him. She knew he wasn't right for her, especially not immediately after breaking up with Maricela. *Two days ago he was in Madrid with his lover*, she reminded herself.

She grabbed her sweater and purse and walked back towards the kitchen to pack her laptop. Jeremy stood in front of a table next to the sofa where she'd put a small, framed photograph of her with Tomás and Landon. The three of them were standing at the surf's edge, Landon's long arm holding the phone for their smiling selfie. White-capped waves were behind them and a seagull flew across the pink-tinged sky.

"You look so happy," he said quietly.

"It was a nice day," she agreed. "We took that the weekend before I flew to Spain. You know how the sunset makes the eastern sky turn all sorts of beautiful colors. We lucked out with that one, and then the boys bought me that frame to go with it." Jeremy looked at her without speaking, the silence lengthening.

Abruptly, he set the photo down and turned to the door. "Let's go conquer the world," he declared.

They walked in silence out of the apartment complex, Azalea careful to avoid accidentally grazing Jeremy's hand. *This is what captured me last time*, she thought. *He's charming and thoughtful—and relentless in getting his way.* Too focused on her inner monologue, Azalea walked a block without noticing a thing around her.

It was just a nice gesture, she thought. *Not red roses and champagne. Just a friendly bouquet.*

"So I didn't forget you asked me to bring you a bottle of wine."

Azalea started as Jeremy broke into her reverie.

"It just felt weird buying something for you while I was there—"

"With her," she finished for him. "It's okay. Truly. I just kinda threw that out on Thursday—I didn't really expect you to bring me back anything." Azalea looked sideways at Jeremy. "Seriously. Just forget about it—not a big deal."

"It's a big deal to me, Azi," he responded. Jeremy slowed, then stopped. "If I tell you I'm gonna do something, I'm absolutely going to do it. You have to be able to trust what I say." She wondered if he meant that as a jab—her word hadn't proven trustworthy after all. He frowned and shook his head. "Anyway, I'll make it up to you."

The day progressed quickly once the pair arrived. Denice walked into Azalea's office right behind her with a list of topics in her ever-present notebook. Jeremy immediately huddled with his sales team in a conference room, prepping for the big day. The energy in the office was palpable as everyone knew the importance of Friday.

After Denice finished running down her last-minute to-do list, she paused for a breath. "Sorry—that was a bit of a tidal wave," she laughed. "So how was your long weekend? Do anything fun?"

Azalea sat back in her chair and considered. Fun? She had enjoyed La Sagrada Familia—until she was struck painfully by her loneliness. She was accosted by a half-naked Maricela at the beach. She had a meltdown in church and then found out her friend's brother was arrested on domestic terrorist charges.

Fun wasn't the word for it.

"It was nice," she said. "How about yours?"

Denice had spent the weekend "on self-care," she said. "You should try it sometime." She leaned forward with an excited look. "Azalea, I'm telling you, Aire de Barcelona is ah-may-zing! I floated in these incredible underground Roman baths, had a massage— which was fab—and drank some of the best wine I've ever tasted." She sat back and closed her eyes. "It was seriously heaven." Her eyes snapped open and she grabbed Azalea's hand. "We should go after the launch!"

Azalea laughed at her friend. "Sounds wonderful," she answered.

"That doesn't come close to describing it. Let's book it for Saturday! We deserve something wonderful after all this work." Azalea nodded, pensive. Maybe a Saturday devoted to herself would be just the thing to bring her out of her funk.

"Sounds wonderful," she repeated. "Let's book it."

Denice jumped up and headed for the door. "I'll book us for one o'clock on Saturday," she said. "Chances are, we'll be out late celebrating on Friday and I'll want to sleep in."

Azalea grinned at her exuberant colleague. "Okay, Denice," she said. "That will give me time in the morning for a beach run."

Denice scowled. "Do you ever relax? Never mind—don't bother answering. I know what you'll say." With a laugh, she turned and walked out to the lobby where she called out for Guillermo, already moving on to the next topic.

Azalea turned to her computer and typed in "Aire de Barcelona." The reviews were five stars and the photos gorgeous. Saturday would be wonderful. She thought that floating in a Roman bath and a massage was just what she needed. And a glass of wine at the spa was surely better than a bottle from Jeremy.

She looked out across the lobby to the executive conference room. Javier was at the whiteboard writing, Ricardo speaking with big hand movements.

Jeremy turned to look and their eyes met. He winked…and Azalea smiled.

Launch week raced by and the office was in a state of controlled chaos, with deliveries arriving nearly every hour. Ricardo and Javier's sales team, usually working from home or at clients' sites, took up spots in the conference rooms as they made phone calls or met with the senior sales leaders. The systems engineers set up their demos in two rooms where they could showcase Fowler Enterprises products and Guillermo and Denice flitted throughout the office, rearranging chairs and tables as new ideas struck them.

Azalea tried to stay out of their way—her role on Friday was to serve as the head of corporate communications, sitting in on Jeremy and Ricardo's meetings with the industry press and analysts. Each day, she ran through the briefing documents with the two men, ensuring they were prepared to address each guest's focus areas with salient points and ready answers for any questions. Azalea was in her element, performing her role with ease and encouraging the team to excel.

Even with Maricela hovering about, always finding a reason to interrupt their sessions.

She'd walk into Azalea's office, ostensibly to ask questions, and always speak in Spanish to Ricardo—although he was from Miami and spoke perfect English. She knew Azalea couldn't follow their conversation, while Jeremy understood every word. Every day she came in around ten o'clock, dressed to perfection, seemingly over her breakup. Azalea watched her, impressed with her control.

On Thursday, everyone wore casual clothes. Jeremy announced on Wednesday afternoon that he would be in jeans and ready to lend a hand for any last-minute set-up work, and everyone followed suit. Denice arrived in skinny jeans, a loose sweater, and Converse sneakers. Azalea opted for cropped jeans, a fitted white t-shirt, and ballerina flats. She pulled her hair into a ponytail and wore little makeup. As she walked to the office that morning, she relished the ability to walk quickly and fearlessly on the cobblestone streets.

When she arrived at eight o'clock, Guillermo and the interns were already unpacking boxes of brochures and putting together the folders she'd ordered for each of the attendees. She smiled brightly at them. "A bit early for you two, huh?" she asked. The Spanish interns were unused to arriving at the office so early and she caught both of them mid-yawn.

"*Lo siento*, Azalea," said Carlos, quickly covering his mouth. She laughed and shook her head.

"*No me importa*, Carlos," she said. "Just two more days and you can get back to your regular schedule." There was something to be said for the Spanish workday, with its late morning start. And some companies still adhered to the *siesta*, closing for hours in the late afternoon, only to reopen at a time when most Americans would be heading home for dinner. *Poor kids are gonna need a nap this afternoon*, she thought, stifling a grin.

Azalea put her things in her office and went back into the lobby to find Denice directing the florist. After the previous week's cancellation, they'd had to reorder the small vases of yellow and white peonies for strategic areas of the office. A huge arrangement stood on the front desk and Denice was showing the florist where to place the smaller vases. "So what do you think?" she asked Azalea.

"Gorgeous! They look fantastic, Denice. You made a great choice with the decorations." Azalea looked around the lobby, with its normally open space now filled with tables where the food and gifts would be displayed. "It's really coming together," she said appreciatively.

"There is one not-so-little problem," warned Denice.

"Oh, dear. That doesn't sound good."

"We lost our breakfast caterer. Last minute emergency and we need to find someone who can fill in. I'm researching like mad."

Azalea pondered, then smiled. "What about La Rosa de Barcelona? I don't know if they cater, but it's worth a call. Their coffee and pastries are fabulous and we probably don't need anything more than that."

"Ooh," responded Denice, warming to the idea. "I love that place! That's the one with the cute barista, right?"

Azalea rolled her eyes. "He's probably 25 years old, my friend."

Denice laughed. "I'll call this morning. Wish me luck!" She looked down at her ever-present notebook. "Now if those damn separatists don't do anything stupid," she growled. "I'll shoot them myself if they screw up the launch again."

Azalea nodded. She wondered if Lorena had been able to see her brother and resolved to call her. She said a quick prayer for Eduardo and his sister, feeling a pang of guilt that she'd told Lorena she would pray for him. She was so busy all week, she barely had time to think of anything but the launch.

Except Jeremy.

Each morning she admired the bouquet he'd brought her, the scent still lingering in her kitchen. All week he seemed to find reasons to touch her shoulder, her hand—nothing blatant, but somehow intimate nonetheless. She felt certain no one in the office noticed, but her senses were heightened whenever they were in the same room. *Focus on the job, Azalea,* she told herself.

It was getting harder every day.

15

Azalea wandered around the office, checking in on all the stations—the two conference rooms for the demos were nearly complete. The systems engineers looked serious as they pounded away at laptops and connected to the big screens on the walls. She smiled at them and left them to their work.

She nearly bumped into Javier as she walked out of one room. He was holding a cup of coffee and it jostled in his grip—just enough to splash on Azalea's white t-shirt. She jumped back, but it was too late. Dark brown drops spattered and Javier stared at her breasts.

"Oh, damn, Azalea," he muttered. "I'm so sorry—" He raised a hand as if to wipe away the stains, but she slapped it away.

"Seriously, Javier?"

He had the good sense to look down before he burst out laughing. "I'm sorry…really, I'm sorry." He covered his mouth with his hand and shook his head. "I know it's not funny. It's just—" he stifled another laugh. "You should have seen your face, *Bella*!"

Azalea couldn't help but smile. "Not exactly beautiful now, am I?" She wondered if she had a sweater in her office. She couldn't walk around with coffee stains on her chest all day. She slapped at his arm as he continued to laugh and walked to her office.

"Of course not," she muttered, as she looked around. She had kept a sweater hanging on the back of her door for a couple of weeks but had taken it to the apartment to launder and hadn't brought it back. She looked down at her shirt—there was nothing for it but to walk back to the apartment to change.

Denice walked in, opening her mouth to speak, but stopped and stared. "What happened to you?" she asked.

Azalea grimaced. "Javier happened to me," she answered. "We bumped into each other in the hall. He thought it was hilarious."

"Well..." began Denice, grinning.

"Not you, too," said Azalea. "It's not funny and I don't have another shirt or sweater here. I'm gonna go back to the apartment and change." She stood up and grabbed her purse to leave. "I'll be back in half an hour."

The two women walked across the lobby just as Maricela walked in. *So much for casual day*, thought Azalea. Maricela was wearing skin-tight black jeans and—*of course*—her ubiquitous high heels. Her hair was swept into a chic ponytail with wisps framing her face. She wore a crisp white blouse, unbuttoned over a white tank top and tied at the waist. Her makeup, as always, was impeccable, and Azalea felt like she'd just rolled in the mud in comparison.

Maricela's eyebrow went up as she looked at Azalea's chest. "Had a little accident?" she asked.

Denice looked back and forth at the two women. "Um...hey, Azalea, why don't you just put on one of the t-shirts we ordered? I ordered a few spares and then you don't have to go back to your place to change."

Azalea continued to look at Maricela as Jeremy approached the trio. "Good mor—" he stopped, looking at Azalea's shirt. "You okay?" he asked, concerned.

"She's fine," broke in Maricela. "Apparently she has a bit of a drinking problem."

Azalea's eyes flashed, then she turned to Jeremy. "Javier ran into me in the hallway and spilled his coffee. I'm just gonna change in the restroom." She looked back at Denice. "Where are the shirts?"

Denice nodded toward the front desk. "Just behind the desk. Let's go find your size." The tension was palpable and Azalea wanted nothing more than to run away. But the contempt on Maricela's face stopped her and she forced herself to walk to the desk.

"You sure you're okay, Azi?" asked Jeremy. He followed her to the desk and took her arm, glancing down at her chest. "You didn't get burned?" Azalea turned to look at him and caught Maricela's eye roll. Clearly, she wasn't happy with Jeremy's concern.

"I'm fine," replied Azalea. "Just…fine."

Azalea slipped on the dark blue t-shirt and tucked it in. Navy wasn't exactly her best color and the bathroom lights didn't do her any favors, she realized. She thought about Maricela, wondering how it was possible to be that perfect every single day. *How early did she get up in the morning to get ready?* she wondered. She smoothed her hair back and redid her ponytail, noticing the gray hairs starting to peep out along her hairline. She'd been so busy, she hadn't taken the time to touch them up, and now she was less than twenty-four hours away from a big day where she wanted to look her best.

Jeremy doesn't seem to mind. The thought came unbidden. She touched her skin, still feeling the spot on her arm where he'd clasped her, worried she'd been hurt by the hot coffee. Azalea stared at herself in the mirror, the conflict plain on her face. *This happened last time,* she reminded herself. He was charming and tender—and then he was masterful at dictating everything about their lives.

But maybe it's different this time?

Azalea shook her head. *There is no 'this time,'* she thought harshly. *He was in bed with Maricela just days ago, for God's sake. Stop acting like an idiot. Flowers and a kind word don't erase the past.*

A knock on the bathroom door startled her. "Azi?" called Jeremy. "Are you all right?"

"I'm fine," she replied as she walked out the door. "Good as new." She smiled brightly, determined to put her tangled emotions aside.

Jeremy held the office door open for her, his hand light on her back. "Should I fire Javier?" he joked, his fingers sliding across her shoulder as she passed him. Azalea met his eyes and turned quickly away.

This was getting out of hand.

Azalea sat at her desk and resolved to put Jeremy out of her mind—at least for today. She thought instead about Denice's weekend, so different from her own. *When was the last time I did something special for myself?* She didn't have much time, but she resolved to make the most of her evening. Maybe she could get a blowout in one of the trendy Barcelona salons. She decided to make an appointment after work and then treat herself to a nice dinner and a bath.

She searched online and found a posh place about fifteen minutes from the office. The client photos were gorgeous—dark-haired beauties with a variety of looks. She made up her mind without another thought and dialed quickly. She scheduled an appointment for five o'clock, figuring she'd done everything she could to prepare for tomorrow and could leave the office a bit early. *If I've forgotten something, it's too late now anyway.* She quickly did the math—she could be done at the salon by six and then find a nice café nearby for dinner. She could be back to the apartment by eight, in the tub by eight-thirty, and in bed by ten. She sat back in her chair, quite pleased with herself.

"You look pretty happy," commented Jeremy as he walked in. "I'm glad you're not too upset about your shirt." He sat down and leaned against her desk.

"It's okay," she replied. "It was an accident and thankfully I don't need to look nice today."

"Well, you always look nice to me," he answered, suddenly serious. Jeremy leaned forward, his elbows on her desk, hands clasped under his chin. "So what about having dinner with me tonight?" He looked down at his own jeans and t-shirt and glanced up. "Obviously nothing dressy," he finished with a smile.

She looked at her former fiancé. Their time together over the past couple of months had been confusing at best. He was still the strong and handsome man she'd fallen in love with, but he also still assumed everything would always go his way. He'd finally begun to acknowledge her as a professional, praising her and relying on her knowledge and expertise as they prepared for the company's big launch. But he'd been involved with Maricela as recently as the previous weekend and Azalea wasn't certain she wanted to get in the middle of that drama.

Thankfully, she wasn't available.

"I'm going to take it as a very positive sign that you're thinking about it," he said. He sat back in his chair, tilting his head to appraise her carefully. "A week ago you would have immediately turned me down." He pulled out his phone and began searching. "So where shall we go?" he asked.

"I can't," said Azalea. "I booked a salon appointment after work and I'm gonna spend the evening getting ready for tomorrow." She smiled crookedly. "Thank you for asking, but I can't."

Jeremy sat his phone down on her desk and gazed at her for what seemed minutes. "I'm still taking this as a positive sign," he concluded. He stood up and put his hands on her desk, leaning in. Azalea sat perfectly still, unsure if she should pull away or lean in to meet him. Her eyes flicked out the door but saw no one nearby. Jeremy didn't look away, continuing to watch her. He leaned even closer when at last he spoke.

"Very positive."

And then he was gone.

16

Azalea stepped out of the taxi in front of the salon. It was even nicer than the photos online and she wondered if she should have stopped at the apartment to change clothes first. She felt underdressed and awkward as she stepped up to the front desk where she was met with a perfectly coiffed, beautiful woman.

"*Hola*," she began. "*Tengo un*…uh…." Azalea wracked her brain for the word for "appointment."

The young lady smiled and helped her. "An appointment? You are Azalea?" She pronounced Azalea's name with the Catalan accent: *Ah-thah-leah*. "I'm Felicia. Come with me." She walked around the desk to lead Azalea to a station with a handsome young man. "This is Asier," she said. "You can practice your English," she told him with a smile. "This is Azalea."

Asier motioned for Azalea to sit in the chair. It was white leather with glistening chrome, one of ten chairs lined up on the marble floor. Instrumental jazz was playing unobtrusively, and Azalea settled into the chair, determined to relax and enjoy herself.

"So you don't speak Spanish?" asked Asier.

"*Mi español es muy pobre,*" she confessed. "*Mi papá es de Méxi-co, pero no lo aprendí.*" She wondered if she said that correctly—all the words were right, but she had no idea if the sentence made sense. She must have been at least somewhat correct because he nodded. "I like to practice English," he said. "Maybe you practice *español?*"

Azalea grinned. "*Sí!*"

Asier began to remove the band on her ponytail. "So what you want me to do today?"

"*Solamente un*…um…oh, no," she rummaged through her mind. She was quite sure she never learned the Spanish word for "blowout." "*Como se dice* 'blowout'?" she asked.

The young man laughed. "Blowout is fine," he answered, "*pero tú no quieres colór?*" He fingered the gray along her temple.

Azalea looked at herself in the mirror. Tomorrow was a big day and she wanted to look her best. But if she were honest, what was really going through her mind were thoughts of Maricela. She undoubtedly would pull out all the stops tomorrow and be spectac-ular. Azalea was certain the beauty was over ten years younger and there was no possible way to compete with her. Would Maricela use tomorrow to entice Jeremy? *And why do I care?*

She thought of her mother and her beautiful silver hair. Susana likewise had let her grays show through her black tresses. Both women were stunning, and both had chided Azalea for her refusal to stop coloring her hair every six weeks.

She sighed and then smiled, decision made. "No, just the blowout."

Asier grinned and asked, "Okay, Azalea…straight or curls?"

She cocked her head and answered, "*Que recommendas?*" This one she knew, thanks to Esteban.

"*Rizos, chica linda! Como* Beectoria Secret!" Asier began twirling her hair around his finger. "*Rizos de la playa…muy* sexy."

Azalea laughed. "This is for a work event," she protested. "I don't want to be sexy."

The stylist looked puzzled. "A woman should always be sexy, Azalea. *Siempre.*"

"Okay," she said. "*Rizos.*"

Why not?

After the most heavenly shampoo experience in her life, Azalea returned to Asier's station, her long hair wrapped in a thick white towel. Felicia met them and asked, "How was that?"

Azalea sighed. "It was divine." She realized she had finally relaxed and was enjoying herself.

Felicia nodded. "Asier is the best," she assured Azalea. "So what can I get you to drink? We have white and red wine, Cava, espresso, and sparkling water."

Azalea thought for a moment but Asier broke in. "Cava," he said firmly. "Something special for the special lady." He winked at her as he began to unwind the towel.

She smiled. "Cava it is."

As they waited for Felicia to return, the stylist began mixing a cocktail of serums and lotions, deftly distributing them through Azalea's hair. Whatever they were, the mixture smelled glorious. When Felicia brought her glass, Asier began speaking in rapid Spanish to his colleague. Felicia nodded and told Azalea, "He's going to make your hair a little curlier than you want tonight because you'll sleep on it and it will be perfect in the morning." Azalea nodded. "His English isn't so great, and he wanted to be sure you understood exactly what he's doing."

Azalea smiled at Felicia and looked up at Asier in the mirror. "*Gracias. Es perfecto.*"

Twenty minutes later, her hair was dry and Asier began with the curling iron. Another impossibly gorgeous man approached them. "*Hola, Bella,*" he said to Azalea. He continued in richly accented English. "You're in good hands today. This *guapo* is our best stylist."

Asier grinned. "This is *mi novio*, Diego. His English is much better than mine."

Diego scoffed. "Only because I use it more. You don't practice enough."

Asier stopped curling Azalea's hair. "*Estoy practicando ahora!*" he protested.

Azalea nodded. "*Es verdad,*" she agreed. "*Estamos practicando ahora.*"

"*Pues…*" began Diego with a sly smile. "*Practica conmigo, Bella.* Let's start with an easy one: *Como te llamas?*"

Azalea took the challenge. "*Me llamo* Azalea," she replied, pronouncing her name in the American way.

Diego lifted an eyebrow. "No, no, no," he replied, shaking his head, curling his lip, and scrunching his nose as if he'd smelled something bad. He put a hand on his hip, cocked his head in a perfect Hollywood glamor pose, and looked at her through dark lashes. "*La Belleza de los ojos verdes y dorados se llama Ah-thah-leah.*" Azalea and Asier burst out laughing and soon Diego joined them. "Seriously, Azalea," he continued. "Those green and gold eyes of yours… they're stunning. Why don't you let me do something with them?"

Asier told Azalea, "Diego is the salon makeup artist. He can make you even more beautiful."

Azalea looked at her watch. It was nearly six o'clock and she was starving. "I don't think I have enough time tonight."

Diego flicked a hand at her as he walked away. "*Momentito, Bella. Momentito.*" He returned with a handful of items and a sheet of paper with a drawing of a woman's face. "What are you wearing tomorrow?"

"I have a simple black dress," began Azalea but stopped when she saw the horrified look on Diego's face.

"*Dios Mio, que lástima!* Are you going to a funeral, *Bella*? It's springtime in Barcelona! You need to wear green—something to bring out those gorgeous eyes." He shook his head in disgust. "Black?" he repeated.

Azalea mentally reviewed her closet. "I do have an olive green blouse I could wear with a skirt or slacks," she said reluctantly. She'd been planning to wear the black sheath since she got to Barcelona months ago. It was one thing to change her hair the night before—it was entirely too much to change her clothes, too.

"*Mira,*" he intoned as Asier continued working on her curls. Deftly, Diego outlined the drawing's eyes with an olive green eyeliner pencil. The green was subtly flecked with gold. He added neutral shadows on the eyelids noting, "I know this is a work event, so I'm not going to make you look too glamorous." He touched the cheeks lightly with a peachy blush and finished the look with a melon-colored lipstick and gloss. He looked approvingly at his work and then back at Azalea. "You can do this yourself. Only one more thing," he added as he stepped back to his design station. He returned with a small pot of concealer and dabbed it without asking under her eyes. Azalea looked in the mirror and smiled. The circles under her eyes were gone and she looked immediately refreshed. "That's nothing like the concealer I use," she said, surprised.

Diego's eyebrow lifted and he blew her a kiss. "I'm a genius. Go ahead. You can say it."

Azalea grinned. "You're a genius."

Azalea left the salon feeling amazing. She walked in tired and tense, but Asier and Diego—and the glass of Cava on her empty stomach—had left her feeling relaxed yet energized. Felicia was right; her curls were a bit tighter than she wanted, but Asier told her firmly not to touch them and to sleep on them just as they were. She bought all the cosmetics Diego had used on his drawing, making sure she bought two of the concealer pots. The men hugged her and kissed both of her cheeks before she left, and she added a fifty percent gratuity to the bill. What else did she spend her money on?

She walked down the street, looking in windows as she decided where to eat. She saw a small bistro with tables outside and was about to cross the road when she glimpsed a dress shop on her right. In the window display hung a celery green dress. It was sleeveless with a V-neck and an empire waist. The fabric was a lightweight wool, perfect for the cool Barcelona spring. Azalea stood at the storefront, staring.

Her stomach rumbled and she decided eating was more important than shopping. But before she crossed the street, she looked at the door. The shop didn't close until nine o'clock. If she were still interested after dinner, she'd stop in.

Azalea sipped her water and looked around. The other tables were full, people stopping for an early dinner before heading home. She had decided on "*Un taso de agua, por favor*" instead of a glass of wine, and was nibbling on a piece of bread when her phone lit up. It was a text from Tomás.

Hey Mom

Azalea answered, delighted to hear from her son. *Hey love, what's up? Miss you.*

Kinda sad. You know Em's new puppy?

She thought back to the photos of the darling rescue dog Tomás had sent.

Yes, she responded. *What about him?*

He got out somehow last night and we can't find him. No one has seen him around her place and she's a mess. We put out flyers today and posted online but no responses.

Her heart sank. Tomás really seemed to be falling for this girl and Azalea was sure his big teddy bear heart was hurting.

I'm so sorry, love, she wrote. *I wish I could do something to help.*

Thanks Mom, he answered. *Landon is out driving around. He took the morning off work to help out.*

Azalea's heart swelled. She was always glad when her boys took care of each other, but wished she were with them.

Anyway, gotta run. Just wanted to say hi and let you know what's up

Saying a prayer, honey, she typed. *Let me know what happens. I miss you boys and can't wait to meet Emily. Maybe you guys can fly to Florida when I get back or I can come out to Colorado?*

That would be great, Mom. You're gonna love her. I think I already do.

By the time Azalea finished her dinner, she was relaxed and contemplative. Her day had started lousy, but really—a stain on a shirt during a workday at the office wasn't the worst thing that had ever happened to her. She got through the day enduring Maricela's sidelong glances and smirks, Javier's suppressed laughter, and Jeremy's…what? What was it from Jeremy? She'd felt certain he was about to kiss her in the office, he'd leaned so close.

Would I have stopped him? She wasn't entirely certain.

And now, in the cool Barcelona evening with the sun setting and the streets again beginning to fill with people, she felt happy. *Alive.* She raised her hand and looked at the waiter two tables away. "*La cuenta, por favor*," she said, smiling. While she awaited her bill, she gazed around. Couples and families strolled along the street, looking at the shop windows, others sitting at tables sipping wine and eating tapas. She felt the familiar pang of longing, but this time didn't feel the acute sorrow. She'd love to be one of those couples, lazily wandering along the cobblestone streets of this beautiful city. But now she was—content? Was that it?

She pulled the drawing out of her purse and looked again. What Diego had applied wasn't difficult. She was certain she could do it herself and felt a bubbling excitement at the thought. She'd look and feel fantastic tomorrow. Not to compete with Maricela.

For herself.

"*Buenos noches*," greeted the saleswoman at the dress shop.

"*Buenos noches*," responded Azalea. "*Hablas ingles? Lo siento... mi espanol es muy pobre.*"

The woman smiled. "*Un poco*," she answered. "What are you looking for?"

Azalea chuckled. What was she looking for? Inner peace? Confidence?

"I'd like to try on *el vestido verde en la ventana, por favor.*"

The woman grinned. "*Muy bien, señorita!*" She walked to a nearby rack and then looked back at Azalea before thumbing through the sizes. She handed two different ones to Azalea and motioned her to follow.

"*Gracias*," said Azalea as she stepped into the dressing room.

She slipped on the first dress, but it hung loosely on her—not at all like she hoped. She needed hips and a more ample bosom for it to fit well. Sighing, she took off the dress and placed it back on the hanger. She looked in the mirror, suddenly deflated. What was she thinking? *Stick to the black sheath*, she told herself.

Are you going to a funeral, Bella? Diego had goaded her.

She unzipped the second dress and put it on. The fabric slid across her skin and fell into place, perfectly fitting her athletic body. The light green of the gabardine hung close without looking painted on as Maricela's dresses did. She could move easily, and the color set off her dark curls and light eyes. Azalea was astonished that she could look and feel so pretty. So confident.

The knock on the door startled her. "*Está bien, señorita?*" called the saleswoman.

"*Si, si, es perfecto*," replied Azalea, stepping out of the dress. She put her jeans and t-shirt back on and carried the dresses out. "I'll take this one," she told the woman.

"*Momentito*," cautioned the woman. "*Mira!*" She walked to the far wall of the small shop and held up a pair of slingback shoes. Camel-colored patent leather, they went beautifully with the dress. The heels were high but not too tall, and Azalea decided to try them on. She slipped off her flats and put on the shoes, walking in front of a floor-length mirror on the shop floor. Even in jeans she could see the shoes were gorgeous. She grinned and nodded at the smiling saleswoman. "*Fabulosos*," said the woman. "*Y tienes una bolsa?*"

Azalea laughed. She was going to end up spending a week's salary at this point, but she realized with a start that she didn't mind. She followed the shopkeeper to the purses and selected a forest green clutch. Ordinarily, she threw her wallet into her backpack or carried the black handbag the boys had given her three Christmases ago. This purse was large enough for her wallet, mobile phone, and lipstick…and not much else. It was elegant and set off the outfit beautifully.

Azalea smiled. "I'll take it," she said. "I'll take it all."

17

By the time Azalea's alarm went off at six-thirty, it was a relief. She'd awakened three times during the night, each time certain she'd overslept. She'd fallen back asleep quickly, but now she was very ready to start her day.

She looked again at the sheet Diego had given her. She tapped cream under her eyes and then applied the concealer. As before, her eyes brightened and she looked more alert. *This stuff is magic*, she thought. She followed his directions exactly, murmuring, "You *are* a genius, Diego" as she completed the application.

Azalea was struck by how positive she felt. This was going to be a good day. And not because she felt pretty. Or not *just* because she felt pretty. She felt strong. Competent. Ready to tackle the day's challenges—even the prickliest journalist couldn't ruffle her confidence.

Azalea laughed out loud. Timothy Reynolds and his outsized ego be damned—he was no match for her. Not today.

After she added two coats of mascara, Azalea stepped back to look at herself in the mirror. She picked a lace thong and matching bra to wear under her new dress. She wasn't much for exotic lingerie—the duo was simple and elegant. *No one else will see it,* she thought. *But I know it's there.*

She spritzed herself with fragrance and slipped into her new dress and shoes. As she ran her fingers through her curls, her phone lit up with a text. It was Tomás.

Hey Mom! he wrote. *We found Dexter!*

That's wonderful! she typed. *Is he ok?*

A moment later, two photos appeared side by side. On the left, a puppy of indeterminate breed sat with matted hair and a sheepish look. On the right, the same puppy was clean and sat on Tomás's lap.

He's adorable, she wrote. *I'm so glad you found him. Looks like he had a bit of an adventure!*

Yeah, Em's over the moon, wrote Tomás. *She loves this guy.*

A few seconds passed and he added: *She likes the dog, too.*

Azalea snorted a very unladylike laugh. *Oh, honey,* she wrote, *I'm very happy for you.*

Thanks, Mom. I know it's a big day for you. Go be your brilliant self!

I will try, she typed. *I love you so much.*

Going to bed now, he wrote. *Love you!*

Azalea took one more look at her reflection and shook out her curls. Asier was right—they fell perfectly after sleeping on them. She slipped her phone into her tiny clutch, grabbed her laptop bag, and headed for the office.

Ready to go be her brilliant self.

Azalea strode into the office, flushed from her walk. She'd come straight to work without stopping for her usual coffee, knowing there would be plenty once the caterers arrived. She took two steps in before being met by Denice who blinked at her, mouth open.

"Azalea!" she exclaimed. "Oh, my."

Oh no oh no oh no…it's too much. I overdid it.

Azalea debated whether she had time to run back to the apartment to change. Why on earth did she listen to anyone else? She knew she should have stuck with her tried and true, boring but professional look.

"You look incredible," breathed Denice. "Just beautiful." She shook her head, eyes wide. "I don't mean you aren't normally gorgeous, but geez...."

Guillermo approached with a clipboard in hand, clearly in a rush to ask Denice a question. He opened his mouth but stopped abruptly as he looked at Azalea. "Wow," he began, then seemed to catch himself. "You look...very nice today," he finished lamely. He turned to Denice and asked her to sign off on a delivery, casting sideways glances at Azalea, who stood awkwardly.

"I'll just go put my things in my office," she said. "Be right back to help." She walked to her office and opened her laptop, placing her new clutch in her desk drawer. She logged on and realized there were nearly two hours until the event started. She couldn't decide if that seemed incredibly short or interminable.

Denice came in and asked, "Big day, huh?"

"A bit of an understatement, don't you think?"

Guillermo knocked, still holding his clipboard. "The breakfast service is here," he announced. "Do you want to talk to the caterer?" The women followed, both nodding. As they walked to the lobby, Denice looked over her shoulder and murmured, "You really do look fantastic." Azalea smiled her thanks.

The three of them walked into the lobby where they met the caterer and two of his employees. They were setting up coffee urns and platters of pastries on the tables along the wall. Esteban looked up, his expression brightening. "Thank you for this opportunity," he said, grasping Azalea's hand.

"Thank you for taking on a job at the last minute."

Azalea felt he held her hand just a bit too long but was unwilling to pull it away. The young man seemed to realize he was still holding on and brusquely spoke to Guillermo. "Let me show you what we've brought," he said, turning away from the women.

Denice looked sideways at Azalea with a sly grin.

"Not a word," warned Azalea.

They followed the two men as Esteban showed off his bounteous spread. There was the traditional *pan dulce,* colorful *conchas* and *empanadas.* There were fruit tartlets and *bocadillos* with thinly sliced ham and cheese. He pointed to one tray filled with squares of something dense and smelling of *canela.*

Is that bread pudding? thought Azalea. *In Barcelona?*

"I wanted to add something a little different," he said. "This is a recipe from the States. It's called—"

"Bread pudding," interjected Azalea. "It's my very favorite dessert." Esteban's face lit up at her comment. "My mother used to make it when I was a girl."

"I hope you will like it," he responded. "I added lot of *canela*."

She nodded. "That's just how my mom used to make it. Lots of cinnamon."

"So what's going on over here?" asked Jeremy. He approached the small group, his eyes lingering on Azalea.

She stepped forward and introduced the two men. "Esteban, this is Señor Fowler. He's the owner of the company. Jeremy, this is Esteban, the owner of La Rosa de Barcelona, our caterer."

Jeremy reached out to shake the younger man's hand. "*Mucho gusto*, Esteban." He looked back at Azalea, nodding toward her office. "Do you have a moment?"

"Of course," she answered, and he turned away without a backward glance. She followed him to her office and they stood in front of her desk. Jeremy was dressed in what she knew was an expensive bespoke suit—he had it made the year before when he opened the Fowler Enterprises office in Venezuela. The navy wool hung perfectly, his crisp white shirt adorned with a tasteful almost black tie, shot through with subtle yellow, nearly invisible threads.

Unless you knew they were there, she thought.

Azalea loved bright colors and had once bought Jeremy a daffodil-colored silk tie. She paid a fortune for it and was excited to see him wear it. He thanked her but explained he only wore dark, plain ties: "Nothing flashy," he told her. He was wealthy but not ostentatious, preferring to let the cut of his suits and his keen mind do the talking for him. She watched him put the yellow tie into a drawer and never pull it out again. Before his Venezuela office opened, she tried again, purchasing him the dark tie with the yellow threads. Until that day, she never saw him wear it.

Jeremy noticed her looking at the tie and smiled. "I wanted something special for today," he said, stepping back to look at her. "Looks like you did, too. I never thought I'd be glad you turned me down for dinner, but if this is the result, I can't say I'm sorry." He smiled. "You look absolutely stunning, Azi."

She started to speak but turned at the sound of people in the lobby. The sales team was arrayed in a circle, their words indistinct, but appreciative. In the center of the group stood Maricela. "Let me by, *guapos*," she said teasingly. "I need to put my things away before everyone arrives." Jeremy frowned, looking at his watch. He glanced at Azalea, then strode into the lobby.

"Nice of you to join us," he said drily. "The early arrivers will be here at any time." Denice and Azalea had planned the morning to begin at ten o'clock but knew some of the attendees would come straight from the airport and arrive early. Javier walked past Maricela, and Azalea noticed how his hand managed to glide across her lower back as he passed. *"Buenos dias, jefe,"* he said, nodding to Jeremy.

Jeremy ignored him and looked at Maricela. "Put your things away and then gather everyone. I want five minutes together before people arrive." He turned and walked into the main conference room where he stood at the window, looking out at the plaza below. Azalea noted the smug look on Maricela's face as she walked toward her own office. She was wearing a yellow dress that matched perfectly with the peonies situated around the lobby and conference rooms. *How does she do that?* wondered Azalea. Maricela's hair was stick straight today, glossy and thick. Her Louboutins were skyscrapers and Azalea marveled yet again that the woman didn't fall over while walking. Her dress fit as if she were poured into it, and her ever-present gold bangles shone against her dark skin. Every eye watched as she sashayed her way across the lobby.

"Señorita?" Esteban's voice cut through Azalea's thoughts. *"Quiere usted un cafecito?* And I saved you a piece of the bread pudding, just to be sure you get to try it. I hope I compare well *con la hornada de su madre,"* he finished shyly.

"Trátame de tú," responded Azalea. "And I'm sure it's wonderful. Thank you so much for saving me a piece." She took the proffered plate and smiled. "And *si*, I would love a *cafecito. Con leche y azucar, por favor."* She stood while Esteban poured her coffee and added cream and sugar.

He handed it to her and said, "*Perdóname, señorita.* I don't mean to insult—my English is not great. But you are very beautiful." He colored slightly. "I hope that is okay for me to say."

Azalea smiled. "*Gracias.*" She sipped the coffee. "Mmm, this is excellent."

"The best beans in Spain," he said proudly. "My father roasts them ever since I was a boy. I'm glad you like it."

Azalea glanced up to see Jeremy looking at them across the lobby. "Well, I'd better get to work," she said. "It's a very big day for all of us." She smiled again and walked to her desk, determined to try the bread pudding before the crowd arrived.

"Looks like you made a friend," said Jeremy as he walked into Azalea's office. He unbuttoned his blazer and sat down. She was busy chewing but grinned.

"You have to try this," she said between bites. "It's so good!"

He reached across the desk to wipe a crumb from her lower lip. "You'll need to touch up your lipstick, I think," he said.

She dabbed a napkin at her mouth and took a last drink of coffee. "Okay, I'm gonna run to the ladies' room." She reached into her drawer where she kept a small bag with toiletries. She added her lipstick and gloss and stood. "Be right back," she said, walking around her desk.

Jeremy stood as she passed, then reached out to smooth a stray curl from her cheek. "I've missed you, Azi," he said gruffly. "I need you today. I'm better with you and I want you by my side."

Azalea stood still, hardly breathing. *I need you today.* Surely this was just about the launch, she told herself.

"I'm here, Jeremy," she said, squeezing his hand. "You're going to be amazing and the press is going to love you." She turned to go but he held on.

"And you, Azi? What about you?"

Azalea met his eyes, then looked away. "I'll meet you in the conference room."

It was all she could manage to keep from running to the restroom. In the bathroom, she quickly brushed her teeth and reapplied her lipstick. She looked in the mirror, appraising her appearance and reminding herself that today was all about the work—about her skill and experience, about the months she toiled making this happen. She was a consultant paid to launch this company and she was going to do just that. Nothing more.

She turned to leave the restroom but stopped as Maricela walked in. The taller, younger woman looked her up and down, leaving no doubt as to her opinion. "So," she purred. "The little mouse decided to come out and play. I didn't know you had it in you."

Azalea's eyes narrowed. Pride and competitiveness flared in her, but she tamped them down. She wasn't going to play junior high games with this woman.

"You don't know me at all, Maricela," she said flatly. "I'm here to do my job."

Maricela's laugh bounced off the bathroom walls. "Ah, right," she responded. "You just go and…do your job."

Azalea brushed past her and left the restroom. Denice caught her eye as she walked into the lobby and asked, "You okay?" Azalea nodded brusquely. She put her things back in her desk, picked up her notebook, and headed for the conference room.

Like Tomás said: *Time to be my brilliant self.*

18

Jeremy stood at the head of the table with his back to the window. Everyone stood around the table excited for the day to start. He looked at each of them, his glance lingering on Azalea before skimming past Maricela, who walked in last. "So we made it," he said, opening his arms wide. "No more protests. Just a bunch of European journalists, although I'm not so sure that's any better." The team laughed at his wry joke. "I have every confidence we all know what to do today. Let's prove to these people that Fowler Enterprises is the company to watch in Spain and that we are here to make a difference." He scanned the room. "Daniel, your demo looked great last night. Well done." Daniel beamed at the praise, his colleagues thumping him on the back.

"Javier," Jeremy looked sternly at his European sales director. "Today is the day you prove to me that I was right to steal you from my competition."

Javier grinned. "*Sí, jefe!*" he saluted.

Jeremy continued, "Maricela will work with you on the key account meetings today. I'm sure the two of you can close at least one deal together, can't you?" Azalea wondered if she were the only one to catch the subtle warning beneath the public question. Javier and Maricela nodded.

"*Por seguro*, Jeremy," she answered. She casually flipped her hair over one shoulder. "*No hay problema.*"

Jeremy looked emotionlessly at her, then turned to Denice and Guillermo. "The place looks fantastic and I'm very aware of all the hours and hard work you've put into making this event happen. Thank you both." Denice inclined her head while Guillermo grinned.

Jeremy rubbed his hands together, then clapped twice. "All right," he said. "Let's launch!"

The team clapped and walked excitedly out of the conference room. Azalea moved to Jeremy's side, reaching for his arm. He turned and she leaned in to speak privately. "That was really nice. You inspired and praised them and they are going to be fantastic today." She smiled warmly. "Well done."

He looked long at her before nodding and heading for the smaller conference room where they would meet their first guest.

Before she followed him, Azalea looked around the lobby for Esteban. He was standing to the side of the tables, looking across the room at her. She walked to him and said, "That bread pudding was wonderful. It was just as good as my mom's."

Esteban beamed. "*Gracias, Bella.*"

Bella.

Esteban, Diego, and Javier had all called her *Beauty*. She smiled and turned toward the conference room, reminding herself that with her beauty came brains and experience. Today was going to be a good day.

A very good day.

Azalea was in the zone. Between the comprehensive research Lorena and the team at Ambos had delivered, Jeremy's perfectionism, and Azalea's insistence on rehearsing, the interviews flew by with the analysts and journalists taking copious notes and leaving with smiles. During one short break, Lorena ran in with an update: Network World's German office was sending a new writer; their usual staffer was out sick. It happened that morning, so the writer would join them after lunch. Lorena had a single sheet with the replacement's recent articles and Azalea and Jeremy spent the break reading and making notes.

"She's new and she's young—just out of university, I believe," Lorena told them. "She may be deferential or she may try to show off what she knows. I haven't worked with her before."

Jeremy was reading Anna Weber's latest article on his phone and looked up at Lorena. "She writes well," he noted. "Make sure we add her to our list of media even after…" he looked down at his notes to find the other journalist's name, "…Derek returns." Lorena nodded in agreement.

Denice walked in. "How are things going over here?" she asked brightly. "The demos are flawless, Jeremy. Everyone seems very pleased."

Jeremy stood and stretched his long frame. "That's great, Denice." He looked at Azalea. "We only have a minute until the next session. I could use a walk and some water. You?"

Azalea nodded. "Same here. I'm very ready to move a bit." The four left the conference room, with Denice in the lead.

As they walked out the door, Jeremy turned slightly and whispered, "Wanna go see your new boyfriend?"

She tilted her head, raising her eyebrows. "Seriously?" She mock punched his arm, determined to keep their interaction lighthearted, but Susana's warning rang in her mind: *Be careful.*

Jeremy looked sideways at her as they walked into the lobby. A dozen guests milled about, chatting, drinking coffee, and looking through their gift bags. Denice and Guillermo had put together a collection of Fowler Enterprises swag into small gym bags, perfect for traveling. It wasn't a cheap assortment, but Azalea had argued that they didn't need many of the items and it was worth spending money on those who took the time to come to the event. "Plus," she contended, "Most attendees are flying and they don't want something bulky. Nobody needs one more coffee mug or water bottle." Jeremy had agreed—*What CEO needs to approve expenses like this?* she wondered—and they ordered the nicer gifts.

Denice stood at the front desk and spoke over the crowd. "We're ready for you to move to your next session, everyone. We'll have this one and then lunch will be served."

Jeremy looked at Azalea. "So much for a quick break. Guess it's show time."

Azalea looked at the nearly empty tables—clearly the guests had enjoyed their breakfast. "I'll be right there," she said. "I'll grab us some water."

Jeremy looked across the room at Esteban, who had begun to clear the tables in readiness for the lunch caterer, then looked back at Azalea. "Don't be too long," he said and then turned away toward their conference room.

She looked at his retreating back and marveled that a man who was on a private jet with his lover not a week earlier was now jealous of a baker young enough to be her son. It was hard not to feel just a bit giddy at the attention. *But this is always about winning*, she cautioned herself. She couldn't help the surge of confidence, though. Here she was, a middle-aged divorcée. But she was also *Bella* in one of the most exciting cities in the world, at the top of her professional game. Desirable, pursued, and smart. *Damn smart*, she whispered as she approached the table where Esteban worked.

"Thank you again," she said. "Everything was wonderful and," she spread her arms wide, taking in the empty tables, "clearly everyone loved it." She reached out a hand and Esteban took it.

They shook hands and he answered, "*Muchisimas gracias, Bella*. I hope to see you in my café again soon. I'm going to add the bread pudding to the menu now." He smiled. "I'm calling it *La Bella Dulce*."

She smiled and nodded, accepting the compliment with grace. "That's lovely, Esteban. I look forward to seeing you soon."

Azalea took two bottles of water and walked back to the conference room, entering just as Jeremy, Ricardo, and Timothy Reynolds were sitting down. The men rose in a gentlemanly triad and Azalea moved quickly to the open seat next to Jeremy and across from the journalist. "Sorry to hold you up," she said, opening her notebook. "I'm Azalea Mora, head of corporate communications. Thank you for coming, Timothy."

"Well, it's not every day that an American company invests this much in Europe—much less Spain," he began gruffly. "You Yanks seem to think technology lives and breathes in Ireland, not the continent." He took a drink of his water and dabbed at his forehead with a napkin. "So why Spain, Fowler? It's bloody hot here, even with the aircon."

Azalea rose from her seat and moved to the wall where she did the quick math. The thermostat was set at 22C. *Double it and add thirty*, she calculated quickly. That was 74 degrees Fahrenheit, comfortable for most, but evidently too warm for the Brit. "I can fix that right now," she smiled as she dropped the thermostat to 19C. She'd freeze, but perhaps it would make the curmudgeon happy. "It should cool down quickly," she assured him.

Timothy humphed and looked back at his notes. "As I was saying: Why Spain?"

Azalea and Jeremy had practiced the answer several times over the previous week and he was ready. "You know that Fowler Enterprises has offices all over Latin America." The journalist nodded as Jeremy leaned back, expansive and open. "I've been following the quality of the software developers in this region. They're the equal of anyone in Ireland, the States, or Latin America. I'm betting our little outfit is simply the harbinger of a lot more tech migration to Spain."

"I'd hardly call Fowler Enterprises a 'little outfit,'" scoffed Timothy. Jeremy inclined his head in tacit acknowledgment of the man's backhanded compliment. "But why Barcelona? You could have picked Madrid...Seville...anyplace else. It's quite obvious this city is a hotbed of separatist activity. You rescheduled your launch already because of that bloody protest last week."

Ricardo stepped in. "And we do appreciate your willingness to come over a week later, Timothy," he said smoothly.

"But what about the next time?" the journalist began heatedly. "These idiots simply made you postpone a demo. What happens when they bomb your building?" The napkin came out again but Azalea refused to drop the temperature further.

Ricardo began to speak, but Jeremy interrupted him. "I feel quite confident that we'll manage the situation, whatever happens,

Timothy. We're bringing jobs to Barcelona—good jobs. Even the separatists can see the value of that. And hasn't that been a focus of your writing in the past year? Making sure US companies don't come over here for favorable tax laws and nothing else? We're here to benefit everyone, regardless of their political persuasion."

Timothy's pen poised over his notepad. "So is that your position? You're not opposed to the separatist movement?"

"I would say I'm neither separatist nor royalist, Timothy. I'm a capitalist." Azalea uncrossed her legs and nudged Jeremy's leg once with her knee in an unmistakable message: *Do not say another word.* She leaned across the table and looked directly in Timothy's eyes. "Surely you didn't fly down here to talk politics. You've been hugely instrumental in the growth of the European networking industry. Tell us what you thought of the demo. How can we best make use of our software to further European leadership in this space?"

Timothy set his pen down and looked over at Ricardo, then Jeremy. "'Hugely instrumental'?" He sighed. "She's good, gentlemen. She's very good. You may want to keep her around."

Azalea bristled. *Keep me around? What am I, a pet?* Jeremy's knee tapped hers, a companion warning. Her smile belied her simmering anger.

After their meeting, Azalea skipped lunch, preferring instead to meander around the lobby chatting with various attendees and the Fowler Enterprises employees. The afternoon crowd would comprise customers and she hoped it would be less fraught than the morning. She looked up to see Lorena and Denice welcoming a woman at the door. *That must be Anna Weber*, she thought, and walked to the front of the lobby.

Lorena introduced them. "Anna, this is Azalea Mora, head of corporate communications. Azalea, this is Anna Weber from Network World Germany." The women shook hands and Azalea asked if she were hungry.

"Famished," replied the young woman. Azalea led her to a café table where she could drop her bag.

"There's quite a spread," she said. "Go ahead and grab your lunch." Anna thanked her and headed for the table laden with food.

Lorena approached and asked, "How's it going?"

Azalea looked around to be certain no one could overhear her. "Great…until that incredibly boorish Timothy Reynolds showed up. He may be all buttoned up in his pinstripes, but he's a jackass." She brushed a curl behind her ear and waved her hand in dismissal. "Enough about him. How are you?" She lowered her voice. "Any news about your brother?"

Lorena grimaced. "The police are certain he is a hardened terrorist. But he's really just a scared boy who got caught up with the wrong people. He swears he has no idea how the gun got into his apartment, and I believe him." She looked around and leaned closer. "Those separatists just used him, Azalea. I know it!" She breathed deeply to control her emotions. "I don't know what we're going to do. His public defender is trying to get him out of jail, but I'm not hopeful."

Azalea squeezed Lorena's hand. "I'm so sorry, my friend."

Anna finished filling her plate and started back toward the café table. "Would you mind babysitting her for a bit?" Azalea asked Lorena. "I'm in desperate need of a few minutes to myself before round two." Lorena agreed, and Azalea smiled in thanks.

She walked to her office and closed the door, leaning back against it with a weary sigh. The morning had gone exceptionally well, with the annoying exception of Timothy Reynolds. But even that interview had been salvaged once she'd made it clear that her knowledge of the European software-as-a-service market was more than a match for his questions. Ricardo had gaped at her for nearly a minute before snapping back into sales executive mode and joining her in pitching the company. Jeremy answered questions authoritatively and with a calm assertiveness. At last, the journalist succumbed to their combined professionalism and admitted he was surprised and impressed and would write an article to that effect.

She was startled by a knock at her door. She opened it to see Jeremy. "Oh! Hi," she said, stepping back to let him in. The look on his face meant something—she just wasn't sure what. "Is something wrong?" she asked.

Jeremy laughed, shaking his head. "Wrong? Ah, my sweet Azi. I could kiss you, you amazing, wonderful woman."

Azalea stared at him. "What?"

He took a step closer, leaning in to whisper in her ear. "Don't worry, Azi. I'm not going to mess up your lipstick." His breath was warm on her cheek as he chuckled. "I just want you to know I think you're incredible and I can't believe I never realized how powerful you are." He stepped back to regard her. "That confidence is so sexy, I can't even begin to tell you."

She felt the blood rise to her face and had no idea how to respond.

"Hmm," he said, cocking his head. "So you are fearless in the face of a sexist journalist but tongue-tied with me. Interesting."

They heard Denice's voice from the lobby. "It's now time for our next session," she called out.

"Time to go," Jeremy said. "Come to think of it, I may have to follow Mr. Reynolds' advice."

"What do you mean?" she asked, her heart in her throat. *What is going on here?*

"I may just have to keep you around."

19

Azalea watched Jeremy leave her office and she closed the door once more. It was a heady experience: Finally getting the recognition from the man she had loved. Putting the arrogant journalist in his place. Seeing the admiration in the eyes of everyone in the office. She knew today was a success and she was largely responsible. She couldn't wait to see the coverage over the next few weeks.

But she had a nagging feeling that she was making too much of it.

She thought fleetingly again of her mother. Azalea's parents were hardworking, salt of the earth types, and her mother would have laughed at her daughter's conceit. Helen Mora would have been incredibly proud but would have told her in no uncertain terms, "Let *me* be proud of you, Azalea. That's my job, not yours."

Her phone buzzed and she looked to see a text from Landon.

Hey Mom. Say a prayer for me!

Her heart dropped—*What was wrong?*

Of course, honey, she typed quickly. *What's up?*

That new account I told you about? Meeting with the VP this morning and I'm super nervous.

Azalea smiled, relieved. Her youngest was charming and wicked smart—that VP didn't know what was coming.

You are going to be amazing, but of course I'll pray. She finished with their special line: *Go be your brilliant self!*

Landon sent a quick selfie, a polished young man in a dress shirt, his hair cropped short on the sides and tousled on top. Her heart caught in her throat—how she missed him.

Thanks Mom. I love you!

I love you, too, Landon. I believe in you.

Azalea leaned against her door again, this time to pray silently for her son. When she finished, she smoothed her dress and thought, *Remember what's important.*

"Thanks, Mama," she whispered, glancing at the ceiling.

The conference rooms were full. The caterers were clearing the lunch tables and she looked at her watch, surprised to see it was after three o'clock. Guillermo approached her with a smile. "Great day, Azalea. Congratulations."

Azalea smiled but shook her head. "Congratulations to all of us, Guillermo. This is a huge win for the entire team." She turned to see Lorena and Anna Weber coming out of one of the smaller rooms.

"I know our last-minute change meant I lost my slot this morning with Mr. Fowler," said Anna. "But is there any chance to get just a few minutes with him this afternoon?"

Azalea looked at her watch; the event was due to finish at four o'clock and Jeremy was in a room with Ricardo and a Portuguese systems integrator. "Possibly," she hedged. "Let me check."

Azalea walked to the conference room where the men were in deep conversation. She knocked lightly and entered, saying, "Please forgive the interruption, *senhores*." She leaned over Jeremy's shoulder and asked if he might spare a few minutes for the German journalist.

Jeremy looked across at the customer and smiled. "I think we've nearly finished here, haven't we, Rafael?"

The two men shook hands and Jeremy excused himself, following Azalea to the lobby where Lorena and Anna stood chatting. "Always time for Network World," said Jeremy, extending his hand to Anna. "Shall we go into a conference room?"

The three sat around the small table and Jeremy spent ten minutes discussing the acquisition and the technology, the jobs Fowler Enterprises would bring to Barcelona, and the local governance. "As you know, Fowler Enterprises is headquartered in the US and I need to be back there. I have every expectation that we'll have a country manager here in the next month." Jeremy answered more questions, smoothly discussing the innovative demos they premiered that day as well as a broad outline of the road map for the next year. After a few more minutes, he looked at his watch and excused himself. "Thank you so much for coming, particularly last minute. I look forward to speaking with you again."

They rose and returned to the lobby where all the attendees had gathered. Denice stood at the front of the room and thanked everyone for coming. Jeremy added his thanks and wished them all safe travels. The group left, stopping to shake hands or share hearty goodbyes before leaving for the airport. Within fifteen minutes, the room was empty save the Fowler Enterprises team.

Jeremy looked around. He smiled broadly at Javier and Ricardo. "Well done," he said. "I'm very, very pleased." Azalea knew that was high praise from Jeremy, but did the fiery Latinos? He nodded a tight-lipped thank you to Maricela, who stood proudly between the sales executives. Smiling at the receptionist, he said, "*Muchas gracias, Guillermo. Todo seveía maravilloso.*" The young man beamed.

"And Denice," Jeremy began, shaking his head. "Where do I begin? We couldn't have done this without your leadership and organization. Thank you to you and your team." Denice inclined her head in thanks.

Jeremy looked at Azalea and she held her breath. *Please don't say anything weird*, she thought wildly. *Please don't make this about us.*

"I've never worked with a more competent communications pro in my career. Whatever good coverage we get in the next month will be due to you and Ambos." He nodded at Lorena. "Thank you and your team, Lorena. You gave us the intelligence we needed to excel today." Azalea slowly let out her breath and smiled. She looked at Lorena and winked.

"*Por supuesto*, Jeremy," answered Lorena. "*Fue un placer.*"

Jeremy laughed. "Well, if you think that was a pleasure, then you'll really enjoy tonight. Everyone gather your things—I'm taking us all out for tapas and drinks. We have reservations at Dr. Stravinsky's at five o'clock." The entire room gasped and began clapping. The trendy Barcelona bar was known for its distinctive drinks and appetizers. As the team began gathering their things, Jeremy approached Azalea.

"Please tell me you aren't going to bail out on this gathering, Azi," he said.

"Of course not," she answered. "The team completely excelled today—they deserve this." She smiled. "I wouldn't miss it."

"Will you ride over with me?" he asked.

Azalea hesitated.

"It's just a car ride, Azi."

Denice approached with a grin. "Sorry to interrupt, *jefe*," she said. "Azalea, will you grab a cab with me? I didn't drive in today because I was pretty sure we'd be drinking tonight." Azalea glanced sideways at Jeremy, questioning.

"Why don't you both ride over with me?" he said, looking pointedly at Azalea.

"Great! Let me grab my things," said Denice, hurrying off.

Jeremy smiled wryly at Azalea. "You don't have to look so smug."

It seemed the entire bar was filled with Fowler Enterprises employees, everyone enjoying adult beverages. Azalea ordered a sparkling water with lime and sat in a corner to watch her colleagues. Maricela and Javier snuggled tightly into a booth, each drinking something Azalea couldn't identify. They seemed to have abandoned their furtive behavior, with Javier's arm around Maricela and her hand on his thigh.

Denice slid in next to her. "So that's no big surprise," she said, nodding at the two. "I kinda thought she was with the boss for a while—they seemed pretty chummy. Guess I was wrong." She took a long swallow of her cocktail, chunks of pink sugar floating in the foam. She closed her eyes. "Mmm," she murmured. "This is so good!" She looked at Azalea. "What are you drinking?"

"Oh, I'm pretty boring," she admitted, laughing. "Just some sparkling water for me."

Denice quirked an eyebrow. "The boss is buying and you're drinking *water*?" she asked.

Azalea grinned. "I didn't eat any lunch," she said. "It's much better on an empty stomach." She moved to change the subject. "So how do you think it went?"

Denice looked hard at her. "Are you serious? We *crushed* it. I'm almost thankful we had to delay a week. Fowler Enterprises reigned today." The ordinarily garrulous Denice was becoming even more so as she finished her drink. She looked quizzically at Azalea. "What does it take to get you excited? How are you always so calm?" she asked.

Jeremy approached the two of them and asked, "May I join you?"

The women nodded, and he pulled a chair up to their table. "Everyone seems to be having a great time," he said, looking around. "A nice chance to blow off a little steam after a stressful couple of weeks."

Denice answered, "I know my CEO doesn't need my compliments, but I'll give them anyway. Getting that extra day off last week and having a group workday yesterday were genius moves. You've brought this team together so well and they love you."

It was true. Jeremy had adeptly managed the entire office, giving them both the responsibility and the encouragement to pull off a successful event. As Azalea pondered, he replied. "Thank you, Denice. Your CEO does need compliments. And I appreciate them very much." Azalea's eyes flicked to his face, realizing the statement was made for her ears.

"Well, if you're still buying, I think I'll have another of these," remarked Denice, rising. Jeremy laughed and nodded. She smiled at Azalea. "And I'll see you tomorrow in the lobby at twelve-thirty."

Jeremy looked between the two of them. "Oh? What are you two doing?

Denice described the spa day they had booked, including the massage and floating in the Roman bath, then left the two of them for the bar.

"Sounds like a wonderful day," he said to Azalea.

She nodded. "She went last weekend and has been raving about it. We thought it would be a fun treat after all the hard work."

"You deserve it, Azi," he said. He looked pointedly at her glass. "Still don't drink at work events, huh?"

She smiled, nodding. "Some things don't change." It was one of her professional rules: no alcohol at work events. As she described to him years before, she'd seen far too many women trying to keep up with their male colleagues at the bar after work, failing and making fools of themselves. "How on earth would I expect someone to treat me with respect the next day if I've been a drunken idiot the night before?" she'd asked him.

"So…" he began. "I don't know about you, but a fancy cheese platter isn't enough after a day like this. Any chance you'd join me for dinner?" He looked directly at her. "I'd really like to take you to dinner, Azi."

The tension between them was palpable. She knew her heart was far from settled, although it appeared his was clear. *It's just dinner*, she thought. *We'll grab something to eat, chat awhile, and that will be it.*

"Okay," she answered at last. "Okay."

Jeremy smiled and stood, offering her his hand. "Your carriage awaits, milady."

Azalea looked up at Jeremy, not taking his hand. "Please don't take this the wrong way," she began, "but I don't—"

"You don't want us to leave together," he finished for her.

"They're my colleagues," she said quietly.

He nodded. "And I know how important your privacy is." He straightened, looking around. "Okay, look, Pedro is out front with the car. Why don't you go out and I'll make my quick rounds to say goodbye and settle the bill? I'll meet you out there in ten minutes." He smiled at her. "I get it, Azi. It's all right."

20

She stepped outside into the cool night air and looked around. Pedro was leaning against his car at the curb. She approached and said, "*Buenos noches*, Pedro. I'm supposed to meet Mr. Fowler here—"

"*Si, señorita*," replied Pedro, opening the door for her—*As if he expected me,* she thought. Azalea slid into the back seat and waited. After a few moments, she felt her purse vibrate and opened the elegant clutch to retrieve her phone. It was a text from Landon.

I did it, Mom! I got the new contract!

Elated, she texted back. *I am so proud of you! Congratulations. I hope you are doing something fun to celebrate.*

Tomás and Emily are taking me to dinner after we're all off work, he wrote. *Em's bringing her roommate Amy. We've gone out a couple of times—she's a really nice girl. Should be fun!*

Azalea was still smiling as she answered. *Have a wonderful time, Son. I love you and I can't wait to hear all the details.*

Pedro opened the door for Jeremy as she finished. "That's a pretty smile," he commented. "What's got you so happy?"

"One sec," said Azalea as she finished typing. *Say hello to Tomás and give each other a gigantic hug from your mama.* She looked up, still smiling broadly. "Landon just scored a big sale with a very important customer." Then she stopped. "I'm sorry. You don't need to hear me babbling about my kids." She looked up as Pedro pulled out into traffic. "So where are we going?"

Jeremy smiled. "It's a surprise," he answered. "And I don't mind you babbling. Landon's such a charismatic kid—it doesn't surprise me."

Azalea looked long at her former fiancé. "That's kind of you to say." Neither of them spoke again for a few minutes and Azalea wondered if she should try to fill the silence or just be still.

At last, Pedro pulled to a stop. Azalea looked out the window and her eyes widened in surprise. They were at the Monument Hotel, home of the Restaurante Lasarte. She'd read about the restaurant and its award-winning chef—there was no possible way to get in last minute on a Friday night. She looked back at Jeremy, but he had already exited and was walking around the car to open her door. Azalea took his hand and stepped out.

"*Gracias*, Pedro," he said. "*Te llamaré cuando terminemos.*" He offered Azalea his arm and she took it, still slightly disoriented. They walked to the front door where a white-gloved doorman ushered them in. The woman at the desk smiled. "Señor Fowler! *Bienvenidos.* Your table is ready." She walked them to a table covered in white linen, set with china and silver, and decorated with candles and a bouquet of red roses. A bottle of Cava chilled in a bucket next to the table.

Jeremy held out Azalea's chair and she sat, her mind reeling. Clearly, this hadn't been a spur of the moment idea on his part. Getting reservations at this restaurant was a minor miracle, and having it set up so—*romantically?*—confused her.

Jeremy sat across from her as the waiter came to pour their drinks. The delicate flutes sparkled in the candlelight. "Will you share a glass with me, Azi?" he asked. "This isn't a work event—it's just us."

Somberly, Azalea nodded and Jeremy held his glass up for a toast. "To you," he said softly. "To the most amazing woman I've ever known." He clinked his glass against hers and they sipped, eyes never leaving each other.

At last, Azalea looked away. It was all too much to process and she needed to break their gaze. "It's beautiful," she said. "I don't really know what to say. This is a bit more than I expected."

Jeremy nodded. "It's okay, Azi. I wanted something special for tonight."

"How on earth did you get a reservation?" she asked. She took another sip and added, "And what if I didn't agree to come?"

"I knew you'd say yes," he answered simply. "And the reservation wasn't difficult. I make it a priority to meet the right people everywhere Fowler Enterprises operates."

A faint pang of dismay echoed in her mind. *Why is he always so sure of himself?* she wondered. But her flickering discomfort dissipated as she looked once again at the beautiful setting. *He's really trying,* she thought. *Stop being so critical.*

"So tell me more about Landon's job," he said. "And what's going on with Tomás? Still the perennial student?"

Azalea smiled. The boys were her pride and joy, and they were both doing well. It was a relief to talk about something else—something safe. "I guess I haven't told you," she started. "They moved to Colorado in January."

"Colorado? What's in Colorado?" he asked. Just then, the waiter returned with the first course. "I hope you don't mind," Jeremy said as the waiter arranged the starters. "I ordered the Lasarte menu for us. We'll get to try a lot of their best cuisine and some lovely wines."

"Of course not," she answered. "It's an adventure." The waiter bowed slightly and left, and Jeremy took her plate and began to serve her from each dish.

"So," he repeated, "what's in Colorado?"

Azalea closed her eyes for a brief moment and said a quick prayer. She opened her eyes and Jeremy was looking at her, a hint of a smile on his face. "Still my devout Azi," he said. "I would have prayed with you if you'd asked."

She looked long at him, gauging his seriousness. "I'll remember that."

"Aha," he said with a grin. "That means there will be a next time. And now…let's eat. And tell me: What's in Colorado?"

Azalea laughed and began eating. The waiter reappeared with a new wine for them to try and she at last was able to describe her sons' decision to move. They chatted amiably and she began to relax. The food was excellent, the wine perfectly paired.

"Enough about my boys," said Azalea. "What about you?"

Jeremy smiled and reached for her hand. "I'm great. Everything is exactly the way it should be."

Azalea sat still, unsure how to respond.

Jeremy squeezed her hand then pulled away, taking another bite of the prawns. "This is delicious," he said. "How do you like the food?"

Thankful to change the subject, she responded enthusiastically. "It's incredible. It's no wonder they have three Michelin stars."

The two sat companionably for the next hour, talking about the food and Barcelona. She asked about Fowler Enterprises, and he described his most recent trip to the office in Brazil and the unrest in Saõ Paolo. "It's getting dangerous in so many places in the world," he said.

"Were you worried while you were there?" she asked.

"No," he admitted. "I have a great relationship with the authorities there, just like here. It's important for my business to get to know the mayor and even higher government officials." He dabbed his lips with his napkin. "Stability is key to business success and I'm not about to lose because some group doesn't like the government." The waiter came back to clear their plates and deliver their final course, an assortment of petit fours along with crystal dishes of sorbet. A slightly sweet wine accompanied the dessert, and Azalea thought briefly that she was thankful not to be driving that night.

The two lingered over their sweets and Jeremy seemed to make a decision. He set his spoon down and looked solemn. "I want to tell you why I got involved with Maricela," he said.

Azalea stopped mid-sip and set down her glass. "You don't need to explain anything to me, Jeremy," she said. "It's none of my business."

"Maybe not," he replied, "but I want you to know. She worked for me years ago but then left the company. She came back after you—after we broke up." He drank deeply from his glass, then looked away. "She made it very clear what she wanted, and I guess I liked being chased." He looked back at Azalea. "I'm sorry."

"Sorry?" she asked, astonished. "For what? You had every right to fall in love with someone else, Jeremy." *Do I tell him I know about their earlier relationship?* Azalea wasn't sure, but she dove in. "Maricela told me you two had been a couple before we met. She accused me of being responsible for both of your breakups."

Jeremy sat back, frowning. "Wow. That must have been awkward."

"It was," she admitted. "I had no idea you'd known each other before. It was a little hard to feel sorry for her after how she's treated me the past few weeks."

"I saw that. I'm sorry. She's not a bad person, but she can be pretty vindictive." He reached for her hand. "I'm not trying to justify her behavior—"

"It's fine—I'm a big girl and it was more annoying than anything." She didn't pull her hand away and continued. "Anyway, I'm the one who should apologize. I'm terribly sorry for what I did to you."

He stroked her hand with his thumb. "I understand…at least now I do. Before? I didn't understand it at all." He lifted her hand to his lips. "But now? Maybe—"

"Please don't," she whispered. "This has been so lovely. Please don't say anything more."

He nodded slowly, then took his hand away. He paid the bill, texted Pedro, and helped her from her seat. She again took his arm, and they walked outside to await the car.

Jeremy walked Azalea to her apartment door. They stood awkwardly until he reached for her hand and kissed her gently on the cheek. "Thank you for having dinner with me," he said.

Azalea smiled crookedly and squeezed his hand. "I wasn't sure I should. This whole thing has been a bit…." She searched for the right word. "Odd? I mean, no one has ever bought a company just so he could take me to dinner."

"I had to get your attention somehow," he answered. He looked away, then took both her hands. "Could I come in? I'm not quite ready to say good night."

Azalea's stomach knotted. It *had* been a lovely evening, but alarms began to ring in her head. Jeremy obviously wanted to rekindle their romance, wanted her back in spite of her jilting him. She wanted to believe he'd changed, that he wasn't the same man he'd been for their two years together. That somehow they could have a true partnership, based on equal respect. He and Maricela were over, and he was moving heaven and earth to be near her. That meant something, didn't it?

She nodded and opened the door.

21

Jeremy took off his jacket and laid it across the back of one of the dining room chairs. "After all that wine, do you have any coffee? Maybe some decaf?"

She moved to the drawer and pulled out two red pods. "Still drink it black?" she asked.

He chuckled. "It's only been a year, Azi. I haven't changed that much."

Should that worry me?

She made two cups of coffee, adding cream and sugar to hers, and brought them to the table where Jeremy stood.

"Shall we sit on the sofa?" he asked.

She nodded and walked to the living room. He sat on the love seat, leaning back against the cushions as he loosened his tie. He patted the seat next to him. "Sit with me."

Azalea slipped off her shoes, then sat gingerly on the seat, her heart beating fast. She was torn between enjoying his company and worrying that she was opening a door she couldn't close. As they both reached to set their cups on the table, their shoulders brushed, and she flinched.

"Azi." Jeremy looked wounded. "What are you afraid of?"

She looked away, thinking. *What am I afraid of?* She rolled her shoulders back, aware of the tension beginning to knot along her neck. "I'm not sure. I don't know what's happening here."

Jeremy shifted on the sofa and beckoned her to him. "Turn around," he said softly. "Let me massage your shoulders."

She looked at him, unsure. The thought of his hands made her flesh tingle and her head swim. Azalea realized that her next move might set her back on the course she'd left nearly a year ago.

I just want to be loved. Is that so wrong?

He reached for her. "Come here, Azi. Let me do this for you."

She turned and leaned against him, reaching back to pull her long hair over one shoulder. Jeremy slid his hands up her bare arms and then began to massage her shoulders, his thumbs pressing the muscles along her neck. "Relax," he breathed.

Other than the morning he'd brought her flowers, it had been almost a year since they were completely alone. Her mind was a jumble—but her body began to respond. She tipped her head forward and a moan escaped her as her muscles began to loosen.

"You're so tense," he murmured. "I know how hard you've been working." His hands slid down her shoulders to her shoulder blades and he deftly massaged the stress from her back. "You're the reason we succeeded today, Azi. I'm so proud of you."

Proud of me? A tendril of worry whispered in Azalea's mind, but his hands moved back up to her neck, then into her hair. She felt his lips behind one ear, softly kissing her as he slid his hands down her arms.

"Azi," he whispered, his voice deep. "We're so good together...." His hands moved to her waist, and he pulled her closer to him. She was keenly aware of his desire and realized with a start that she wanted him, too.

Azalea turned to face him, her body taut with indecision. They gazed at each other for a long moment, and then she decided, sliding her arms around his neck. Their kiss took her breath away. *It's been so long*, she thought. *I've been alone so long.*

As they pulled apart, Jeremy took her face in his hands. "I've missed you, Azi." He ran his fingers through her curls and pulled her to him again, kissing her deeply.

"I've missed you, too," she breathed.

He buried his face in her neck, holding her tight. "I need you, Azi. I need you right now." He pulled back and gazed at her, his longing plain. "Please don't say no."

Every nerve in her body screamed at her to say *Yes*, but still she hesitated.

What am I doing?

It's different, she convinced herself. *It has to be.*

She pulled away, then stood, not taking her eyes from his. Jeremy sat very still as she reached back to unzip her dress. His eyes widened as it slipped from her shoulders and fell to the ground. She stood in her bra and panties, a slight shiver running through her as she contemplated making love with him at last.

"You are so beautiful." His voice was husky as gazed at her. Then he stood and carried her to the bedroom. "I love you, Azi. I have always loved you."

Azalea pressed her cheek to his chest. She could hear his heart beating and tightened her arms around him.

"I love you, too," she whispered.

I do. I'm sure I do.

Azalea stretched languidly, her eyes closed against the sun she felt warming the drapes. She slept later than she wanted to, but it was Saturday and she had nowhere to be until she met Denice in the lobby. Rolling over away from the soft morning light, she sat up suddenly, clutching the comforter.

Jeremy.

She jumped up, wrapping her robe around her chilling body.

Where is he?

In the kitchen, she found a note propped against the coffee maker.

Good morning, my beauty. I hope you slept in and are reading this late. I had some work to do in the office but didn't want to wake you. Please don't worry—no one saw me leave. Your privacy is secure!

I'll call in a bit and we can figure out what we want to do for the rest of the day.

You were right. It was worth waiting for.

Love you, J

Azalea walked back to the bedroom in a daze. She could still feel his hands in her hair, his mouth on hers when she finally gave in. She ran a fingertip lightly across her lip, remembering the moment she reached for him. *Why now?*

For two years Azalea had insisted that they delay intimacy, that it was important they build a trusting relationship that wasn't based on sex. She opened her heart and shared with him the pain she experienced from her ex-husband's infidelity. It was the one area where she never gave in and, astonishingly, the one area where Jeremy hadn't been demanding. He thought it was quaint and he reached the point where he simply teased her about it. Once they got engaged, Jeremy had asked again that she share his bed, but when she told him that "it was worth waiting for"—*I actually said those words!*—he acquiesced and simply refurnished her beautiful separate bedroom in his Orlando mansion. She loved him so much, especially in the beginning. But even when he proposed, she had an inkling that sex would become a connection she couldn't sever.

But now she wondered, *Why did I wait so long?*

For months she'd been lonely, far from home and friends. Last night she drank too much and let her guard down. *Don't put this on the wine*, she rebuked herself. *You made this choice completely sober.*

His hands. His mouth. Azalea's face flushed at the memory. She looked at the chair in the corner of her bedroom, her lacy bra and panties strewn on the seat. *And I thought no one but me would see them.*

She was awash in emotion—it had been years since she'd had sex and the thrill of it engulfed her. *But have I lost something?*

The apartment felt oppressive, and Azalea realized where she needed to go. She dressed quickly, grabbed her headphones, then whispered a prayer that she wouldn't run into Jeremy in the elevator or the lobby.

Azalea ran for the beach. She ran and ran, turning the music up loud.

At last, she stopped and stood staring at the ocean. She slipped off her shoes and walked into the surf, the cold water biting at her legs but cooling her run- and emotion-heated body. She looked at her watch—ten-thirty. She'd run for an hour and was no nearer to clarity than when she began.

Her mind whispered that she made a mistake. Her heart? All she wanted at that moment was to run back into his arms. To immerse herself in his caresses, his passion.

It had been years since she'd allowed herself to feel this deeply. Years since her ex-husband had betrayed her and shredded their marriage vows. Azalea took a shuddering breath as she waded deeper into the water.

I just want to be loved.

Azalea's phone jolted her out of her reverie. It was Jeremy.

"H-hello?" she stuttered.

"Babe, where are you? I don't have a key to your apartment and you're not answering the door." He sounded almost frantic. "Are you okay?"

"I'm okay," she said quietly. "I'm at the beach. I went for a run."

Jeremy was quiet. "Azi," he began, then hesitated. "Come back."

Azalea stood silently as the waves lapped against her calves. She shivered in the cold water as she pondered her next words, knowing they portended far more than a simple return to the apartment.

"I'm coming."

Jeremy sent Pedro to pick her up. She sat quietly in the back seat, still trying to process last night, what she'd decided and what it meant. Pedro stopped at the entrance and Azalea thanked him absentmindedly. She went up the elevator and found Jeremy standing at the front door of her apartment. He looked relieved and she responded with a timid smile as she opened the door.

The door had barely shut when Jeremy's arms were around her, pulling her close. His lips found hers and she melted into his kiss. As they separated, breathless, she was surprised to find that she was crying.

"Baby…what's wrong?" he asked.

"I don't know," she admitted. "I'm just...overwhelmed, I guess. I'm confused and I'm happy and I'm scared...." She trailed off, looking away and then back at him.

He took her hands and squeezed, then pulled her into his chest. Stroking her hair, he said, "I'm only happy, Azi. This is exactly the way we're supposed to be and nothing is going to separate us again." He suddenly pulled her tight. "Nothing."

Too tight, she thought.

Azalea put her hands on Jeremy's chest and pushed back slightly, looking up at him. *Slow down*, she thought. *Please slow down.* Then it hit her. She had less than an hour before Denice arrived.

"I need to shower. Do you want to go grab us some breakfast before I have to leave to meet Denice?"

Jeremy grimaced. "Damn. I had forgotten you were doing that today. No way you can cancel?" She frowned and shook her head. "I figured we'd just spend the day in bed," he confessed.

Too tempting.

"I'll only be gone a few hours," she said. "And I did promise. She'd be upset—and I really do want to go." She looked up at him, tilting her head, the tears still glinting in her lashes. "Maybe we can go together next time?"

Jeremy smiled. "Fine. I'll let you go but come straight back to me. I'll just work in my apartment. We have a lot of time to make up for, my love." He kissed her lips, her nose, and her eyelids. "A lot."

Azalea pressed her cheek to his chest, marveling at how comfortable it felt. She reluctantly pulled away and headed for the shower. "I'll text when we're on our way back," she said. Jeremy nodded and left the apartment.

She showered quickly and put on a simple flowing skirt with a tank and sweater, slipping her feet into sandals. She knotted her hair into a simple bun and applied a quick coat of mascara to her lashes and a gloss to her lips. She looked at her reflection. *Do I look any different?*

I'll let you go, he said.

I'll let you?

And what had he said last night? *It's only been a year, Azi. I haven't changed that much.*

But...*Azi, I love you.*

I love you, too, she'd said. She remembered his hands, his body, the way he'd loved her and the way she'd responded.

She had a sudden rush of memory, thinking about the young couple in the elevator at La Sagrada Familia.

I just want to be loved.

22

Azalea's hair created a nimbus around her head as she floated in the warm salt water. Denice's description and the website hadn't done the place justice, she thought.

The woman at the front desk explained that they could move from bath to bath at will, as each had a unique advantage for the body. Azalea considered moving to the cold pool but was so utterly relaxed she couldn't manage the effort.

Denice sat next to her after visiting the jacuzzi. "Ahh…" she sighed as she slid into the water, the candlelight flickering on her face as she lay back to float. "This is even more magical than I remember it."

Azalea stood up, the water running down her face. "I'm so glad you invited me." She leaned against a wall, then sunk down until the water met her chin. "I have just about melted into this bath."

An attendant silently beckoned them and the two women stepped up onto the stone floor. "The only thing that could get me out of there is knowing we have an hour-long massage," whispered Denice. Azalea smiled and wrapped her robe around her. She felt languid and sleepy, her earlier anxiety a faint memory. Instead, she imagined what it would be like to share that warm bath with Jeremy, their bodies wrapped around each other....

"Hey—you there?" Azalea realized she'd not heard anything Denice had said.

"Sorry. It's just so relaxing, I sort of zoned out." She was thankful the woman couldn't read her mind.

The attendant led them to the dressing room area where she explained quietly that they should take off their swimsuits, rinse off, and put back on their robes. The serene music and the susurrus of low voices felt like a caress as they walked to the massage rooms.

"Hola," said a young man. "*Me llamo Pablo.*" Azalea had to lean in to hear him speak. He motioned for her to turn around and he removed her robe, then pointed to the table. She lay on her stomach, and he placed a light sheet over her.

The room was warm and smelled of flowers. Pablo began working on her upper back, spreading a warm oil over her skin. "Tell me if you want a different pressure."

Azalea was drowsy and hardly heard him. As he worked on her muscles, she daydreamed about the massage Jeremy had given her the night before. "Let me do this for you, Azi," he said. *But was it for me?* It was obvious he wanted her. It was so confusing, trying to decipher his motives and her own responses. Jeremy was still Jeremy. He was strong, intelligent, handsome, and charming.

And he knew how to get what he wanted.

But I wanted it, too, she thought. *I wanted that intimacy. I wanted to finally let go and feel something, something passionate and real.*

Unbidden, she wondered how their lovemaking compared with him and Maricela.

Pablo softly told her to turn over and held the sheet up as she rolled onto her back. She lay still as he massaged her shoulders, neck, and arms. Before he reached her calves, she fell asleep, her emotions leaving her drained. When he finished her legs and feet, she awoke to feel his hands massaging her head through her thick hair. The redolent floral oil was glorious, and she fantasized about

Jeremy lying next to her, smelling her hair when she returned to the apartment.

"I hope you enjoyed the experience, *señorita*," said Pablo. "Take your time coming out. There is water and tea just outside the room, and we will bring wine and chocolates to the lounging area."

Azalea murmured, "Thank you," and arched her back as he left the room. She ran her hands down her arms, still lightly covered with the fragrant oil. Reluctantly, she stood and put on her robe, leaving the room just as Denice was leaving hers.

The two women walked to the lounging area where they drank deeply of the cold water. An attendant brought them each a glass of wine that caught the light of the candles set around the room.

Denice held out her glass. "To us," she said. "To two small, fabulous women." Azalea laughed and raised her glass, lightly touching Denice's.

"To us," she answered.

It was four o'clock before Azalea and Denice returned to the apartment building. They were quiet and relaxed, yawning the entire way, marveling at how early it was. After two hours in near dark, it felt surprising to drive in the sunlight.

They took the elevator up together. "So what are you up to tonight?" asked Denice. "Please don't tell me you're going to work."

Azalea shook her head. "No way. I'm not going to waste everything we just did on working. I'm going to put on my pajamas and curl up on the sofa with a book." She hoped her face didn't betray the lie. She smiled. "Thank you again for today. It was really lovely."

"I had a great time," said Denice. The doors opened on the fourth floor and she smiled. "Enjoy your book. See you Monday." She walked off, waving.

Azalea leaned against the wall of the elevator and closed her eyes. She couldn't remember the last time she'd felt so relaxed. But now she felt the butterfly wings of excitement in her stomach. She felt uncomfortable texting Jeremy at the spa—she hadn't wanted Denice to notice. But now she pulled out her phone and texted: *I'm in the elevator. Are you ready?*

His response came in seconds. *Are you kidding? The question is: are you?*

Oh, yes. She answered. *Hurry.*

Azalea answered the door with a smile. Jeremy walked in, a puzzled look on his face.

"What?" she asked, wondering what was wrong.

"You're still dressed," he said, then laughed.

She playfully slapped at his arm and he grabbed her hand to pull her in for a kiss. "I missed you," he said.

"It's only been like four hours!" she protested. He slid his hands down her shoulders and arms. "Your skin is so soft," he said. "And you look very relaxed. Was it as good as you hoped?"

"It was incredible," she gushed. "We have to go together—you would love it." Azalea walked around the kitchen counter and asked, "Are you hungry? I can fix something or we can go out."

Jeremy looked incredulous. He strode around the counter and lifted her easily, ignoring her protests as he walked to the bedroom. "The only thing I want right now is you."

Azalea opened sleepy eyes and gazed at the moonlight streaming in the window. It lent a magical quality to the air around her, casting shadows in some areas and highlighting others. Jeremy stroked her shoulder and asked, "You awake?'

"Mmhmm," she answered, snuggling back into him. He buried his face in her hair and said, "You smell so good."

Azalea reached back to stroke his hip. "The whole time the guy was massaging oil into my scalp I was daydreaming about you smelling my hair. Is that weird?"

"I don't know how I feel about another man's hands all over you." He pulled her closer and kissed her neck. "Did he do this?"

Azalea laughed. "Don't be silly...."

"Or this?" Jeremy turned her to him, his hands sliding across her hips. "Or this...?"

The sun woke her and Azalea threw an arm over her eyes. "It's so bright...what time is it?" She rolled over but the spot next to her was empty. "Jeremy?" she called.

Jeremy walked naked into the bedroom and slid in beside her, kissing her forehead. "I'm here. Just didn't want to wake you—you were sleeping so soundly."

Azalea curled up next to him, her head on his chest. "Couldn't you sleep?" she asked.

"I slept later than usual," he answered. "Lots on my mind."

Azalea moved away so she could look at her lover. "Are you okay? Is something wrong?" A faint sense of trepidation crossed her face. *Was this a mistake?*

Jeremy smiled as he touched her cheek "Nothing's wrong, love. I just don't think you can understand what it's like to be me right now."

She waited, eyes wide.

"I've watched how Javier trips all over himself at the office to be around you. There was that caterer—that guy didn't stop staring at you all morning." He kissed her lightly. "And then there's your amayyyzing massage therapist," he said, dramatically drawing out the adjective.

Azalea frowned. "Oh, c'mon," she chided. "Getting a massage is like going to the doctor—he's like a medical professional."

"How many medical professionals rub hot scented oil on your naked body?"

Azalea scrutinized him, wondering how serious he was. "Are you—" she began.

"Marry me."

She stopped. *What?*

"Jer—"

"Marry me, Azi. We can do it tomorrow. I'm actually supposed to have lunch with one of the district judges tomorrow. I know he could make it happen. We could go to the courthouse here in Barcelona and get married tomorrow. I'd say today, but it's Sunday and they aren't open."

Azalea stared at him, not knowing what to say. At last, she pulled away and sat up, plumping a pillow behind her and pulling the sheet up under her arms. He reached for the sheet and pulled it down, exposing her breasts. "Don't cover up," he said gently. "I want to look at you just like this—naked in the sunlight, hair all tousled, mascara smudged." Azalea reflexively raised a hand to her eye, but Jeremy caught it before she could wipe anything away. "Don't do that," he said. "You look perfect, and I want to remember this moment exactly as you are."

She gazed long at him, uncomfortable. He repeated, "Marry me, Azi."

Azalea's mind spun. This was all too fast. She felt sluggish and stupid, unsure how to respond. "What about the boys?" she asked weakly. "What about my friends?"

"We just tell them we eloped," he said smoothly. He reached up to stroke her breast, then slid an arm around her, pulling her down toward him. He smoothed her hair away from her face and kissed her.

She leaned back, her hand on his chest. "This is exactly what I was afraid of," she said, tears beginning to form. He looked surprised but then tenderly wiped them as they fell from her lashes.

"What are you afraid of?"

"This is why I didn't want us to make love before we got married. I feel so…so…*vulnerable*. So raw. I can't think straight. You're asking me to marry you after we've been together less than two days—"

"Azi, we've been together for two years."

She closed her eyes. *I can't think straight when he's looking at me like that.*

"It sounds like you're asking me to marry you because other men find me attractive. Maybe I'm wrong, but that's what it feels like. That's no reason to get married. And—"

Jeremy stopped her with a passionate kiss. His hands entwined in her hair, he pulled her closer. "I want to marry you because I love you. Because we should already have been married for a year."

And there it was—that sense of guilt that she'd destroyed something precious, that she'd hurt him and now needed to make amends. But was that any reason to say yes now?

"Just give me some time," she pleaded. "I'm not trying to hurt you."

"I'll wait," he said quietly. "But not right now." He slid his arms around her, his mouth finding hers. "I want you, Azi. I want every part of you."

They did finally leave the apartment, heading out to the plaza for an early dinner. Azalea stopped at the apartment office to request a second key and handed it to Jeremy over *montaditos* and calamari. He smiled and tucked it into his wallet. The day was cool, just warm enough to sit outside. They walked to the beach and strolled along the walkway, holding hands and watching the waves. In the gathering twilight, she slowly began to relax.

Jeremy refrained from any deep conversation. They talked about Barcelona, how much they both loved the city. She told him about her regular running path and how it compared with her Florida beach runs. She told him about the church she'd found and how much she'd enjoyed the sermon.

"Would you go back?" he asked.

"I would," she answered. "But I'm only here for a few more weeks. Not really time to get too involved."

"I'd like to go with you," he said. "It means getting up on Sunday morning instead of the middle of the afternoon, though." He squeezed her hand and laughed. "Not that I'm complaining."

Azalea smiled and slid her arm around his waist. He put his arm around her shoulder, pulling her close as they walked. "I'd like that," she answered. "Next week would be nice. I've missed being in church. I guess I've missed a lot since I've been here."

"Not anymore," he said confidently.

This feels right, Azalea told herself. *This is what I want.*

They walked in comfortable silence until they came close to the apartment. Azalea released his hand and she looked around.

"People are going to find out, Azi. We can't keep it secret forever."

She looked sideways at him, nodding. "I'm sorry," she said. "I just don't want anyone in our business." She looked down, then back up with a sad expression. "And it's awkward if anyone knows you were with Maricela."

Jeremy sighed and nodded. They entered the elevator without another word.

23

Jeremy's alarm went off at five thirty Monday morning and Azalea groaned. He kissed her and said, "Go back to sleep, babe. I'm gonna shower and get ready at my place. I'll see you in the office."

"Mmhmm," she mumbled and rolled over.

"Te amo, Bella," he whispered, kissing the back of her neck. Azalea smiled, groggy and still half asleep. She knew she didn't have to get up yet. They took turns, and today Esteban rose two hours before she did to start the baking. She'd get up at six to start the coffee and prepare the café to open at seven. Their earliest customers were usually there when they opened, typically the expats. The locals didn't roll in until late morning, so Esteban would make sure he had a second batch of his delicious pan dulce ready for the later crowd. She worried that she added a few pounds as a result. Not that he minded. He loved everything about her, he said.

And she believed him.

Azalea woke with a start, her alarm playing far too loudly. She fumbled for the phone to turn off the song and lay back, her heart racing.

It was her dream Esteban again. She didn't think of dreams as magic or prophecy—she figured they were just an expression of her subconscious. But this was the, what? Third time she'd dreamed of this man and this café? She felt so at home in these dreams, so comfortable with him. She'd never imagined owning a café, but in her dreams, it was as natural as breathing. Not a job, like her marketing work. More like just *life*.

She longed to stay in bed and think through everything that had happened in the past three days. *Or maybe just daydream about Esteban. That's easier.* Instead, she made herself get up and shower. She stared at herself in the mirror, wondering again if she looked any different. She certainly felt different. All weekend she felt loved and pampered.

But when Jeremy proposed, she felt uncomfortable and confused.

Azalea knew she had to make some decisions, and soon. Her contract with Fowler Enterprises was up in a month and she would go home to Florida. *Unless I suddenly buy a little café,* she thought with a wry giggle. She'd made enough money with her contract to cover her expenses for several months, so she wasn't in a hurry to get back to work. Maybe she would take a couple of weeks and go to Colorado to visit the boys.

She gazed in the mirror as she brushed her hair. "They're grown men," she said to her reflection. "They have their own lives." She knew she was simply postponing the most important decision. What would she do about Jeremy?

She accepted his marriage proposal once. *He's a good man,* she thought. He seemed to have changed—at least in some ways. He was noticeably appreciative of her and he wasn't shy about expressing it. It nagged at her that he had been so sure of himself—sure of *her*! Certain enough to spend well over a thousand dollars at the restaurant Friday night when she assumed they were only going out for a quick meal.

And the odd jealousy he showed bewildered her. *I just don't think you can understand what it's like to be me right now.* That was strange and a little disconcerting. He brought up Javier—which was ridiculous given how cozy the sales exec was now with Maricela. He mentioned Esteban, who was no older than her sons. And the massage guy? She had fantasized about Jeremy throughout the entire experience. It was absurd.

She was surprised at how practical her thinking had become. Waking up alone seemed to have brought her back to herself. *Or was it waking up with Esteban?* she wondered with a smile.

She finished getting ready for work and packed her laptop bag, tossing in her wallet. She wondered when she'd use her new clutch again. *It is beautiful,* she thought. *But it's for special occasions.* She put it away in her drawer.

Is that what this weekend was? Just a special occasion?

Gripped with a sudden sadness, Azalea left her apartment and walked slowly to the elevator. She decided she didn't have the luxury of thinking about her love life this morning. It was time to put on her work brain *I wonder if any of the analysts wrote over the weekend.*

Azalea walked into the office and went straight to her desk. It was early enough that she didn't expect to see anyone, especially since the launch was over. She opened her laptop and began surfing for coverage. *It's only Monday morning,* she chided herself. *Nothing is going to be out there yet.*

Anna Weber's name popped up in her search. *Hmm…that was fast,* she thought, clicking the link. The article started with a positive tone, citing the new company's commitment to the European market, the strength of the technology, and…

"CEO Jeremy Fowler's stereotypical American swagger can be either charming or off-putting," she read. "Yet the Fowler Enterprises products have met the rigorous standards for the Spanish market, and the company seems poised to capture significant market share. Customers embraced Fowler and his sales pitch, and many jumped at the opportunity to become reference accounts. It remains to be seen if the CEO's confidence will carry the company beyond this honeymoon phase of development."

She frowned at the screen. *Who edited this drivel?* she wondered. After fifteen years in the tech industry, she was very used to their publications. Jargon-laden and awash in acronyms, most articles could put her to sleep in minutes. But this was more like a gossip magazine piece than the normal tech pub.

She was surprised to find herself feeling defensive. "Stereotypical American swagger?" she scoffed aloud. "What a load of crap."

"What's a load of crap?" asked Jeremy as he walked into her office, two coffee cups in hand. "I saw you walk in without coffee so I thought you might want some," he offered. She smiled and thanked him, but her scowl didn't lift completely. "So? What's got you so upset?"

"This stupid article by Anna Weber," she snapped, inexplicably angry. "Very little about our products but plenty about your charm."

Jeremy lifted an eyebrow. "Oh?" he asked.

"Well, she says you're either charming or off-putting," she hedged. *What am I so worked up about?* she wondered.

"And what did she say about you?" he asked.

"Me? Why would she say anything about me? All I did was introduce her to you."

Jeremy smiled broadly, seeming to enjoy her discomfort. "What exactly bugs you about this, my sweet PR maven? She doesn't say anything terrible about us, does she? And isn't any coverage better than none? She must have thought a lot about us to write and post this right after the event."

"I don't know why I even let her come once their regular writer got sick. She's brand new and obviously doesn't know how to write a decent piece about technology."

He laughed aloud.

"What's so funny?" she asked, miffed.

"You are," he said. "I haven't seen you like this before. Would you feel better if she didn't mention me at all?"

Azalea stopped—*What is bothering me?*

"I don't know," she admitted. "I'm honestly not sure what bugs me about this." She looked back at her screen and then at Jeremy. "It just seems so unprofessional."

"You know what's really unprofessional?" he asked. She looked up at him, confusion on her face.

"This," he said, and walked around her desk to kiss her. She pulled back, stunned at his brazenness, but he pulled her close, refusing to concede. "I love you," he murmured, his lips pressed to hers. "I'm going to marry you and I don't care who sees us."

He finally released her and smoothed a stray lock of hair from her eyes. He pulled out a handkerchief and wiped the corner of her lip and then his own. "Sorry I messed up your lipstick," he said.

Azalea remained quiet as he sat on the corner of her desk, his demeanor casual and confident. "I'm going to lunch with Judge Moreno today, so I'll be gone a couple of hours. But we can go out to dinner tonight." She nodded, unsure how to respond. "Oh, c'mon, Azi," he remonstrated. "Baby…relax. It's all going to be fine. I love you. You love me. Everything is going to be just fine." He touched her cheek with one finger. "And don't worry about our journalist friend. It's a fluff piece and there will be lots more coverage this week, I'm sure. Let's just hope Timothy Reynolds doesn't talk about my charm."

She smiled at that. The thought of the irascible Brit saying anything apart from a technical review was amusing.

"I'll let you get back to work, love. But don't be surprised if I come to bother you from time to time." He smiled. "I can't stand to be apart from you anymore." He stood, smoothed his slacks, and picked up his coffee cup. "I love you, Azi. Do not forget that." He stood still at her doorway, waiting for her response.

"I love you, too," she said.

Please don't let anyone have seen that, she prayed.

Jeremy returned to the office late, his lunch with the judge having gone longer than expected. He came into Azalea's office, but she was on the phone and he simply winked and smiled before heading to a meeting with Ricardo.

She was a bit disappointed that Tomás didn't join Landon on their weekly phone call. It was afternoon in Spain, but morning in Colorado, and she cherished their Monday conversations. Her eldest had opted instead for a breakfast date with Emily, the girl he'd been seeing, but she knew they'd catch up soon. She asked Landon about Tomás and he described his brother's new relationship. "She's actually pretty awesome, Mom," he said. "I think Tomás might be in trouble with this one."

For her part, Azalea regaled him with stories of the flamboyant Javier. Landon was a sales guy and knew the type, and they laughed merrily at her anecdotes.

"Just be careful, Mom," cautioned her youngest. "I think he's got a crush on you."

Azalea laughed. "No worries, Son. I'm not interested."

Landon cleared his throat. "And what about Jeremy? Did he get there?" Azalea had told both the boys about the Fowler acquisition. Neither of them had said much, but she could tell they weren't thrilled with the news.

"Yeah, he's here," she said, her tone casual. "It's fine. He's just the CEO of my biggest client."

"It's gotta be weird, Mom. I don't like it, to be honest."

"It is a bit weird," she admitted.

Weird isn't the word for it.

She quickly changed the subject. "But I'm a whole lot more interested in you! What's going on with your new client?"

Landon's smile was obvious in his voice. "They're new but they're hungry," he enthused. "I have a good feeling about this one." He stopped abruptly. "Oh, geez—I gotta go, Mom. They're calling me. I love you!"

"Love you, too, honey. Talk soon."

The rest of the afternoon went smoothly, with no additional articles showing up. Azalea called Lorena and made plans to meet in person on Wednesday to review any coverage and strategize for follow-up communications.

She looked across the office through the glass window into the conference room where Jeremy sat with Ricardo and Javier. The three men were deep in conversation. Ricardo wanted to get home to Miami—he'd been in Barcelona for weeks and missed his family. Javier, she assumed, was just as eager to have his boss out of Spain so he could be the top sales executive in country. She wondered how soon Ricardo would leave and made a mental note to ask Jeremy that evening.

Going out to dinner and talking about work is a good plan, she thought. She was concerned about his lunch with the judge, hoping he hadn't discussed a quickie Barcelona wedding. She wasn't ready to have that conversation again.

Her phone buzzed with a WhatsApp message, and she looked down to see a photo from Lauren.

Look at your hibiscus! The text had a photo of a beaming Sara with a pink bloom behind her ear. Azalea smiled. She loved those flowers and in spring they bloomed like crazy. This year they seemed even bigger than usual. *But perhaps that's because I've been gone so long*, she mused.

They're beautiful! she wrote back. *I miss them almost as much as I miss you guys!*

When do you come home? wrote Lauren. *I know it's soon—but don't hurry on our account! We love these weekends at the coast. Sara sends a hug, too xo*

Four more weeks in Barcelona, wrote Azalea.

Have you made any friends while you're there? What do you do with your time off work? How's your Spanish?

She realized wasn't ready to talk to her friends about Jeremy. She wasn't even sure what she would say. *Hey, I know I told you guys I realized Jeremy wasn't the right guy for me, but I've changed my mind.* She could imagine their reaction. They'd been so proud of her for calling off the wedding. At best, they'd be confused. At worst? They'd be disappointed, maybe even angry.

And her boys? What would Tomás and Landon think?

She didn't need to wonder. She knew they wouldn't approve.

I love you, too, she told Jeremy just that morning.

Hastily, she got back to her texting with Lauren.

I run on the beach and there are lots of beautiful places to visit. And great food! Still working on the language.

Let's talk soon. I'm trying to decide if I should quit my job and would love your advice.

Of course! Happy to help.

Gotta get back to work, messaged Lauren. *Love you and miss you!*

Azalea responded: *Same xo.*

24

Six o'clock rolled around without Azalea noticing. She felt rather than heard someone watching her and looked up to see Denice at her door. "Hey, Denice," she said. "I've been so busy today I haven't seen you at all. What's up?"

"Not much," she replied, sitting down and stretching her legs. "Long day. I found out today I'll only be here another week, so I was busy starting to tie up loose ends."

Azalea shot up in her chair. "One more week? Said who?"

Denice chuckled. "Who do you think? Jeremy. I do report to the CEO, you know." She rolled her shoulders. "I'm actually glad. It's time for me to get home. I love being here, but I miss my own bed and kitchen."

Azalea nodded. "I know what you mean. I love running on this gorgeous beach, but I miss mine. I think I'm ready to go home, too."

Denice lifted an eyebrow. "Even with all these hot Spaniards checking you out?" She laughed. "You were quite the belle of the ball on Friday. It was kind of a 'Maricela who?' situation."

Azalea fought back a laugh. "Denice!" She shook her head and gave in to a giggle.

"Well, it's true," insisted Denice. "Every man in this office was gaga over you." She smirked and said, "Including our boss."

Azalea could feel the flush on her cheeks. She looked down at her phone and exclaimed, "Oh, wow—it's after six already? This day has just flown." She busied herself packing up her laptop. "I'm gonna get out of here and see about a quick run before the sun goes down. What are you up to?"

"I'll be done shortly. Now that I know I'm leaving, I'm just figuring out what needs doing and what I can pass off to the team." Denice looked long at Azalea. "Don't get so flustered." She glanced across at the men in the conference room. "Single, rich, smart, and handsome. Would it kill you to relax and have a little fun?"

Azalea opened her mouth to answer but Denice laughed and walked out of her office.

She stared after her friend, then looked across at the conference room. She wondered: *Would it kill me to relax and have a little fun?*

Jeremy and the sales execs were still in the meeting when Azalea left the office. She wanted to let him know what she was doing without being obvious, so she packed up and popped her head into the conference room. Looking at the three men equally, she said, "Do you guys need anything before I head out?" She looked out the window. "It's a beautiful evening and I'm gonna get a run in before the sun goes down, but happy to stay if you need me."

Ricardo spoke first. "Nah, get out of here, Azalea. Go enjoy your run. I can't wait to be running in Miami soon." He nodded at Javier with a grin. "Leave things here to this *chistoso*."

The joker in question laughed. "That's *Señor Chistoso* to you."

Jeremy smiled at them and then looked back at her. "I think we're good here. We won't be long either."

She smiled, the message delivered. "Well, then *buenos noches, caballeros. Hasta mañana.*" She closed the door behind her and left the office.

Once in her flat, she changed into her running clothes but by the time she was ready to head for the beach, Jeremy arrived. He tossed his backpack on the sofa and ran a hand through his hair, looking thoughtful.

"Long day?" she asked.

He strode to her and gathered her into his arms. Gazing down, he studied her face without speaking. Azalea asked, "Is something wrong?"

"Do you have to go running tonight?" he asked simply.

Azalea looked sideways at him, wondering what prompted the question. "I'd really like to," she said. "It's always the best way for me to process a day and get rid of stress." She smiled. "And there's going to be far too much of me to hold if I don't get my workout in."

He grimaced. "Don't even say that. You're beautiful." He pulled her to him, kissing her until she had to pull away, breathless.

"Jeremy? What is it?"

He suddenly let her go. "It's nothing," he said. "I just can't stand a minute we're apart." He kissed her again and stepped away. "I'll rustle up dinner while you're gone. Please be careful," he cautioned.

She laughed. "Careful of what? It's still daylight—I'll be back before dark." She stroked his cheek. "I'll be fine and I promise to be careful." She was always mindful of her surroundings when she ran, but the beach was still full of people in the early evening. She hadn't had any uncomfortable moments in all the months she'd been there. *What was he worried about?*

He seemed to shake off his mood and swatted her playfully on the behind. "Go! Before I change my mind." She laughed and headed for the door.

Azalea jogged lightly on the sand and thought about her day. Day one after the launch was predictably busy, with her time spent following up with analysts and journalists, sending thank you emails or answering questions. She had the one odd experience that morning after reading Anna Weber's piece—*Why did that bug me so much?* she wondered again. And then Jeremy's outrageous, surprising kiss, right in the office. She was irritated and embarrassed. And yet when he stood there awaiting her response, she simply told him she loved him.

Not again, she thought. *Am I going to lose myself to this man?*

No. She'd talk to him about it when she got back to the apartment. She needed to set some ground rules before things got out of hand.

She glanced at her watch and stood up. She needed to start running back if she were to keep her promise.

As she ran down the beach, her thoughts drifted back to their nights together. The warmth of his body and the eagerness of her response. The desire in his eyes when he looked at her across the lobby—even in the office he couldn't hide his longing. She couldn't pretend she didn't enjoy the physical intimacy. Yet her initial regret resurfaced. *I can't think clearly when I'm daydreaming of his hands all over me.*

She jogged the blocks from the beach to the apartment, dodging people out for an evening stroll or on their way to the various restaurants along the way. She waved at the doorman and headed up to her flat. When she got to the door, she realized she left her key inside on the counter, once again thrown off her routine by Jeremy's kisses. Annoyed, she shook her head and knocked.

Azalea looked around, realizing how it would look if someone saw her knocking on her own door with Jeremy letting her in. She quickly pulled her phone out and began to text: *Forgot my k—*

He opened the door, puzzled. "I was wondering who on earth would be knocking on your door tonight." He spoke lightheartedly, but with an undercurrent she didn't like. *Am I not allowed visitors?* she wondered.

She walked in and hurriedly closed the door. "I forgot my key," she said, pointing to the kitchen counter. "You distracted me before I left," she said, playfully hoping to diffuse her discomfort.

The tension vanished and he smiled. "Sorry," he said, clearly unapologetic.

"I'll just take a quick shower," she said, only then noticing the dining room table. Candles flickered and the table was set. "What happened to just 'rustling up dinner'?" she asked. "Do I need to shower and dress properly?"

"You don't need to dress at all," he said, coming toward her.

She pulled back, "I'm all sweaty," she grimaced. "You don't want to hug me now."

"I want to hug you and lots, lots more, my love," he said, putting his arms around her. He kissed her forehead and undid her ponytail. Her long hair cascaded down her back, and he gripped it with both hands, kissing her hard. "Don't be long," he whispered. "Or I just might join you."

Azalea looked up at him, considering. *Would it kill you to relax and have a little fun?* Denice's words rang in her ears.

"'Just might'?" she challenged. "That doesn't sound much like a man in love."

He stared at her, then laughed and scooped her up, carrying her to the bathroom. "Challenge accepted."

When his alarm went off at five-thirty the next morning, Azalea was dreaming of showering with Jeremy. *Was there anything so luxurious, so sensuous as having your hair washed while simultaneously rubbing bath gel all over your lover's body?*

She was deep in the throes of her dream when he brushed back the hair along her neck, her thick curls still damp from the previous night's shower. His lips close to her ear, he whispered, "Sleep well, my love."

Half asleep, she rolled over to face him. Her eyes flickered open as she realized he was leaving. "No…don't go yet," she murmured. He smiled and said, "I'm gonna go upstairs to get ready. Just go back to sleep and I'll see you in the office." He stroked her cheek. "I think you were having a pretty nice dream, so you might want to get back to it."

Azalea slid one bare leg over his hip and pulled him close, "I said, don't go yet."

His eyes widened. "Who are you?" he whispered, his voice hoarse. "And what have you done with Azi?"

25

Azalea reached for Jeremy but felt only empty space. Her eyes flew open and she jerked upright. *What time was it?* She found her phone and groaned—how had she slept through her alarm? It was eight o'clock—she was usually in the office by now.

She rose and took a quick shower to wake completely. All she wanted to do was lie in bed—*When is the last time I did that?* she wondered. She looked again at her phone. It was going to be unseasonably cool, so she pulled out a black turtleneck and black cigarette pants. She didn't have time to dry her thick hair, so she looped it into a chic French twist and secured it with black enameled hair sticks. Once years ago, Landon had asked why she was wearing chopsticks in her hair. She smiled at the memory—her little boy had thought it hilarious.

Thirty minutes later, she was ready to head to the office. Her makeup was simple, but as she looked in the mirror, she felt…what? Sophisticated. Attractive.

Sexy.

She swiped on the classic Dior red lipstick and grabbed her jacket as she walked out of the apartment, a swing in her step.

She stopped at the café on the way but didn't see Esteban. She made it to the office at nine o'clock, just as Guillermo arrived. He held the door open for her, and she smiled her thanks as she walked in, then glanced surreptitiously around for Jeremy. She didn't see him, so she unpacked her bag and started her computer.

There was an email from Lorena, letting her know more post-launch coverage was on the way. Ambos had also secured a guest opportunity for a new tech blog and wanted to ghostwrite it for Jeremy. She quickly scanned the publication and agreed—it was relatively new, but the blogger seemed to know his stuff. She was about to respond to Lorena when Jeremy walked in.

"Ah, you stopped for coffee already," he said, setting down another cup on her desk. "I wasn't sure if you would since you were a bit…late this morning." He grinned at her. "Sleep well?"

"I slept just fine, thank you," she answered primly, glancing behind him to see Ricardo approaching. Jeremy still had his back to the sales vice president and he mouthed *I love you.* Ricardo stood in her doorway and asked, "So? Anything new today?" He was eager for good news that would allow him to turn the new office's sales completely over to Javier.

"You're just dying to leave us, aren't you?" she teased.

Ricardo laughed but then turned serious. "I have enjoyed my time here," he said. "But I'm homesick for Miami. I miss my wife and my kids. Two months is very long. I'm ready to go home."

"Well, I can't speak for sales, but PR is coming along," she said. "Jeremy, Ambos got an opportunity for a guest blog post with a new outlet. Ambos will write it and have a draft by tomorrow for our review."

He smiled and nodded. "Great," he said. "Now let's get ten more."

She rolled her eyes. "Yes, sir!" she said, saluting smartly.

Jeremy stood and motioned Ricardo to come with him. "Let's go look at the numbers from yesterday and see when we can get you out of here." Ricardo turned to leave and Jeremy looked back at Azalea. Again, he mouthed the words: *I love you.*

The day flew by, with additional emails coming from Ambos. It seemed every journalist was posting a piece on the new company, either that week or the next. Timothy Reynolds called Jeremy directly to clarify a technical question. His article would appear online the following Monday, and in print two days later. The launch was a success.

Jeremy left the office at four, letting her know he had an appointment with Judge Romero. *Again?* thought Azalea, but only smiled and waved as he left. Feeling guilty for coming in late, she stayed until nearly seven, when she was surprised to see Maricela walk into her office and sit down.

"Maricela," she said politely. "What's up? I was just about to leave." To punctuate her point, Azalea put her laptop in her bag.

"You seem very happy these days," said Maricela.

Azalea looked at the woman. They hadn't interacted much since their launch day confrontation in the restroom. Maricela was now involved with Javier, which left her little time to taunt Azalea. *Why was she here?*

"It's hard not to be happy," she said, putting on her best professional voice. "The launch was flawless and we're hearing very good things from the press and analysts. And I understand the sales team is making some promising connections." She didn't notice the double meaning until it slipped out. *Oh, well,* she thought.

"It appears you're making some 'promising connections' of your own," said Maricela.

Azalea stood, shouldering her bag and taking her jacket from the back of her chair. "I guess we're all having a successful week," she said, refusing to rise to the bait. "If there's nothing else, I'm heading out." She stood pointedly at her door, unwilling to walk out with the haughty woman following her. Maricela sat for another moment, her eyes unreadable. Then she stood and, without a word, left Azalea's office.

Azalea took her time locking her office door to avoid walking right behind Maricela. Not for the first time, she wondered why the younger woman reveled in provoking her—or why she let it bother her so much. The woman was a gold-digger: first, with Jeremy, now with Javier. Maricela's grief over losing Jeremy was a sham, Azalea convinced herself. Angry over losing a rich husband, perhaps. But she felt certain there was no real love there.

At least she hoped not.

Jeremy hadn't returned to the office and she walked back to the apartment as the sun slowly descended. She opened her door, set her things down on the counter, and flipped on the lights.

And was stunned to see flowers all over the flat.

They were everywhere: On the dining room table, the kitchen counter, the coffee and end tables in the living room. She walked into the bedroom where a huge bouquet lay on the middle of the bed between the pillows. There were more arrangements on the dresser and yet another on the bathroom counter. There was even a single yellow rose—*her favorite!*—on the floor of the shower.

Azalea walked back into the kitchen and noticed a card propped against the vase on the dining room table. She opened it and read,

To my new and improved Azi, my sexy Latin lover…my wife to be. Enjoy the flowers. Their beauty doesn't even come close to yours. I love you

-J

Azalea looked around again, overwhelmed. So was this what he was up to this afternoon when he left the office? It was so thoughtful, so extravagant, so—

New and improved? What was that supposed to mean?

Suddenly deflated, she went to her room to change.

Jeremy arrived half an hour later. Azalea was curled up on the sofa with her laptop and looked up as he entered. "So?" he asked. "Do you like them?" He set his things on the dining room table, walked to the sofa, kissed her, and sat down next to her. She smiled and nodded, unsure how to answer. She was still trying to process her wildly disparate feelings. Was she loved and cherished? Or was she being molded and praised when she met his expectations?

Jeremy took her laptop and set it on the coffee table. He pulled her legs onto his lap and leaned onto her, burying his face into her stomach. She gently ruffled his hair, then leaned down to kiss him. It was an awkward movement; they were tangled a bit, and he sat up and pulled her into his lap. "You seem quiet this evening," he said, wrapping his arms around her. "Is everything all right? I'm sorry I left you alone."

Azalea's brows furrowed. "I'm fine by myself, you know," she said gently. "Don't feel like you need to be with me all the time. I'm very used to quiet evenings with a bath and a book."

"Well, the bath sounds nice," he said, holding her close. "But honestly, I don't feel like you *need* me to be here. I just hope you *want* me to be here." He kissed her neck and stroked her hair, his hands slowly caressing her shoulders. She leaned back into his chest, closing her eyes. *Why does this have to be so confusing? Why can't I just let him love me?*

"Of course I want you here," she said, although she wasn't entirely sure. She turned her face to him and smiled. "The flowers are absolutely wonderful." She touched his mouth lightly with a finger. "Even if they are a bit extravagant."

Jeremy nibbled at her finger. "Nothing is too much for you, Azi." He sighed and pulled her tighter, laying his cheek on the top of her head. "I realized I didn't know how to keep you last time. I'm not going to make those same mistakes."

She tensed, but was wary of her emotions. "What do you mean, 'keep me'?" she asked lightly. "I'm not a possession." She stopped, wondering if she'd said too much, gotten too heated. *Don't be ridiculous*, she told herself. *I can't get sucked into this life again.*

And this time it's harder. So much harder.

He was silent for a moment and she moved to sit up, leaning against the opposite side of the sofa. He reached down and pulled her legs into his lap and began to massage her feet. He gazed long at her before answering. "I didn't mean 'keep you' like a possession," he began. "I meant keep you happy. I didn't know what would make you happy before. I think I'm learning now." He slid his hands up her legs and leaned over to kiss her. "Don't you think so?"

Azalea slid her arms around him and he stood up, pulling her to him. "Babe," she started, "Being happy isn't just about great sex."

"It is pretty great," he said, smiling.

"Listen to me," she retorted. "Yes, it's amazing. But I need to know that you respect me—that you, I don't know…admire me? That you think I'm smart and capable and…." He stopped her with his lips. She thrummed with desire coupled with frustration—was he even listening to her? And how often would her body betray her by giving in to him?

"Why don't we go take a hot bath and I can tell you just how much I admire you..." he kissed her neck, "and respect you," and kissed her nose. "And how smart I know you are?" He kissed her eyelids and she leaned into him—and then broke away.

"I'm serious," she said, looking at him with a pained expression.

He took her hands and stepped slightly back. "I know you are, Azi. I know. And I know I can be way too overbearing." He chuckled. "I'm self-aware enough to know that. And I'm working on it, I truly am." He looked at her frankly and said, "I need you, babe. I want to be a better man and you help me do that. It's why I want you to marry me." He sighed. "When I'm not fantasizing about making love to you, I'm thinking about you next to me in that conference room, with us this powerhouse couple taking over the world. You want me to be patient, but it's hard. I want you and I need you and I'm not used to having anyone make me wait for anything."

Azalea held onto his hands. "That's very honest of you," she said. "But I can't make that decision now. I just can't."

"I know," he said, putting his arms around her and laying his cheek on the top of her head. "I know. But I have to believe that you will."

26

After they made love, Azalea slept fitfully, finally settling down when Jeremy left the next morning. As usual, he was up early, kissed her, and went to his apartment to shower and get ready for the day. She rolled over and went back to sleep, waking when her alarm went off at seven.

She felt lethargic, moving through her morning routine almost robotically. There was a cloud about her head, the weight of it palpable. She couldn't look any direction without seeing the lavish flower arrangements and she found herself wondering why they began to irritate her. He'd never done anything like that when they were engaged.

What spurred such a grandiose gift this time? she wondered. It appeared to be a reaction to their lovemaking. She had thrown herself into their intimacy with abandon—and he seemed to be rewarding her. Why else the single rose in the shower? Why the card explicitly describing her as lover? Azalea felt a knot in her stomach, hating the thoughts barraging her. She'd been delighted last week at his effusive praise. He had seemed to finally see her as a powerful, intelligent woman and it had excited him. *That confidence is so sexy, I can't even begin to tell you*, he had said. He longed for her—claimed her as his own. But did he truly love her?

More importantly: *Do I love him?*

Why else did she yearn to share her bed and her life with him? Why did she look for his approval at work? She had genuinely missed him after breaking up with him. She could see the good in him, especially now as he confessed to wanting to be more. She could appreciate that—she was always looking for ways to improve, to grow, and to learn. This was a new way of existing for him. It only made sense that there would be fits and starts. Could she be the woman he needed to help him overcome those inevitable challenges?

She stared at herself in the mirror, hairbrush hovering. In a moment of brutal self-awareness, she asked herself, *Why haven't I told Susana or the boys that we are back together?*

She glanced at her watch. It was seven-thirty and she needed to hurry if she were going to make it to the office by eight. She dressed without thought, pulling on grey trousers, a pale pink tank, and a matching cardigan. She added a final swipe of mascara and opted for a rose-colored lipstick.

Putting aside her troubling thoughts, Azalea walked briskly through the side streets and across the plaza. She didn't plan to stop for coffee, but as she walked past the door an elderly couple walked out, carrying their steaming cups out to the patio. The smell was rich and inviting, and Azalea went in. She wondered if she should buy Jeremy one. He'd thoughtfully brought her coffee this week and she decided to return the favor. She shoved her worries and confusion down, purchased two coffees, and headed for the office.

As Azalea approached the door, she heard Denice behind her. "Let me get that for you," she said, stepping in front of Azalea and opening the door. She looked at the two coffee cups and smiled. "Rough morning?" she asked.

Azalea laughed. "Nah, Jeremy bought me coffee yesterday so I thought I'd return the favor." She hoped it came off casually, but Denice's smirk said otherwise.

"I half expected you to be serving it to him in be—"

184

"Denice!" broke in Azalea. She shook her head, wondering how many people in the office were thinking the same thing.

Denice chuckled. "Relax. It's just obvious he's crazy for you." Azalea frowned and walked toward her office deep in thought. "Good talk," called out Denice with laughter in her voice.

Azalea put the cups on her desk and set down her laptop bag and purse. She headed for Jeremy's office and met him coming out as she approached. "Good morning," she said. "I thought I'd return the favor." She handed him his cup and he took it with a smile.

"Well, aren't you thoughtful," he said, glancing behind her as Guillermo walked by. Once the young man had passed with a "*Buenos dias*," Jeremy nodded toward his door, beckoning her inside. She followed with a quizzical look, and he closed the door behind her, turning to face her as soon as the door shut. He reached behind him to set his cup on the desk, then took hers and set it down next to his. Before she knew it, his arms were around her and he was pressing her against the door, his mouth on hers. She tried to push away, but she had nowhere to go. "No one can see us," he whispered. "I just wanted to thank you for the gift."

"It's just a coffee," she protested around his kiss.

"No, Azi," he answered, his hands sliding down her shoulders. "It's you. It's everything about you. I can't think about anything but you and everything you do is a gift." He stood back a bit, brushing a stray hair out of her eyes. "I love you, Azi."

Once more, he waited for her response. Her body was screaming at her to wrap her arms around him right there in the office, but her thoughts were a jumbled mess. "Jeremy," she began, and he put a finger to her lips.

"I know, I know." He sighed. "We're at work, I'm your boss, this isn't professional, blah blah blah...."

Enough, she thought. *I do love him.*

She stopped him with a passionate kiss. Moving them slightly toward the wall so she was sure no one could see them, she pressed her body to his, feeling him respond. "Don't start something you can't finish," she whispered, reaching down to stroke him lightly.

His body shuddered and he pulled back, an astonished look on his face. "Azi—" he began.

Her breath came quicker, and she had a brief fantasy of them on the top of his desk. "I do love you," she whispered, willing it to be true. She pulled away, reluctant to separate. "But I can't concentrate if you keep doing this."

"Me?" he said, surprised. "I think you just escalated things pretty dramatically, my love."

She glanced down, then looked at him, all wide-eyed innocence. "You'll probably need a minute before you can leave your office, but I'm going back to work now."

"Good God, woman. What am I going to do with you?" Jeremy's look was inscrutable as he opened the door to let her out.

Azalea walked back to her office, completely forgetting her coffee cup on Jeremy's desk. She opened her laptop and resolved to concentrate on work, but her body still resonated with their encounter. They were acting like teenagers, she thought.

But taking charge like that feels good.

Jeremy came into her office later that day to invite her to lunch.

"I can't," she answered. "Lorena will be here soon. We may need some time with you later this afternoon to talk through some press opportunities."

"Can I bring you anything?" he asked.

"No, thanks. She's picking up sandwiches on her way in."

He stood in her doorway, gazing at her without speaking. At last, he said, "And dinner? What are your plans?"

She smiled up at him, sensing the shifting dynamics. She'd been bold that morning, far more than she'd ever been. It had startled and excited him, but now he seemed almost tentative. "Whatever you'd like," she said. "You tell me."

His face brightened. "Let me give it some thought," he said with a grin. "I'm sure I can come up with something you'll enjoy."

She laughed. "I have no doubt. You are a very resourceful man." Their flirtatious banter caused a flutter in her stomach as she imagined "something she'd enjoy."

Jeremy whispered, "I love you," and walked out the door.

Minutes later, Lorena arrived and the two women settled down to eat and talk.

"The coverage is starting to come in all over Europe," said Lorena. "Tecnología is running a piece tomorrow, and that Portuguese tech blogger Manuel Silva is writing this afternoon." She took a sip of her water and continued. "We've sent thank you notes to everyone who attended, sorry to have missed you notes for those who didn't, and answered all the questions that have come in." She looked up from her notebook. "I don't think it could have been more successful."

Azalea jotted notes while Lorena talked. She set her pencil down to take a bite of her *bocadillo*. "Mmm…" she said. "I will miss these when I leave." She set down her sandwich and looked at the public relations executive. "I can't thank you enough for all the hard work. Your team executed flawlessly. I'm eager to see what comes next."

"Well, we've been pitching all the majors, plus some outliers that are up and coming. There's also a speaking opportunity I wanted to tell you about. There's a conference in Madrid next month and one of the panelists is an Ambos client. He had to cancel and I'd love for either Jeremy or one of your senior tech guys to fill in. It's a great conference and would be good visibility."

Just then, Jeremy returned. He popped his head into Azalea's office, his lunch in hand. "Sorry to interrupt, ladies," he said. "I just wanted to say hello and thank you again, Lorena." Azalea was surprised—CEOs didn't normally deign to acknowledge their PR team. She suspected the comment was made for her benefit, but Lorena beamed. "You're very welcome," she said. "It's been a real pleasure working for you and your team."

"Well, I'll leave you to it," he said. "I've got a few calls, but I'll be available in an hour or so if you need me." He smiled and headed for his office.

Lorena looked at Azalea. "That was a surprise," she said.

"A nice one," Azalea agreed.

The two continued reviewing their plans, and Azalea agreed to find a Fowler Enterprises replacement for the panelist. She didn't think Jeremy would appreciate sharing the stage; he was more of a keynote kind of guy, she thought.

After an hour, the two were ready for a break. They decided to walk out to the plaza for a cup of coffee and a stroll before meeting with

Jeremy. Before they could get up, though, Jeremy walked in. His posture was tight and his face hard. Azalea was immediately on guard, but Lorena appeared not to notice.

"Oh, Jeremy," she said. "We were just going out for a quick break and thought we could meet with you shortly. But if now is better—"

He glared at her. "I've been on the phone with Judge Romero," he said flatly. "It seems there was more to the separatist 'rally'—" he spat the word, "than we originally knew. The police have found a terrorist who planned to target businessmen." He stopped and stared daggers at her. "Foreign businessmen." He took a deep breath.

"My name was on that list, Lorena. The list they found in *your brother's* apartment."

Lorena blanched and looked wildly at Azalea before returning to Jeremy. "It wasn't him," she began. "I know he got mixed up with some bad people but he would never do anything like—"

"Stop." Jeremy's harsh retort cut through her defense. He spat out his next words. "Ambos' services are no longer required. We will pay your final invoice as of today, although I am quite certain you've broken our contract in numerous ways, not the least of which is not to allow your client to be murdered."

Azalea spoke up. "Jeremy, he's just a boy. He didn't know what he was getting into."

He rounded on her, eyes wide. "You knew about this?" he hissed. He glared at Azalea and then turned back to Lorena. "Get out. Get out now. We are finished."

Lorena glanced at Azalea and grabbed her things. "Jeremy," she started.

"Get. Out."

Lorena all but ran out of the office and Jeremy rounded on Azalea.

"How could you?" he asked. "How could you betray me like this?" His voice was low and dripping with venom. "You know, after you betrayed me *the day before our wedding*…I hated you. Your complete callousness—your selfishness…." Jeremy's voice dropped even deeper.

"I thought you changed. I thought you were different now." He ran his hand through his hair. "I was telling my sister just yesterday that you had finally come to understand what it meant to be with a man in my position, that you had evolved to truly be a partner—"

Azalea was shocked to hear her chair crash against the wall. She hadn't realized that she'd bolted out of it.

Finally come to understand? Evolved?

"You talked to Sophia about me?" she asked, incredulous. "She despises me."

He looked at her, astonished. "Who are you? Are you listening to yourself? *My name was on that list and you knew about it.* And you're worried about my sister?"

"I didn't know anything about a list," she insisted. "I knew he'd been arrested but he's just a dumb kid. Lorena assured me—"

"*Lorena* assured you? The terrorist's *sister assured* you?" He turned around and closed the door hard, then spun back to face her. "How could I have been so blind? You are nothing like the woman I thought you were. *Nothing.* I believed you, Azalea. I believed your whole transformation lie. I really thought you understood what I needed." He shook his head. "I can't believe I thought you could be my wife."

Jeremy's words pierced her and burned away every shred of confusion. *So now he calls me Azalea?*

Fury overtook her. Her emotional dam broke and she found she could no longer hold back. "Is that how you see me?" she asked. "Am I your Eliza Doolittle to brag about with Sophia? Or wait—is that too pedestrian an example for you in your lofty ivory tower? Perhaps I'm Galatea to your Pygmalion? Is that sophisticated enough for the Fowlers?" She looked down at her hands as she leaned on the table, breathing deeply to calm herself.

But Jeremy wasn't through.

"You also are dismissed," he said. "I will pay for the apartment for another forty-eight hours and your flight home." He turned as if to leave but then looked back. "And give your laptop and keys to Denice. She'll see to getting them back to our IT department."

It was too much. All her emotions coalesced into a single thought and she suddenly, improbably, began to laugh.

Azalea folded her arms and shook her head, feeling almost giddy. "You arrogant bastard," she said, less with anger than with mirth. "*I'm a consultant* and it's not your laptop." She reached into her pocket and pulled out her office keys, tossing them onto the table. "I'll be out of the apartment tomorrow. And now, if you'll excuse me, I'll just grab *my things* and be off."

She walked around her desk, slammed her laptop into her bag, grabbed her purse, and stalked out without a backward glance.

27

When Azalea pushed open the door to her flat, she didn't even remember walking there. Her hands were still shaking as she tossed her bag onto the kitchen counter.

What just happened?

She strode into her bedroom and began opening drawers and throwing things onto the bed. Looking around, she saw all the flower arrangements and she had a ferocious desire to grab every vase and smash it on the ground.

She opened her closet door and yanked out her suitcases. *How on earth am I going to fit everything in these two cases?* she fumed. *Why did I bring so many shoes?*

Leaving the chaotic mess behind, she stalked back into the kitchen and opened her laptop bag. *I need a hotel room,* she thought. *I'm not staying here one more night.*

She started searching for a hotel room in Barcelona but her hands were shaking so badly she mistyped the words over and over. She angrily pushed her laptop across the counter and then had to dive to grab it before it flew off and smashed on the floor.

"Stop!" she shouted. Azalea buried her face in her hands. "Enough."

She sat back and tried to take stock of her situation.

Breathe in for the count of four, hold for four, exhale for four, hold four more.

It didn't work. She took a ragged breath and then pulled a notebook from her bag.

Life is like a math problem, she told herself. *Throwing a fit isn't going to help. Set up the problem, isolate the variables, and solve for* x. She began to write.

What I need
Place to stay
Another suitcase
A flight home
A new job

She erased *A new job*, preferring to concentrate on immediate needs. She sat back and again attempted the box breathing. *C'mon, Azalea,* she thought. *You can do this.*

When her heart rate finally slowed, she pulled her laptop to her and typed *hotels in Barcelona*, this time without any mistyped words. She perused the list, eliminating anything close to the office or the apartment complex. When she left, she wasn't returning and she had no interest in running into any of her former colleagues.

The Hotel Arts was expensive but gorgeous. She'd stayed there years before with Susana and she found herself reminiscing as she looked at the website photos. Her practical side said she only needed someplace safe with a bed. Another part of her, hurt and still in shock, decided that she deserved something nice. She entered her information and booked a room for two nights. *Surely I can get out of here by Friday,* she thought.

Now that her lodging was secured, Azalea looked around the apartment, feeling slightly less disoriented. She again gazed at all the flowers but was able to see them without rage overtaking her. Now, she just felt wrung out.

She knew she should pack and get to the hotel, but everything in her longed to go to the beach. It was her sanctuary, her refuge.

Suck it up, she thought grimly. Tears stinging her eyes, she walked back to her bedroom and began to pack.

Somehow, Azalea got all her clothes into the two suitcases and a large beach bag she bought at a kiosk in the plaza. She figured tomorrow she would have time to repack more efficiently and wouldn't need the extra bag. She was thankful not to see anyone she knew as she left the apartment complex, hailing a taxi for the Hotel Arts.

As expected, her room was lovely. Looking out from the tenth-floor window, Azalea gazed longingly at the expanse of beach, still peppered with tourists. She was surprised to find it wasn't even six o'clock. It felt as if hours and hours had gone by, yet it was still light outside. She opened a suitcase and dug out her running gear. She had time to get to the beach and she hoped it would settle her. She left her phone on the nightstand and headed out.

Within minutes, Azalea was on the sand. She began to run but found her chest too tight to breathe properly. Instead, she stopped and took off her shoes and socks, wading into the cool water until it reached her knees. The rhythm of the ocean would ordinarily soothe her, but today her mind was a whirling mess.

She thought back over the day, feeling emotional whiplash as she remembered that morning, naked in bed with Jeremy, then his passionate kiss against the office door and her bold sexual advances. His playful flirtation later in the morning and then his fury at Lorena...and at her.

My name was on that list and you knew about it.

Azalea stopped walking, suddenly cold. *That must have been terrifying to learn,* she thought. An unexpected sorrow hit her—should she have told him about the gun they found in Eduardo's apartment? She hadn't known a thing about a list, but perhaps she should have told him what she knew.

Would it have made a difference?

She began walking again, oblivious to her surroundings. What had he said to her?

I believed you, Azalea. I believed your whole transformation lie. I really thought you understood what I needed.

And then she realized: It wouldn't have made a difference. Jeremy was still Jeremy. Self-absorbed, yet passionate and kind when it meant he got what he needed. Despite Susana's judgment, she didn't think he was a bad man. He never had anyone teach him how to care for someone besides himself. When his parents died and his aunt and uncle shipped him and Sophia off to boarding school, the message was clear to the young Fowlers: *No one is going to take care of you, so you have to do it yourself.* Once, she had pitied him for his upbringing, convincing herself that their marriage would give him the love and support he never experienced. But after two years of finding that he would just continue to drain her love and give only to get, she had enough.

Why did I think this time would be different? she wondered. *I have been a fool.*

She looked up at the setting sun and headed back to her room. She wasn't hungry, but she ordered room service anyway and took a quick shower while she waited. She was combing out her hair when she heard the knock. She thanked the young woman, then took the tray and set it on the bed, at last looking at her phone.

There were three texts from Denice.

What happened???? read the first.

Are you OK? read the second.

Azalea PLEASE CALL ME read the third text, delivered while she was showering.

Azalea sighed. She didn't have the energy to talk with Denice, so she texted back: *I'm fine. I was sacked. I'm not really up for talking tonight. How about tomorrow? Hoping to fly home on Friday.*

Denice's response was immediate. *He is livid—I was worried about you.*

Please don't worry, Azalea wrote. *Truly—I'm fine. I've moved out of the apartment but I'm here for a couple of days. Let's talk tomorrow, OK?*

OK, wrote Denice. *Please take care of yourself.*

Azalea set her phone down, lifted the silver top off the dish, and was surprised to find she was hungry. She pulled the tray closer and leaned against the pillows of her bed to eat. Restless, she looked at her phone again. There was a new message, this time from Susana.

I miss you, hermana xoxo

Flooded with a need to talk to her best friend, Azalea did a quick calculation: It was two o'clock in Florida. She answered: *I miss you so much. Can you talk?*

Azalea's phone rang in seconds.

"I have thirty minutes between meetings," said Susana. "Perfect timing. How are you?"

Azalea was quiet. "'*Mana?*" asked Susana. "What's wrong?"

"Oh, Suze," began Azalea, "I messed everything up." Her voice broke and she fought back tears. "I should have listened to you...." She trailed off as she began to cry.

Susana's voice was soft and concerned. "What happened, honey? Did that *cabrón* hurt you?"

"I honestly thought he'd ch-changed," said Azalea, her breath catching as she struggled against the tears. "We were getting along so well and he kept talking about how valuable I was and how I was doing great work. And then he broke up with his girlfriend—"

"It's ridiculous that he has a girlfriend already," broke in Susana.

"Well, we *were* apart for a year," said Azalea. "I didn't mind, even though she was constantly baiting me and trying to rub it in that she was living with him—"

"They were living together?" Susana's voice rose, her contempt and impatience clear.

"Suze...I know this all sounds terrible. And I should have been talking to you about it for the past few weeks. There are a million details I'm leaving out. There was a separatist rally and this one crazy faction targeted Jeremy and some other execs.... I know I'm babbling. It all happened in slow motion and at the same time it was so fast. It's like that stupid boiling frog story you always tell. It all just snuck up on me and suddenly I was in bed with him and he was proposing again."

The silence lasted for several seconds. "Suze?" asked Azalea. "Did I lose you?"

"You didn't lose me, '*mana*. I'm here." Susana exhaled, hard. "I'm not going to pretend I don't want to strangle my best friend, but I'm here. And I love you and I don't want to make this any worse by being upset with you." She quieted for a moment and Azalea knew her friend was calming herself. "How can I be the best friend to you right now? You know I would do anything in the world for you. If you need me to fly over there, I will be on a plane *mañana*."

Azalea leaned back against the pillows, tears sliding down her cheeks. "You don't need to do that," she said softly. "I'm coming home."

"Okay, I have fifteen minutes." Susana's voice was matter of fact. "Give me the down and dirty version."

Azalea began, jumbling everything together as quickly as she could. Susana made appropriate noises throughout her recitation, finally interrupting her friend. "Listen, *'mana*—give me five minutes to get out of this meeting and I'll call you right back." Azalea could hear her typing.

"It's okay," she said, sinking back on the pillows and taking a long drink of her wine. "I'm not going anywhere tonight."

"Never mind," said Susana. "I just sent someone else from my team. I'll catch up with him later. So finish your story. The kid had a list of names in his apartment?"

"I guess so. That's what Jeremy said. It's why he was so angry." She looked out the window at the dark sky, now flecked with stars. "He must have been so scared," she said softly.

Susana's intense response made Azalea sit up straight. "Listen to me, Azalea: I'm sorry he was scared. I'm sorry there are terrorists who think it's a good plan to target American businessmen. But don't for one minute let that change the fact that he was manipulating you and trying to turn you into the perfect little Stepford wife." Susana's voice dropped. "I cannot believe he set you up like that with the restaurant."

Azalea thought about her friend's assessment. *Was it a set up?* "I didn't make good choices, for sure," she began.

"Azalea. *Escúchame, hermana.* He told you he knew you'd say yes. He set up the whole night just to get you into bed. He didn't manage that *for two years.* I don't mean to hurt you, but this is all about keeping score for him. The bimbo girlfriend, buying the company…all of it. He's a narcissist and a manipulator and a complete jerk. I hate that he did this to you and I hate that you're hurting but I am so damn glad it happened and now he's out of your life for good." Susana was breathless as she finished, and Azalea imagined her friend stomping around her office, her fiery personality on full display. Despite her tears, she smiled.

"You are the best friend in the whole world," she said. "I'm sorry for disappointing you."

Susana harrumphed. "Don't be daft—isn't that what you always say?" She sighed heavily. "You never have to worry about disappointing me, my friend. I adore you and you're stuck with me. *Tu eres la hermana de mi corazon.*" Azalea could hear the smile on Susana's face. They'd been friends for decades, through trials and triumphs, and they'd always been there for each other.

"And there is one piece of good news in all this," said Susana.

Azalea frowned. "That's hard to imagine but tell me."

"At your age, at least there's no way you're pregnant."

The two friends burst out laughing, a salve to Azalea's heart.

They talked late into the night and Azalea finally slept. When she awoke, the sun was well into the sky and her room was uncomfortably bright. She groaned and rolled over, pulling one of the pillows over her eyes.

She longed to go back to sleep but knew she wouldn't. She slept until nine o'clock—far later than her usual weekday morning. With a heavy sigh, she rolled onto her back and looked at the ceiling. *So this is day one of my new life,* she thought. *Time to make some plans.*

She showered quickly and dressed, her hair wrapped in one of the lush hotel towels. She stood a long time in front of the mirror, her reflection drawn and tired. Fighting back tears, she called for room service.

28

Azalea picked at her breakfast as she searched for a flight back to the States. She found an outrageously priced flight to Orlando from Barcelona the next day. She didn't care—Fowler Enterprises could afford it and she just wanted to go home. Now it was time to text Denice and get it paid for. *No way am I going to expense this one,* she thought. She picked up her phone and saw that she missed a call.

It was from Jeremy, leaving no voice mail and no text. She scowled, wondering if she should just block his number. She certainly wasn't going to answer his calls.

A text from Denice popped up: *Hey, are you up? Can you talk now?*

I'm up. Just having breakfast in my room.

OK if I call?

Sure.

Denice's call came through seconds later and Azalea put it on speaker so she could continue eating. "Hey, Denice," she said.

"'Hey, Denice?' Seriously? That's how you answer?" Denice's voice was sarcastic. "What the hell happened?"

Azalea finished chewing her croissant and wiped the jam from her lips. "So apparently some violent faction of the separatists had a plot to harm foreign businessmen," she began in a monotone. "Turns out Lorena's little brother got mixed up with the group and they found a gun and a list of names in his apartment." She sipped her coffee, then sighed. "Jeremy's name was on the list."

"Oh, my God," breathed Denice. "That's horrible! But why fire *you?*"

Azalea closed her eyes, wondering again if she should have told him. "Because Lorena had confided in me that her brother got arrested. I didn't know anything about the list. She was a mess—her brother's just a kid who got in with the wrong crowd. When Jeremy found out I knew about Eduardo—that's Lorena's brother—he came unglued."

Denice was quiet. "Unglued is the right word," she said at last. "He was furious. Scary mad. He prowled around the office for an hour after you left and then he just took off without saying anything to anyone. Even Ricardo was surprised.

"He's not back in the office this morning and he hasn't called anyone," she finished.

He called me.

"I can't think about him right now," Azalea said. "I need to book my flight home and I need your help. There's a flight to Orlando tomorrow but it's over two thousand dollars booking it this late. Can you book it for me? No way am I spending that much money and then trying to get reimbursed." Would Jeremy refuse to pay? No, he'd told her yesterday he'd take care of her flight home. *He may be furious, but he'll honor his word*, she thought.

"Sure," replied Denice. "Send me the details. I'll book it right now and put it on the company card." She paused. "I'm so sorry it came to this. I guess you won't be working for Fowler on any other projects now. But I'm happy to be a reference for you. You've been an incredible resource for us so many times.

"And you've become my friend," she finished.

Azalea looked out the window. She gazed across at the horizon, the deep blue of the ocean meeting the azure sky. "Thank you, Denice," she said at last. "I'll always remember our spa day and all the good work we did together. Let's have dinner when you get back to the States, OK?"

"I'd like that," answered Denice. "Okay, gotta run now. Tomorrow's my last day so I'm finishing up here, too."

"Oh, geez…I'm sorry," said Azalea. "I wasn't even thinking of everything you're going through. I sincerely appreciate your help. When are you heading back?"

"I'm taking a week's vacation to wander around Spain," she answered. "I'll fly back in about ten days."

"That sounds lovely," said Azalea. "Safe travels."

"You, too." answered Denice.

Azalea hung up and looked around the room. She felt overwhelmed by everything she needed to do. Now that Denice was handling her flight home, she had to figure out how to get all her things into the two suitcases. She knew she could go buy another one and just pay to check an extra bag, but she wasn't eager to drag three bags around in either a taxi or walking through the airport.

She emptied everything onto the bed, compressing her clothes tightly into sausage-like rolls to fit. It didn't matter if they were wrinkled in transit—she just wanted to get them all in. She stared long at the beautiful green dress. Was it really only a week since she bought it?

Rolling it up, she made a nice nest for the photos she had brought with her.

Where is my photo with the boys? she thought, searching the pile. She had brought three photos with her to adorn her apartment, but the one from the living room table wasn't there. She searched through her things but only found the other two. Abruptly, she remembered right where she set it, on the table next to the sofa—

Where Jeremy picked it up and admired it.

Stupid, stupid, stupid, she muttered. There was no way she was leaving without it. The picture could be reprinted, but the frame was from her sons. Her boys, her treasures. She couldn't just forget about it.

She still had the key to the apartment. Jeremy said he would pay for it through Friday, so technically it was still hers and she could go back to retrieve the photo. She looked at her watch. It was the middle of the day—a workday—so she was reasonably certain she wouldn't run into anyone she knew. Maricela, Denice, and Javier would all be in the office or at customer sites. Surely Jeremy would have gotten to the office by now. No matter how angry he was, there was work to be done and he wouldn't let the company falter. She could get in and get out quickly, she reckoned. Do a once over in the apartment to be sure she hadn't left anything else behind.

Refusing to worry, she grabbed her purse and headed downstairs to find a cab.

Azalea gazed out the taxi window, soaking in all the beauty of Barcelona. The sky was the cornflower blue she remembered from her childhood crayons, dotted with pillowy white clouds. She watched people walking along the sidewalks as she passed, stopping to chat with friends or sitting at one of the dozens of outdoor café tables. Despite the traumatic ending, it was a beautiful city, and she knew she would miss it.

The taxi stopped in front of the apartment building and she paid and thanked her driver. She stepped out, noting how warm the day had become. The doorman's face lit up with a smile as he recognized her. "*Señorita!*" he exclaimed. "Welcome home." She smiled, not willing to disappoint him with the news that this was the last time they'd see each other. But then she changed her mind, tired of keeping secrets. "I'm going back to the States tomorrow," she said. "Thank you for always welcoming me—you put a smile on my face every day."

He made a mock frown and shook his head. "You will be missed, *señorita*," he said glumly.

She smiled and headed for the elevator, saying a quick prayer that she would be the only one on it. The door opened to empty space and she rode silently to her floor. *I'll just do this quickly*, she thought. *In and out.*

She walked into the apartment and set her purse down on the kitchen counter, glancing around at the still fresh flower arrangements. She'd forgotten about them and was a bit disconcerted by their presence. It was as if they belonged to someone else, another person—another life. Her eyes drifted to Jeremy's note, still propped against the vase on the dining room table. She felt a fleeting regret and nearly picked it up—but shook off the urge. *There was no love there*, she determined. *Just a desire to make me into what he wanted.*

She took a step toward the living room and realized she wasn't alone.

Jeremy sat on the sofa, holding her frame. He looked at her, sorrow plain on his face. "I'm surprised you forgot this," he said softly.

She stood still, emotions roiling. Anger mixed with hurt, love mixed with regret—she felt them all in what seemed an interminable moment. "I was in a bit of a hurry," she said at last. "I guess I just missed it." She held out her hand. "May I have it, please? I'm in the middle of packing and I need to get back."

He gazed at her without speaking for a long moment before handing her the frame. "You really do look so happy in this," he said, looking at the photo before she took it from him. "I saw that look over the last couple of weeks. With me."

Unsure how to respond, she looked down at the photograph. Her sons stood on either side of her, their arms around her. The three of them shared the same smile. *We all look like my mom*, she thought absently. She looked up at Jeremy, who continued to watch her. "I'm just here to be sure I haven't forgotten anything else," she said, wishing he would leave.

She walked to the bathroom and opened each of the drawers, knowing she wouldn't find anything, but unwilling to talk more with the man she had loved—the man who had thrown her out of the office and his life. *Why is he still here?* she thought. Finding nothing in the drawers, she moved to the bedroom, opening the closet and the dresser drawers quickly and cursorily, again finding nothing. She glanced at the flowers on the dresser but refused to touch them.

He followed her and stood in the doorway. "Did you want to take any of the flowers?" he asked. "They're still so beautiful—"

"Jeremy, why are you here?" she asked abruptly, tired of the discomfort. "This is…*was* my apartment. I get that you're paying for it, but you only had a key because we were together. We aren't together now and this is extremely awkward." She ran a hand across her face, gathering her thoughts. "Look, this is hard enough. I just want to get my things and get out of here. If you—"

In two long steps he was beside her, taking her face in his hands. "What happened to us, Azi?" he asked, anguish in his voice. "Things were so good," and he bent to kiss her.

She stepped back, stunned. "What are you doing? Jeremy, *we are through*. Done." She shook her head, surprised at the tears gathering. She wiped roughly at her eyes. "No more."

"Azi, we can fix this," he began, reaching toward her again.

"No. We cannot *fix* this. We have both said and done things that are unfixable." She looked at him and her gaze softened. "I did love you," she said, her voice quiet. "I wish you nothing but goodness, but this…us…it's not right. We're broken, beyond repair."

He stood still, his face unreadable. *I've got to get this out*, she thought.

"I'm truly sorry I didn't tell you about Lorena's brother. I had no idea about the list and I would never have done anything that put you in danger. I hope you can forgive me." He remained still and silent.

"Goodbye, Jeremy."

Grasping her frame firmly, she walked to the kitchen, retrieved her purse, and left the apartment.

29

Azalea looked around, vaguely puzzled at how she ended up on the sidewalk. Somehow, she had completely missed her elevator ride and walk out of the apartment lobby. She looked at her watch and was surprised to find it was only noon. Time seemed to have slowed to nearly nothing and her knotted stomach forced herself to move. She didn't want to be standing outside if Jeremy decided to leave.

A taxi pulled up, but she waved the driver off, preferring to walk. Slipping her treasured photo into her bag, she headed toward the beach. The day had warmed nicely and she slipped off her sweater, tying it around her waist. As she walked, she savored every flower, every tree, every smiling person she passed. Barcelona was truly one of the most beautiful cities she'd ever visited, and she wondered if she'd ever return. Being hired by Seaside Tech and then Fowler Enterprises for these months had been a dream come true. She was able to do work that challenged and inspired her, and she was proud of her accomplishments.

And deeply ashamed of some of her choices.

She reached the esplanade and walked along the pavement next to the beach, heading toward her hotel. *How did I lose myself?* she wondered. Slipping off her shoes, she walked onto the sand. She felt a deep, aching sadness. She had felt such confidence and pride when she had broken off her engagement to Jeremy a year ago. True, it had been painful. But she had felt a strength that buoyed her beyond the pain. She had decided firmly that love was not for her and was determined to build a life without it.

What happened in Barcelona?

Azalea looked across the beach to the blue waves peacefully lapping at the shore. *I was lonely,* she admitted. *And I was swept away by Jeremy finally seeing me as a partner—not an accessory.* She sat on the sand, wrapping her arms around her shins. Tears balanced on her lashes until one by one they slid down her cheeks.

Her phone rang and she closed her eyes. *Go away,* she thought. *Please stop calling me.* When it stopped, she let out a breath of relief. But when the phone rang again, she took it from her purse to turn it off.

It was Tomás.

She tried to keep her voice from quavering as she answered. "Hi, honey."

"Mom!" Tomás's voice rang out. "Mom, I have some news."

"Are you okay? You sound like you're crying."

"I kinda am," he said with a chuckle. "I hate that I'm telling you this on the phone, but you're on the other side of the world. I'm gonna propose to Em tonight."

Azalea wrestled her anguish into a box in her heart. Her son's news deserved her complete attention. There was plenty of time for soul searching later. Grieving would have to wait.

"Mom? Are you there?"

"Yes, I'm here. I am so happy for you. Landon said she's a wonderful girl. I can't wait to meet her." She stopped and chuckled. "It was the dog, right?"

His laugh was a balm to her heart.

"Well, it didn't hurt that she's a really good dog mom," he admitted. "I feel terrible that this has happened so fast and you aren't here to be a part of it. I honestly thought about waiting until you could meet her 'cuz it just felt weird to propose to someone you haven't even met. But, Mom, you're going to adore her." His voice grew soft. "She's not perfect, but she's perfect for me.

"Mom..." Tomás's voice was soft and boyish. "Would you pray for me? I'm excited but I'm also nervous."

Azalea closed her eyes, tears wetting her cheeks, her personal anguish vying for attention. Again, she tamped it down.

"Lord, please bless Tomás. Calm his nerves and give him the right words to say." She smiled and finished, "And let Emily know she's getting the best husband on the planet!"

Her eldest burst out laughing. "Thanks, Mom. I love you so much."

The two talked and laughed until she said, "Things have changed for me, too. Not quite as exciting as your news, but I'm actually coming home tomorrow." She smiled. "Now I just need to plan a trip to Colorado to visit you boys and meet this fiancée of yours."

"Tomorrow? Isn't that early? Oh, shoot...Mom, I gotta run. I'm late for class and I have to leave campus early to get ready for tonight. I purposely picked a Thursday so she'll be surprised—it's just a normal weeknight, right?" She could hear the smile in his voice. "I love you and I'll call you tomorrow."

"I'll be thinking of you all day and can't wait to hear, honey. Be well, my sweet."

"Love you to the moon, Mom," Tomás said.

"And back," she answered.

Azalea stood and dusted the sand from her backside, then shook her purse. Sand grains flew off the leather. She picked up her shoes and looked at the ocean, her sorrow flooding back. She would miss this sight, this beautiful beach where she spent so many hours running, walking, and thinking. She hoped she'd return one day. There was still so much to explore. She walked toward the sidewalk when she heard a voice: "*Bella*?"

Azalea turned and was surprised to see Esteban. "It is you!" Grinning, he walked his bicycle across the sand. He was wearing board shorts, and his hair and bare chest were wet. "How are you, *señorita*?" He looked quizzically at her outfit. "A bit overdressed for the beach, I think."

207

"I hadn't planned to sit out here but I guess I should have known." She looked around, wistful. "It seems I always end up at the beach."

"So do I," he confessed. "Every chance I get when I'm not working. I grew up here and I love the ocean—no matter what season or time of day." He ran his towel through his wet hair. "But it was a little chilly today!" Azalea marveled at how much he reminded her of Landon. His open friendliness and charm were warm and endearing.

"You must work a lot to keep your place running," she said.

"*Dios mio*," he muttered. "*Si*, I am there all the time. No *siestas* for me," he added, regaining his smile. "I took a break to come and have a swim, but now I have to get back to my flat to shower and get ready for dinner with my *papá*."

"That sounds nice," she answered.

Esteban laughed. "I doubt it. It will be all about how well I am running the café. My father is a wonderful man, but since my mother died, he's all business. We have another café in Cadaqués—it's a couple of hours from here. He runs it by himself and he's sure I'm doing everything wrong with our place in Barcelona."

"Cadaqués?" she asked. Azalea thought back to an article she read about the picturesque village, then frowned. "I've pretty much stayed in Barcelona the whole time I've been here—I wish I had traveled outside the city."

"It's a beautiful little village on the Costa Brava. We moved there when my parents felt Barcelona got too big." He grew thoughtful. "*Mi mamá* tried to get me to stay there but it's just too small for me. When I moved back here I know it was—hmm, I'm not sure how to say it in English. A *tristeza* for her."

Sadness? Disappointment? Azalea wasn't sure of the exact translation, but she got the gist of Esteban's thought. "I think I understand," she said. "My sons moved to Colorado a few months ago. That's several hours from me in Florida and I miss them terribly." She smiled. "I'm sure she was very proud of what you've accomplished here in Barcelona, though."

Esteban grinned happily. "She loved the café here—it's named after her. And every time I would make a change to the menu, my father would grumble but she would be so happy. She said I was becoming *mi propio hombre*."

Azalea laughed. "And what will your father think of your American bread pudding?"

Esteban rolled his eyes, placing his hand over his heart in mock horror and dropping his voice. "*Que has hecho, mijo?*" He laughed and added, "I will find out tonight. After dinner I'm taking him back to the café to try some. If he's honest, he'll agree it's a wonderful addition. If he's stubborn, he will complain." Esteban shrugged. "We'll see."

"I'm sure he'll love it," replied Azalea. "It's delicious and...."

"You should have dinner with us!" broke in Esteban. "You can tell him how much you love the bread pudding and how I did with your event." He nodded delightedly. "*Sí, sí!* You must come."

Azalea shook her head in the face of Esteban's exuberance. "No, I couldn't possibly intrude with your dinner—I don't know your father and it doesn't sound like he would appreciate me being there—"

Esteban interrupted again. "No, this is *perfecto, Bella*. He needs to have some fun. He's done nothing but work for five years. If you are there, we can talk about Cadaqués and about America. About your sons. About *anything* besides the café."

Esteban reached for her hand, almost pleading. "Please. I would be honored if you would join us."

She was shaking her head—but then reconsidered. On her last night in Barcelona, what had she planned? She needed to repack her bags and call Susana to get a ride from the airport in Orlando. And dinner? Room service alone in her fancy hotel. She had nothing that would distract her from her anguished regrets.

Her life had turned upside down and the grief hovered, ready to overcome her. She wanted to simply close this chapter of her life, and yet she was surprised to find Denice's words whispering in her mind: *Would it kill you to have a little fun?*

There was plenty of time for self-recrimination.

"Okay, okay," she decided. "I'll join you."

Esteban beamed. "I only have my bike," he said, "But I can call you a car—"

"Esteban, I'm fine," she broke in, nodding toward her hotel in the distance. "I'm staying at the Arts."

His eyes widened. "Oh—I thought you had an apartment in Las Ramblas."

"I did," she answered. "But I moved out yesterday. I…I'm going home tomorrow." She looked around, taking in the view. "It's my last day in Barcelona."

Esteban looked at her, surprised. "And you're going to spend it with us? *Gracias, gracias, Bella!* I promise you won't regret it." He pulled out his phone and took her number. "I'll text you with the address." He looked up, embarrassed. "Oh! Where are my manners? We can pick you up. *Mi mamá* would be furious with me right now," he finished lamely.

Azalea laughed at his confusion. "Esteban, it's fine. I'll meet you at the restaurant. What time is good?" He continued to protest but she stopped him with her "Mom voice," as Landon called it. "I will meet you. Just text me an address."

Esteban grinned. "*Perfecto*—nine o'clock. I will see you then." He waved and rode off on his bike.

She walked back to her hotel, marveling at herself. *Did I really just decide to have dinner with them?* Being impulsive wasn't like her, but her normal decision making hadn't exactly been brilliant lately. Even if the evening were a complete disaster, she surmised, *I'm going home tomorrow.*

Azalea reached the hotel lobby in minutes and took the elevator to her room. Her phone buzzed and she looked to see a text from Esteban. *"Plata Bistro, 9:00. Mi papá is eager to meet you!"*

She texted back, *"Lo mismo—hasta luego!'*

"What a day," she muttered aloud. *Just keep moving forward,* she thought. *One step at a time.*

After packing and repacking several times, she managed to fit everything into her suitcases. She sent Susana her itinerary and had time for a bath before preparing for dinner.

As she soaked in the tub, she nearly decided to cancel. The thought of meeting someone new, having to chat—*What was I thinking?*

She lay in the warm water and cried, wondering if she'd ever feel whole again.

If she could ever trust herself again.

I can't just stay in this room and cry all night, she decided.

She dressed quickly before she could change her mind again. She picked a full skirt that just grazed her knees and a white pullover. *Stick with simple,* she decided, and put on a pair of gold hoops, her gold watch, and a delicate gold chain bracelet her parents had given her years before. She thought about the flashy gold bangles Maricela always wore. They were as different from her own taste in jewelry as could be. The women were different in every way, yet somehow connected to one man.

Perhaps not so different after all, she thought. She wondered if Maricela were genuinely hurt by her breakup with Jeremy. The tall beauty seemed like she recovered pretty quickly, bouncing back with Javier within the week. *It's so hard to know with her,* Azalea thought. Was she making a point to show Jeremy she was unfazed? Or hiding sincere pain? Azalea felt a surprising swell of compassion—surely even Maricela had feelings.

Why not? she thought and sat down at her laptop to dash off a quick email.

Maricela, I'm going home tomorrow and don't want to leave with any animosity between us. I am truly sorry for your pain and regret any part I may have had in it. I wish you well and hope you will be happy.

All the best, Azalea

She closed her laptop and sat back. She didn't know if it would be received well, but at least she stayed true to herself—and that had become even more important to her over the past day. She wasn't going to lose that again, she vowed.

She started to grab her black purse but then decided on the slim green clutch. "It's the last night," she said aloud. *Time to imbue it with a different memory.* She was just about to put her phone in the tiny purse when it buzzed. An email notice flashed on the screen and Azalea opened it. It was from Maricela.

Keep your pity to yourself, Azalea. I have no need of it.

Azalea blinked, then reread the short note.

And burst out laughing.

Well, that's one loose end nicely tied off, she thought. She gathered her purse and room key and headed out the door.

Tears or laughter, it was her last night in Barcelona.

30

The evening was beautiful, the night sky sparkling with stars. Azalea stood for a moment, just soaking in the scene. In the dark, she couldn't see the waves, but she could hear the surf and smell the ocean. Straightening her shoulders, she said a quick prayer of thanks—she was wounded, but she would survive. *One step at a time,* she reminded herself.

She thanked the doorman for hailing her cab and climbed in. "Plata Bistro, *por favor,*" she told the driver.

As they drove, she marveled again at the differences between the city and her own little town in Florida. People walked everywhere and restaurants were open and lively. *At home they pretty much roll up the streets by nine o'clock*, she mused. *Here it's just getting started.*

The taxi pulled up to the curb and Azalea paid and thanked the driver. She stepped out and was immediately greeted by Esteban. Smiling, he reached for her hand and pulled her in for a traditional *dos besos* greeting. Surprised, Azalea did her best not to pull back—kissing colleagues wasn't her common practice. *Is he really a colleague anymore?* she wondered. *I'm unemployed. Tonight I'm out for dinner with new friends.*

"*Bella*, I would like you to meet my father, Esteban Obregon." He stepped back and held out his hand to an older gentleman.

Esteban? She knew this man.

On her first day in Spain, when she'd been surprised to see the young Esteban at La Rosa de Barcelona, this man—*this very handsome man*—had opened the door for her as she left the café. And then he served her coffee—*Was it only yesterday?* Esteban Senior stepped up and took her hand. "*Mucho gusto, Señorita Mora.*"

She gaped at the two men, then composed herself and smiled. "Please, call me Azalea. It's lovely to meet you."

"Athaleah, then," he said, making the slight bow she remembered from their first encounter. Her eyes widened, but she said nothing. It wasn't her name the way she pronounced it, but in his voice, it was rich and lovely and she found that it didn't bother her at all. *Athaleah*, she thought, rolling the syllables over in her mind.

"Shall we go in? I hope you will like this restaurant." He offered her his arm and she took it, pleasantly surprised at his courtly manner.

The three walked into the foyer, Azalea glancing sideways at the man as she held his arm. They were seated quickly, and Senior pulled out her chair, sitting next to her once she settled. His son sat across from her, smiling. "Thank you for coming," he said.

"Thank you for inviting me," she replied. She looked around and smiled. "It's really lovely." She sensed his father's gaze, and she picked up her menu to hide her sudden nervousness. "So what's good here?" she asked.

Esteban Junior laughed. "Everything! This place has its own garden and all the food is local. The chef is a magician." He picked up his menu and asked, "*Papá? Que quieres comer?*"

The elder Esteban scolded his son. "We speak English tonight, *mijo*. We should be mindful of our guest." He smiled at Azalea, then picked up his own menu and said, "These are traditional *tapas*. We can order several and share them. I understand this is your last night in Barcelona, so perhaps it will be nice to try something new?"

Azalea nodded, looking back at her menu. She noted his Catalan pronunciation—*Bar-the-lona*. It was warm and vibrant, not unlike the city itself. She smiled at father and son, setting down her menu. "I agree," she said. "Why don't you two order for us? I'll try whatever you choose."

Esteban Junior jumped in. "You will love everything, *Bella*." He looked at his father and his face fell. "What?" he asked. Azalea hid a laugh—he sounded like a reprimanded child.

His father's voice was stern. "Don't you think you should call her Azalea?" He turned to look at her. "I expect she might prefer her own name. You are too casual with our guest, Esteban."

My own name.

Not Azi.

The young man nodded. "I did not mean to insult you, *Be*—Azalea. Forgive me if I have."

She smiled at both of them. "I'm not insulted. It's a compliment." She looked at the man next to her. "Your son has been nothing but polite and professional, Esteban. You can be very proud of him." Junior leaned back, grinning.

"See, *Papá*? Professional."

His father shook his head. "*Ay*…this boy," he muttered. "So Esteban tells me you have sons, too. How old are they? And are they as much trouble as this one?"

Azalea laughed. As she was about to answer, the waiter came to their table to take their drink order. Again, she considered her situation. If this were a work event, she would have sparkling water. If a dinner with friends, she'd order wine. The waiter stood patiently awaiting her decision. "I'll start with *agua con gas, por favor*," she answered, not wanting to take more time on internal debate. *Why do I have to make everything so complicated?* Father and son ordered wine and then ordered what seemed like everything on the menu. The waiter left and the two men returned their attention to Azalea.

"Yes," she began again, "I have two sons, Tomás and Landon. Tomás is thirty. He's in graduate school and he works as a teaching assistant at a university. Landon is twenty-eight. He's in sales and works at a technology company. They live together in Colorado."

"Their names are interesting," said Esteban Senior, a thoughtful look on his handsome face. "One is Spanish, the other is English.

Why is that?" He stopped and touched her arm. "I hope I am not being too forward," he hastened to add.

"Not at all. It is a bit unusual," she replied. "My father is from Mexico and the boys' father's family is English. My mother's family is also English, so we thought it would be nice to represent both those backgrounds." She smiled ruefully. "It does cause confusion sometimes, though. Tomás doesn't look Latino at all."

Esteban Senior smiled. "I like that you honor both sides of their heritage." He took a sip of his wine. "Ah…very nice. Are you sure you don't want a glass, Azalea?"

"I'll have some when our dinner arrives," she decided, putting herself firmly in the non-work zone. She found she was eager to listen to his voice and leaned forward, interested. "So tell me about Cadaqués. I've seen pictures but never been there. It sounds beautiful."

The waiter returned with their tapas and interrupted the conversation. Father and son described each dish, and Esteban Senior took it upon himself to serve Azalea a bit from each plate. While the men served themselves, Azalea closed her eyes for a brief prayer, thankful for the surprisingly easy camaraderie. She was astonished and grateful that she seemed to have, at least momentarily, put the angst of the day behind her.

And was surprised to find herself intrigued by the man next to her.

"*A la dama le gustaría una copa de vino*," Esteban Senior told the waiter. "What would you like, Azalea?" he asked.

"What do you recommend?"

"This *garnacha* is very nice," he answered, swirling the deep red wine in his glass.

"Then I'll try that."

As the waiter left, Esteban Senior began describing his village. "It's truly one of the most beautiful places in Spain," he began. "The water is deep blue and crystal clear, and the homes are white and picturesque. It's like a postcard." He continued describing the harbor and how the ocean was dotted with boats every day. As she listened, Azalea angled her chair so she could look at him. He was in his fifties, she guessed, tanned with jet black but lightly graying hair. His dark brown eyes were bright, and his smile infectious. His richly accented English mesmerized her until she noticed his son grinning at them from across the table. The waiter returned with the wine, and she broke off her gaze, returning to her food to cover her sudden flush. •

"And so I have my little flat just above the café," Esteban continued. "I get up early to start the baking before my customers come in." He laughed quietly. "I have to be ready for the American tourists who like to come in early. The locals don't come in until late morning."

Azalea's head snapped up. *My little flat just above the cafe?*

She looked down and dabbed at her lips with her napkin to keep from gawking at Esteban. Flashes of memory assailed her—the little flat above the café in her dream, the handsome Spaniard sharing her café…and her life. She felt her face flush again and excused herself to use the restroom.

As she washed her hands, she looked in the mirror. She reapplied her lipstick with shaking hands and marveled at how she looked. Bright eyes stared back at her, a faint pink tinge on her cheeks. *What is going on?*

Practical Azalea kicked in.

I am unemployed and going home tomorrow. My time in Barcelona is over. Get a grip, she thought roughly. *I was in bed with Jeremy thirty-six hours ago.* Her stomach knotted as she remembered Jeremy's face, first full of rage, then sorrow.

But another Azalea—this unfamiliar woman who dared to be spontaneous and go to dinner with people she didn't even know—remembered her dreams.

She put her lipstick into her clutch and walked back to the table. As she approached, Esteban Senior stood up and held her chair for her. Their eyes locked and he smiled warmly.

The other Azalea stirred and she couldn't help smiling back.

Dinner progressed smoothly, with Senior proving to be a deft conversationalist, his English impeccable. He asked questions about Florida, about her work, and about her life outside the office. Junior sat mostly quiet, eating and smiling as his father and Azalea chatted. At one point, when his father looked down at his watch, he caught her eye and raised an eyebrow. She stifled a laugh and made a mock grimace. *This boy*, she thought, mentally agreeing with his father.

Esteban Senior looked up. "This has been very nice, *mijo*. Thank you for inviting your friend." He looked at Azalea. "I hope we have made your last night in Barcelona a pleasant one."

Junior broke in. "It doesn't have to be over, *Papá*. Azalea would like to come to the café with us, wouldn't you?" He turned his dazzling smile to her, but his eyes implored her. "She loved one of the new desserts I added to the menu. Don't you want a happy customer to join us?" He looked back and forth between the two.

Esteban Senior frowned at his son. "I would be delighted to have your company, Azalea," he began, "but I don't want to impose on your time." He looked at his son and then back at her. Something seemed to change in his face, as if he'd made a decision. He reached out and lightly touched her arm. "Would you like to join us?"

Her face betrayed none of the battle going on in her mind. Her practical side shouted: *You're leaving tomorrow! Are you crazy? That dream meant nothing.*

The other Azalea won.

She looked directly into his eyes. "I would love to."

It's my last night in Barcelona.

31

The three waited outside for the car. Azalea shivered slightly in the cool air and Esteban Senior took off his sport coat and slipped it around her shoulders before she could protest. His hands lingered briefly on her shoulders, then rubbed her arms briskly. She felt herself warming—and not only from the body heat left in his jacket. Embarrassed, she looked over her shoulder and thanked him. "You are most welcome," he said with a slight nod. "The car will be here soon and I'll turn on the heater for you."

The valet drove up, saving her from having to respond. Esteban Junior pointedly avoided her gaze as Senior took her arm and led her to the car. He opened the door for her and she slid into the front seat, murmuring her thanks. Junior slipped into the seat behind her. His father turned on the heater and showed her where the button was for her seat warmer. "It will heat up quickly," he said.

"Thank you, Esteban," she replied. "I've never had seat warmers before." She chuckled. "Not much need of them in Florida."

"It gets cold in Cadaqués in the winter. I'm glad I have them for you tonight," he responded. He put on his seatbelt and pulled away from the curb. "It will be warm in the café, too."

At eleven o'clock, the city was still awake. The sky was clear, a midnight blue canvas dotted with stars. "It's so beautiful here," mused Azalea, looking out the window. "I will miss Barcelona."

Junior laughed softly behind her. "What's so funny, *chistoso*?" asked his father.

"Nothing," he answered. "It just makes me laugh to hear how Americans pronounce Barcelona."

"Esteban," began his father with a stern air, "Please do not—"

Azalea stopped him with a hand on his forearm. "It's really okay," she said with a smile. "I'm embarrassed to say I laughed about the Catalan pronunciation a few months ago." She shook her head, regretting her early remarks, no matter how good natured they had been. "Now I love your accent." She flushed at her comment. How patronizing she sounded! He didn't have an accent—*she* did. It was his country.

"I'm sorry—that sounds terrible. I mean, I love the Catalan pronunciation and I'd like to learn the language—" She trailed off, embarrassed. She had traveled extensively and was keenly aware of how boorish Americans could be when they were abroad. She feared she'd just joined their ranks with her thoughtless comments.

Esteban Senior glanced at her as he turned into the driveway of the café. "Unfortunately, *Bella*, you cannot learn the language in one night."

Bella?

Junior stifled a laugh, turning it into a cough as his father parked. "Okay, *Papá*, Azalea, let's go try some delicious dessert." He opened his door and climbed out, opening her door and offering his hand. As he helped her out of the car, he whispered, "Let's hope you distract him enough so he doesn't complain about the bread pudding."

Esteban Senior walked around to the passenger side, offering her his arm. "Shall we, Azalea?" he asked.

"I'd be delighted," she said with a smile.

Junior opened the café door. A young woman was sweeping the room and looked up as they entered. "*Hola, Gabriela*," said the son. "*Todo está bien?*"

Gabriela nodded. "*Estaba tan ocupada esta noche. Había mucha gente aquí.*" She looked at her watch. "*Ay…es muy tarde.*"

Esteban Senior reached for her broom. "*Vete a casa con tu familia, Gabriela. Puedo terminar de barrer.*"

Junior looked at his father, surprised. Then he smiled and agreed. "*Si, Gabriela. Muchisimas gracias por todo. Que tengas un buen noche.*"

The woman sighed gratefully and handed the broom to the older man. "*Igualmente, Esteban. Gracias, Señor Obregon.*" She headed behind the cash register to retrieve her purse and left the café with a tired, "*Hasta mañana.*"

Junior reached for the broom. "I can do that, *Papá*," he said. "Why don't you just sit and visit with Azalea?"

"No, *mijo*," responded Senior. "I'll get this done quickly. You go ahead and serve us this special dessert." He gestured for Azalea to sit. "And make us some coffee, please."

"*Si, Papá*," responded the son. As his father turned to begin sweeping, Junior looked at Azalea and made a face, miming shock.

She laughed and shooed him away. "*Cafecito con leche y azucar, por favor,*" she said.

"Your accent is very good," called Esteban Senior from across the room. "You won't have to learn that—just the vocabulary." Azalea turned to look at him, sweeping the floor and turning the sign to *Cerrado*.

Her face flushed as she remembered her first dream. Her imaginary Esteban had swept and closed up their café for the evening. They sat at a table together, enjoying coffee and bread pudding. There had been a sense of peaceful companionship, a warmth that left her feeling whole. Nothing sexual—*At least not the first dream*, she reminded herself. Just a profound contentment at being together.

It was just a dream.

He finished sweeping and propped the broom against a wall, then pulled out the chair next to her. "It was good of you to join us," he said. "Esteban thinks very highly of you, and I can tell this means a lot to him."

"It's my pleasure," she began when Junior returned holding two coffees.

"*Cafecito con leche y azucar* for the lady," he entered, "*y espresso oscuro* for the gentleman." He set the two cups down with a flourish. "*Momentito, por favor,*" he added, as he straightened to return to the kitchen. His father shook his head fondly. He may have been stern with his son at various times throughout the evening, but his love and pride in his namesake were unmistakable. He looked back at Azalea who gazed at him knowingly.

"He's a good boy," she said. His father smiled and nodded.

Junior returned with a large tray. On it, there were three small plates with warm bread pudding and another espresso for him. He set the plates on the table, his nervousness barely controlled. Azalea looked at him and smiled encouragingly. "This is my favorite dessert," she told his father. "I was so excited that Esteban brought it to the event. Everyone loved it at my office." She sensed Junior's relief at her compliment. He set the tray on another table and sat down.

"This is it, *Papá*. American bread pudding, but with a Spanish twist." He spread his hands wide, inviting them to try the warm dessert. Azalea took a bite, closing her eyes and sighing. "So good," she murmured. She sipped her coffee and looked at Esteban Senior, who was chewing and looking up at the ceiling, thinking. Junior sat across from them, anxiously awaiting his father's reaction.

Senior looked at his son and smiled. "It's very good, *mijo*," he said. "*Necesita mas canela, pero me gusta mucho.*" He looked at her, abashed. "I'm sorry, Azalea. I said it needs—"

"*Yo entiendo*, Esteban," she broke in with a knowing smile. "I put cinnamon in just about everything." She looked at Junior. "It's delicious, Esteban. I like this version even better than the one you brought to the office. You've added more apples, I think?" He nodded, his relief palpable.

"*Si, si.* It takes a bit longer to bake, but I think it's better now." He smiled shyly at his father. "I'm so glad you like it, *Papá*."

"I need your recipe, *mijo*," Senior responded, giving his son the greatest compliment. "I will add this to the Cadaqués menu next week." He looked sideways at Azalea. "I will call it *La Americana*."

Junior grinned. "I was going to call it *La Bella Dulce*, but *La Americana* is better."

Azalea blushed, her eyes bright at their compliments. "Your customers will love it whatever you call it," she replied.

Junior looked back and forth between his father and their guest, a knowing smile on his face. He took a sip of his coffee and then a hearty bite of the bread pudding. "*La Americana*," he mused. "*El nombre perfecto, Papá.*"

His father didn't correct him.

The three finished their dessert when Junior yawned and pushed back his chair.

"*Lo siento, pero estoy muy cansado.*" He caught himself. "I'm sorry, Azalea. Too tired to remember my English. I hope I'm not too tired to ride my bicycle!"

She laughed. She wasn't tired at all, and was surprised to find herself pleasantly relaxed. "I understand. You probably have to be back early tomorrow—" she looked at her watch—"I mean, today. I should get back to the hotel so you can go home."

"Is that crazy girlfriend still around?" interrupted Senior.

"*Papá!*" remonstrated his son "We broke up months ago. She's gone and not coming back."

"That's what you said last time," commented Senior. He looked at Azalea, apologizing. "I know I should stay out of it, but I do not like that girl."

Azalea chuckled. "Actually, neither do I," she said. Esteban Junior looked askance at her and she inclined her head, chagrined. "I saw you two break up at the airport," she confessed. "It was my first day in Barce—Bar-*the*-lona."

"You were at the airport that day? Why didn't you ever mention it?" Junior was surprised.

"What should I have said? 'Hey, I saw you and your girlfriend have a shouting match at the airport.'" She shook her head. "I'm sorry. I shouldn't even have mentioned it now."

Junior looked at his father. "So now you know, *Papá*," he said with a half-smile. "She yelled at me in the airport and I broke up with her. Gloria is not coming back." He looked at Azalea, then his father. "I realized that day I deserve someone who supports my dreams."

His father looked at him and answered quietly, "Your mother always supported both of us, *mijo*. Find someone like her."

Azalea's eyes grew misty as she gazed at the tender moment between father and son.

Esteban Senior put out a hand. "*Mijo*, go home. I can lock up here and I have my key to the flat. I'll take Azalea to her hotel and come back to the apartment."

Azalea protested, "No, please. I can call a car to take me back. You both get home."

The elder Esteban was shaking his head before she finished, his eyes intent on her face. "I must insist, Azalea. Esteban can ride his bicycle home—our apartment is only two blocks away. I would never send you off in a taxi when I can drive you myself." He looked at his son. "Get some rest, *mijo*. I'll be quiet when I come in."

Junior nodded in thanks and spoke to Azalea. "Safe travels, *Bella*. Thank you for everything." He leaned in for the traditional *dos besos* farewell, and this time Azalea returned the kisses to his cheeks. "I wish you all the very best, Esteban," she said quietly. "You're a special young man and I know you will find someone who sees that, too." His answering smile warmed her heart.

He walked to the back of the café and returned with his bicycle. Father and son walked to the front door and embraced, speaking quietly. Then the older man locked the door behind his son and stood for a moment, silently watching him ride down the street.

32

Azalea sat quietly watching Esteban. She was gripped by a longing for her own sons when she remembered Tomás's call and looked at her watch. It was nearly one o'clock in the morning. She did the quick math—almost six o'clock in Colorado. Her oldest son was about to propose!

She looked up as Esteban returned to the table. He sat quietly next to her, and Azalea spontaneously reached for his hand. She squeezed gently and repeated her earlier words: "He's a good boy."

Esteban nodded and returned her squeeze. Surprised and embarrassed by her bold gesture, she gently pulled her hand away and looked at him. "Tomás is proposing to his girlfriend right now," she said simply. "I haven't met her, but Landon said she is wonderful." She looked away, thinking. "And of course Tomás says she is perfect."

"This is your older son?" asked Esteban.

"Yes," she replied. "He met her when they moved to Colorado, so it hasn't been long. But he seems very certain." A slow smile spread over her face. "I trust him."

"Well, congratulations are in order, then," said Esteban. He lifted his nearly empty coffee cup, and she raised her own for a toast. They finished their coffee, then grew silent.

After a long moment, Esteban broke the quiet. "So," he asked tentatively, "you are not married?"

"No," she said, looking down at her empty cup. "I've been divorced for several years." She looked at Esteban, weighing how much to tell him. *His eyes are so beautiful,* she thought, again surprising herself. After a moment, she dove in.

"I broke off an engagement a year ago. I realized he wasn't the one for me. He was more interested in his dreams than mine.

"Sort of like Gloria," she finished, in a weak attempt to lighten the mood.

Esteban sat back, crossing his legs and folding his hands in his lap. "What happened? I know Americans are less open with their feelings than we Spaniards so I hope that isn't too forward for me to ask."

She sat quietly pondering her response. *I don't know you,* she thought. It felt awkward to share something so personal, yet a bit liberating, too. *I'm going home. What could it hurt?*

And those eyes. He genuinely seemed to care.

"I realized that he didn't want *me.* He wanted the me he could create." The pain, so recent, threatened to bring her to tears.

Esteban reached out to touch her forearm as he looked at her with sympathy. "I'm so sorry. I didn't mean to cause you pain."

She smiled, though her eyes were sad. "It's all right. I'm more disappointed in myself than him. I didn't see what was happening until it was almost too late." She sighed. "At least I didn't have to go through another divorce."

"That was to your sons' father?"

She took a deep breath. "Yes. Unfortunately, it turned out that he didn't value our marriage vows the same way I did. He was unfaithful and it was very, very painful." She shook her head, lost in memory. "I wondered if it were the right thing to do—you know, divorce. I worried about my boys. I worried about them more than I worried about myself, honestly."

Azalea looked at his hand on her arm, then up to see him gazing at her intently. "It was very painful," she repeated. "We were married a long time."

The confusion was plain on his face. "How on earth does a man betray a woman like you?" He slid his hand down to capture hers, but she drew it away with a frown. He looked at her with surprise as she bristled.

"What do you mean?" she asked sharply. "'A woman like me'?"

Esteban leaned forward and spread his hands wide. "Look at you, Azalea," he gestured. "You're beautiful. You're intelligent. You're warm and kind. You're—"

She interrupted him, her tone curt. "So what you're saying is that there is a type of woman who deserves to be betrayed? Someone who isn't beautiful? Someone who isn't intelligent? Is that what you mean?"

Esteban was dumbfounded. "*Madre de Dios*," he murmured.

Azalea looked at her shaking hands. She was suddenly angry at Esteban and herself. She had let herself enjoy his company, had begun to open up to his questions. *Why? Because we both love our sons? Because I'm raw and vulnerable and he's so charming? How could I be so reckless?* She had watched his rough edges soften with his son and witnessed his generosity and pride. She glanced up and was surprised to see his morose face. With a questioning look, he reached again for her hand, holding even as she began to pull away.

"Azalea," he began in a soft voice, "Please. I am very sorry. That was a thoughtless thing to say. There is no woman who deserves betrayal. None." Esteban's voice grew stronger, and he held her hand in both of his. His dark eyes fixed on hers without flinching. "Marriage vows are promises we make before almighty God." He looked down at her hand and absently stroked the finger where she'd once worn her wedding band. Her heart pounded, but she sat perfectly still, waiting for him to go on.

He looked up and spoke with a serious tone. "Forgive me, Azalea. You have taught me something tonight."

She stared at him, astonished. The last thing she expected was an apology. *Who was this man?* Brushing off his comment or defending it was far more likely. Finding a quick way to exit the conversation—that's what she assumed was coming. But an apology? That threw her. She couldn't imagine either David or Jeremy being so humble.

Her hands still trembled. His thoughtless words rankled, yet she believed his apology was sincere.

Esteban sat quietly, waiting for her to respond. His hands held hers and his eyes were gentle. She took a deep breath to calm herself. She hadn't expected him to understand, much less apologize, and she found it difficult to step back from her anger.

At last she spoke. "Thank you," she said quietly. "That means a great deal to me."

Esteban nodded. The two sat awkwardly, unsure where to take the conversation next.

"Thank you," he said at last. "I am sorry for insulting you." He grimaced. "For insulting women in general, it seems."

Azalea looked down at their hands, still clasped together. His earnestness pierced her. She looked up, feeling *What?* she wondered. She had a sudden longing to move closer to him. "You're a good man, Esteban."

He smiled ruefully. "I try very hard." He released her hand and sat back, pensive. "My wife was such a good woman. I spent our entire marriage trying to live up to her example and to be a good role model for our son. Since she died, I've tried to continue but, as you can see," he said with a shrug, "I am not always successful."

Azalea roughly tamped down her emotions. "She sounds like a wonderful woman."

"She was," he answered simply. "We were married for twenty-two years before she died. She was an excellent wife and mother, always encouraging Esteban and me. I was the dreamer." His eyes grew soft, remembering. "All she cared about was making sure our home was a place full of love and laughter.

"She wasn't perfect, but she was perfect for me."

Esteban flinched at Azalea's sudden intake of breath. "Did I say something wrong?" he asked, concern all over his face.

She shook her head and reached for his hand, willing them to reconnect. "No, no. It's just…." She trailed off. "That's exactly what Tomás said to me yesterday about his girlfriend. It's such a lovely thing to say." Embarrassed, she pulled slowly away. "You must miss her very much."

"I do," he replied. "But it's been five years. I can finally look back on all the joy we experienced and be very, very grateful. I look at our son and I see that he has so much of her goodness in him." He inclined his head and smiled. "And I have come to realize that I cannot just live on memories. I'm not ready to give up on living just yet."

Azalea gazed at him, wondering why she kept the conversation going. She needed to get back to the hotel, to prepare for her trip home.

But the complex Spaniard intrigued her. Tentatively, she asked, "So…do you date?"

He smiled. "No." He ran a hand through his hair. "Esteban keeps encouraging me to get out and meet someone. But I just concentrate on my café in Cadaqués and come to Barcelona once every month or so to check in on La Rosa here." He waved a hand to take in the café. "He's doing a great job. He is a good manager and a good leader and he's a wonderful baker." He laughed. "He really doesn't need me to come here and bother him."

"I don't know if I agree with that," said Azalea. "I think our boys still need us even at this time in their lives. When Tomás called me today to tell me that he was going to propose to his girlfriend, it was very special. He's thirty years old, but he still needed to call his mama." She offered a wry smile. "But I know what you mean. Both my boys would like to see me with someone special."

Esteban looked long at her. "Azalea," he began, his voice deep and resonant, "I would like to see you again."

Her heart fluttered. It made no sense, this pull she felt toward a man she'd met only hours before. Her ragged emotions bounced, then coalesced, and she heard herself saying, "I'd like to see you, too, but I'm leaving tomorrow." She looked at her watch and smiled sadly. "I'm actually leaving today."

With a serious, piercing look he reached for her hands. "Would you let me take you to the airport at least?" he asked.

She nodded. "I would like that," her voice near a whisper.

"And perhaps you will come back," he said.

"Perhaps I will."

Esteban held the car door open for her, then walked quickly to the driver's side. "The heater will come on very soon," he murmured, looking as if he wished to say more. She nodded without a word. She wasn't uncomfortable, precisely—but she felt strangely vulnerable. After the past two days, her emotions were still raw.

They drove in silence for several minutes. Then Esteban looked over at her, his eyes intent. As he looked back to the road, he reached over and took her hand, his fingers sliding smoothly between her own. His hand was warm and strong, and Azalea didn't refuse him. He continued to look forward, but she saw the hint of a smile and his shoulders relaxed. She sighed, suddenly realizing how tense she also was. Closing her eyes, she surrendered to the peace and quiet.

As they drove, she thought about how different it felt to sit wordlessly holding hands with Esteban compared to the passion she'd felt only days before with Jeremy. There had been something exhilarating in the way she threw herself into their rekindled romance. *But did I ever feel this serene?* she asked herself. There had been tension, fire, confusion, and raw sensuality—but very little peace. *I may never see this man again*, she supposed, *but this simple moment is something I want to hold onto.* Tears pricked her eyelids as she basked in the warmth filling her body.

Esteban pulled up to the hotel and stopped the car. He turned to her and brought her hand to his lips. Kissing it gently, his eyes met hers. Azalea gazed back, holding her breath. "I don't know what's happening, but I don't want to say goodbye," he said simply.

"I don't either," she admitted. "But I do need to get ready for my trip." She swallowed, embarrassed. "Esteban…I got fired this week. I was supposed to be here for another month, so this is all very last minute."

"Fired? Why?" His handsome face darkened with concern. "Are you all right? I am so sorry."

"It's a long story," she said. "And I'm far too tired to share it tonight." Azalea tried to smile, but it was lopsided and sad. "Thank you for making this such a lovely evening. You took my mind off all my troubles."

He reached up to stroke her cheek, his fingers lightly touching her hair. She closed her eyes and leaned into his touch, wondering what on earth she was doing—yet refusing to turn away. "Azalea," he said at last, "May I at least walk you to your room? I won't interrupt the rest of your night—I would just like to say goodbye properly." His smile was gentle and kind, his eyes bright.

"I'd like that," she whispered.

Esteban parked the car and walked around to open her door. Azalea took his arm and the two walked into the lobby. She held tightly to his arm and he pulled her in a little closer as they entered the elevator. She pushed the button for the tenth floor, and they stood quietly as the elevator glided up.

When it opened, they walked to her door and stood together outside her room. "I'm very glad I have met you, Azalea," said Esteban. "I—I wish you weren't leaving. I feel like we have much more to talk about. I want to know all about you—you are a fascinating woman." He held her hands loosely as he talked, gesturing as he did.

She was torn. Only two nights ago she'd lain in bed with Jeremy, trying to reconcile her feelings with his possessiveness and control. She had a job she loved and excelled at. Today, she was single, unemployed…and *happy*? No. More than happy.

Peaceful.

This is insane.

I don't care.

Making up her mind, Azalea slid her arms around his neck and kissed him.

"I will come back, Esteban," she whispered. He tenderly returned the kiss, stroking her thick hair.

"Don't be long, *Bella*," he answered. He nodded to her door. "Sleep well." Then he turned and headed for the elevator.

33

"Hey, girl—why are you calling me in the middle of the night?" Susana's voice boomed in her ear. "What time is it? It must be three in the morning for you!"

Azalea grimaced. "Yeah…." She trailed off but then began with excitement. "Is now okay? I really need to talk to you." She knew her friend was rarely in bed before eleven but didn't want to impose.

"Of course, 'mana," responded Susana, suddenly serious. "What's wrong?"

"Nothing," answered Azalea. "Things are surprisingly good."

"Now you have me really curious. What happened?"

"I sort of met a man tonight."

Susana snorted. "'Sort of'?"

Azalea grinned and stretched out on her bed. "Okay, I did meet a man. You remember the kid from the café with the bread pudding?" She had raved to Susana about the bread pudding that reminded her so much of her mother.

"Oh, come on. You said he was the boys' age!" Susana didn't hide her disdain. "That's gross."

"No, no, no," responded Azalea. "I met his *father* tonight. His name is also Esteban and he's a widower." She smiled. "A really nice widower."

Susana laughed. "As long as his name isn't Jeremy Fowler, I'm happy," she said. "But seriously, you sound kinda giddy. Tell me everything!"

"So…" began Azalea, but Susana interrupted her.

"Never mind telling me everything. What does he look like?"

Azalea burst out laughing. "Oh, Suze…he's *beautiful*."

"And?" prompted Susana.

"And we just…connected. I don't know. It wasn't like fireworks or anything. I don't even know how to describe it. He feels warm and comfortable."

"Not gonna lie. That doesn't sound all that impressive. Are you sure this isn't just a rebound thing? You did just break up with the antichrist."

Azalea chuckled as she considered her friend's words. "I don't think so," she said at last. "I didn't feel any big infatuation. It was more like this quiet, peaceful feeling. It's hard to describe. I felt so comfortable being with him. And once I got over being angry, I felt really connected to him. And then he held my hand and it felt natural and just so sweet." She closed her eyes, remembering.

"You got angry?" asked Susana, breaking into Azalea's reverie.

"Oh, yeah. We got into an argument," she said. "I forgot about that."

"Sounding less and less great, my friend."

"And then he walked me to my hotel room and I kissed him." Azalea laughed, still surprised at her spontaneity. "I actually kissed him! And then he kissed me back and he left." She marveled again at their interaction. "A complete gentleman. He's going to take me to the airport tomorrow."

Susana laughed quietly. "You sound really smitten, my friend. Are you sure you want to come home?"

Azalea thought before answering. "I'm actually not so sure," she admitted. "If I were still working, I'd be eager to spend more time with him. But without a job and no place to stay, it's not the smart choice."

Susana barked a laugh. "Always making the smart choice. That's my *hermana*."

"Far from it," Azalea said. "I've made so many bad decisions over the last month. This week has turned my entire life upside down. I still have to deal with the whole Jeremy debacle and losing my job. It's not a good time to fly by the seat of my pants." She sat up. "Oh, my gosh…I forgot to tell you: Tomás proposed to his girlfriend tonight! So I need to come home to meet her. I hope she said yes."

"Oh, girl," replied Susana. "Who could turn down that brilliant son of yours?"

Azalea laughed. Her best friend loved her boys.

"So where did you leave things with Esteban?" asked Susana.

"We both want to see each other again," she answered. "He'll take me to the airport, and I guess we'll figure out what's next." She lay back down, suddenly weary. "I have a feeling I'll be coming back to Barcelona soon. He's pretty special, Suze." Her yawn threatened to split her jaw and she sunk down into her pillow.

"Set your alarm before you fall asleep, *chica*," warned Susana. "You'll end up missing your flight if you don't."

Azalea wasn't sure that was such a terrible idea.

Her alarm woke her and she shot up in bed, disoriented. It was only eight o'clock, and she felt like she'd barely lain down moments before. She pressed the snooze button and was asleep before her head hit the pillow.

And awake again in ten minutes.

She turned off the alarm and lay back to think. Her flight left at four, so she wanted to be at the airport by one o'clock. She was never late for a flight and wasn't going to start today. But she was so tired….

She awoke with a start and grabbed her phone. Eleven-thirty! She'd fallen back asleep and now her heart was pounding with the massive adrenaline dump. She nearly ran to the bathroom. Her hair was wild, and she was still exhausted, her eyes red and her skin sallow. She turned on the shower and stripped off her night shorts and tank. She didn't even remember putting on pajamas last night.

After she hung up with Susana, she vaguely remembered brushing her teeth, but that was where her memory failed.

Get it together, Azalea, she thought as she got into the shower.

Five minutes later, she was out and drying off. She looked again in the bathroom mirror and sighed. Ordinarily, she'd just throw her hair into a ponytail and put on mascara and lip balm for the transatlantic flight.

But Esteban was coming.

She went into the bedroom and dressed quickly, pulling on jeans and a sweater. *Good thing I did most of my packing yesterday*, she thought as she efficiently wrestled her last things into two suitcases. Her phone buzzed and she looked to see a text.

I know you're heading home today, it read. *I wish you'd reconsider. I know things are bad but we can work through them. I want to see you, Azi.*

She stood still, staring at the screen and unsure how to respond. She wanted to ignore the text—why wouldn't Jeremy just let her go? They'd made a decisive and ugly break at the office and having him turn up at the apartment had only exacerbated the wound. Yet now, Azalea realized she felt only annoyance at seeing the text. She was through.

Please don't contact me again, Jeremy. I'm going home and it's best that we part without any ambiguity. I sincerely wish you well.

She set her phone down and closed her suitcase. The phone buzzed again and Azalea sighed heavily. "Would you please just stop?" she scowled.

Good morning, Bella.

Esteban.

Buenos días! she typed, her frown vanishing.

I hope you got some sleep. Is 12:30 OK?

That's perfect. I'll be in the lobby.

Hasta luego, Bella.

Azalea couldn't stop smiling. She put on makeup as quickly as possible, tossing her hair into a messy bun—*That's going to have to do*, she thought. Before she left, she took one last look in the mirror. She still looked tired, but her eyes were bright and she wasn't unhappy with her appearance. *You're like a daft teenager*, she chided herself.

Esteban was sitting in a chair in the lobby when she got off the elevator. His smile at seeing her lit up the room and he walked quickly to help her with her luggage. After taking her suitcases, he leaned down to kiss her lightly. "I'm very glad to see you, Azalea," he said. "Very glad."

"I'm glad to see you, too," she answered, smiling. "Thank you for picking me up."

He looked puzzled. "You don't need to thank me. I couldn't imagine not seeing you before you left." He shook his head. "You have captivated me, *Bella*."

She couldn't stop smiling as they walked to the car. Esteban opened the door for her and then put her suitcases in the trunk. He slid into the driver's seat and turned to look at her. He was quiet for several seconds, and she began to feel nervous. At last, he spoke.

"I couldn't stop thinking of you last night," he said simply, his tone full of wonder.

"Nor I you," she confessed.

He kissed her hand and then started the car. They drove several minutes in silence, and she wondered what was best—to enjoy the serenity of the drive or to converse with the short time they had left. Esteban solved her dilemma by glancing at her and asking, "May I tell you something rather serious?"

"Of course," she answered, suddenly wary. They'd known each other less than eighteen hours and she wondered if she'd made too much of their connection.

"I was happily married for a long time," he began. "As I told you last night, my wife was a very special woman. I still miss her." Azalea nodded, her expression serious. "I've been content to be alone since she died. I didn't want to dishonor her memory by being with anyone else."

Azalea's heart sank. *Of course he's still in love with his wife.*

He glanced at her again and took her hand. Turning back to the road, he continued quietly. "But over the past few months I've considered that maybe my Rosa wouldn't want me to be alone. Esteban has told me that for a while, but I've kept myself busy so I wouldn't have to think about it." Esteban looked at her again, squeezing her hand. "I still talk to her, Azalea," he confessed. "I hope that doesn't sound strange."

Compassion flooded her heart. "Not at all," she answered. "She was part of you. I can't imagine how hard it must have been to see her go." He nodded, his eyes fixed on the road.

"It was the hardest thing I've ever done. But each year it becomes a little easier, the pain less. And last night, I talked to her again.

"I talked to her about you."

Azalea sat very still, unwilling to mar the moment with her words.

Esteban pulled into the parking lot at the Barcelona airport. The silence was heavy between them as he parked the car and at last turned his attention fully to her.

"I believe Rosa would be happy for me right now, Azalea. I feel free to follow my heart." He studied her, yet his gaze was almost shy. "I feel a connection to you. I don't know what that means—I don't even know what to do about it. But I can't pretend I don't feel it."

Azalea was awash in emotions. She felt the same way—there was a connection between them. At one level it was real, palpable, and nearly irresistible. At another, she knew it was terrible timing and she couldn't trust her own feelings. The dreams pulled at her, opening her to possibility. At the same time, she berated herself for her decisions with Jeremy. She sat for a long moment with conflicting thoughts racing through her mind and Esteban's face fell. He pulled his hand away and ran it through his thick dark hair. "I'm sorry. I—I shouldn't have said those things to you. I didn't mean to—"

Azalea reached up and placed a finger on his lips. "Shh," she whispered. He stopped and looked at her, unsure. "I can't pretend either, Esteban." *I'm not going to let this slip away,* she thought fiercely. *Bad timing or no, I am not turning from this moment.* She moved her fingers tenderly from his lips and traced his cheek and jaw. "But I also need to tell you something before we go any further." He nodded under her touch and reached up to take her hand.

Here we go, she thought, determined to tell him the truth. "I made a very bad decision this past month. The man I was engaged to last year bought the company I was working for." Esteban's eyes widened but he didn't speak. "He came to Barcelona and I thought he had changed…but I was wrong. I was very, very wrong. I let myself fall back into a relationship that I ended a year ago." She looked directly into his espresso brown eyes. "We broke it off three days ago." Tears formed on her lashes and she forced herself to finish. "I understand if that makes you question me. Even my best friend asked me last night if how I'm feeling about you is a rebound thing. You know what that is?" she asked.

Esteban nodded.

"I thought hard about her question," she continued.

"And?" he asked quietly.

"It's not," she said simply, a single tear sliding down her cheek. "What I've felt in these few hours is something very, very special." She fought her fear that he would choose to end their connection before they had even begun and decided to bare her heart. "Esteban—I *dreamed about you* before I even knew you existed. I dreamed about the café and the upstairs flat. I feel this sense of peace with you. You're kind and tender and—"

Esteban reached up and gently wiped the tear from her cheek. "*Un sueño? Ay, querida,*" he whispered as he leaned across to kiss her. It was sweet and whisper soft but soon became ardent. He unlocked his seatbelt to turn more fully toward her and unlatched hers before enveloping her in his arms. He kissed her tears and she buried her head in his shoulder. They sat awkwardly in the car, neither willing to break the spell or their embrace.

At last, they separated. Each looked at the other with wonder. "We both come with more than a dream, sweet Azalea," said Esteban. "Neither of us is a child. We have our own history.

"I am willing to follow my heart. Are you?"

She lifted her chin and looked directly into his eyes. "It's terrible timing," she said. "We live thousands of miles apart and who knows when we'll see each other again. We live such different lives." He nodded, his eyes probing hers for an answer.

"But yes. I'm willing to follow my heart," she concluded. "Wherever it takes me."

"Wherever it takes *us*," he answered. He stroked her cheek. "And right now, my sweet Azalea, I hate that you are leaving." His smile was wistful. "But I believe we'll be together again very soon.

I'm not giving up just because of some big ocean between us." She smiled and he took her face in his hands. His touch was gentle yet strong, and it felt…*right*.

"We don't even really know each other. But I am eager to get to know you and I hope you will still like me once you know me better," he said with a chuckle. He glanced at his watch and grimaced. "And now, *Bella*, you need to get inside."

34

Azalea sat on the plane, her heart a jumble of emotions. In the space of just a month, she'd reignited her relationship with Jeremy, deepening it and throwing caution to the wind. She'd made herself vulnerable with him in a way she hadn't before—and then suffered the consequences. She had inklings all along she was making a mistake with him but failed to listen to her intuition, instead following what she thought was her heart.

And then she met Esteban. She'd known him a ridiculously short time yet felt a connection so deep it frightened her…and thrilled her. She wasn't a girl—she was a grown woman, not prone to infatuation. Nevertheless, here she was, aglow with feelings she'd never experienced, daydreaming about a future she could never had imagined.

And now she was on a plane leaving him. Would he wait for her? Was their connection enough?

She tried and failed to sleep, finally opting instead to open her laptop. *Might as well get some work done*, she decided. But what work? She had no other clients besides Fowler Enterprises—she'd ended all her engagements when she left for Spain. She paid for the in-flight wifi and opened a browser, ready to start searching through her contacts for possible projects.

Instead, she saw another message from Jeremy.

We've meant too much to each other, Azi. We owe it to each other to at least talk this out. Please don't leave until we can talk.

She scowled. Surely, she had been crystal clear with her refusal.

Another message popped up, this time from Esteban: *I hope you can sleep on the plane, querida. Please call when you land and know I am thinking of you.*

Her heart ached. *Should I have stayed?* she wondered. She still felt Esteban's lips on hers, the feel of his cheek under her hand, the tiniest glimmer of something wonderful in her heart.

What time is your flight? messaged Jeremy. *Can you just wait a day or two?*

Ignoring Jeremy, Azalea wrote back: *I don't think I'll be able to sleep. Last night gave me a lot to think about. I miss you already.*

Last night? What are you talking about, Azi???

Azalea stared at the screen, her heart in her throat. She'd answered Esteban in the wrong window and now Jeremy was responding.

There was no good way to answer.

Azalea felt sick. *How could I have picked the wrong window?* She waited several moments, trying to come up with an appropriate response.

Azi? Would you please answer me? Were you with someone else last night?

Her hands shaking, Azalea typed: *I'm sorry. That was meant for someone else. I was out with friends last night. I didn't mean to confuse you.* She hesitated, not wanting to get into a full-blown conversation, but needing to make her position clear. *I'm already on the plane and I can't keep this up. Let's please end this gracefully.*

Moments passed and a new message arrived, this time with a photo. Azalea lay sleeping, one arm under her pillow, her hair tousled behind her, the sheet loose under her bare breasts.

He took my picture?!

She hunched over her screen, glancing around to see if anyone were looking. She'd been fortunate to have an empty seat next to her—a luxury when booking the last-minute flight. The other passengers were sleeping or watching their own screens, and Azalea took in a shaky breath.

This is how I will always see you, Azi. Beautiful and vulnerable.

A knot formed in her stomach as tears of anger and helplessness pricked her eyes. Her hands balled into fists, and she gritted her teeth.

You had no right, she typed. *Delete that and anything else you have right now.*

I'm not going to do anything with them, Azi. I just want you to know where my heart is. It's in that bed, with you.

Susana's words rang harsh and cold in Azalea's mind: *It's all about keeping score with him.*

She closed her laptop. The knot in her stomach hardened as hot tears slid down her cheeks. She wouldn't answer Jeremy and she couldn't answer Esteban. *How could I have been so blind?* She'd begun to imagine there could be a future for her, one that was pure and lovely.

But no. Jeremy would never let her go and there was no way she would put Esteban through that. He was too good, too honorable. Now that he had at last decided to open his heart, he deserved someone better—someone who wasn't tethered to abysmally bad choices.

Someone better than I can ever be.

Tears of loss now flowing freely, Azalea hardened herself and decided once again:

Love isn't for me.

She pulled her blanket up to her chin, leaned against the window, and tried to sleep, her heart shattered as she imagined how close she'd come to happiness.

When she landed, she steeled herself to message Esteban. *He deserves so much more, someone like Rosa,* she thought with new anguish.

With shaking hands she typed: *Thank you for a wonderful time, Esteban. I will never forget you. I wish you a beautiful life, filled with love. I know you will find it. I'm just sorry it won't be with me.*

Azalea turned off her phone, got through Customs, collected her suitcases, and went to find Susana.

Azalea was able to plead jet lag and the ride home was mercifully quiet. She and Susana promised to get together later that week and she wearily went inside, blowing goodbye kisses to her best friend. After she unpacked, she was certain there was a message from Esteban and probably something from Jeremy, but she couldn't face either.

I can't run forever, she decided at last, and turned on her phone.

The first message was from Jeremy. *I'm sorry you're already going back but I'll be there in another week. We both know there's more for us, Azi.*

It was all she could do to keep from throwing her phone across the room. But almost immediately, the anger gave way to numbness. *Is this my life now?*

She hesitated before opening Esteban's note, the ennui nearly overcoming her. When she opened it, she simply stared, unable to cry.

Azalea, I confess, I am confused. I am also afraid, and I suspect that is what prompted your note. But I will honor your wish and will not burden you with my feelings. I am deeply grateful for the short time we were together and I wish you nothing but joy in your life. I will forever remember you fondly.

For two weeks, Azalea threw herself into life with almost manic energy. She took Denice up on her offer of a reference and began looking for new clients, touting her experience as a global marketing consultant. She took long walks on her beloved beach, visited her favorite café in the village, and met Tomás's fiancée on a video call. She blocked Jeremy from her phone and tried to put both men out of her mind.

One afternoon, a delivery truck brought yellow roses. She looked at the card as the driver held the bouquet and read, *I'm a patient man and I will wait for you to come back. Love, J*

It was too much. She tore the note in half and told the driver to keep the roses. "Are you sure?" he asked, surprised.

"Very sure," she said. "Give them to someone who will appreciate them." She closed the door and went back to her desk, heart pounding and hands shaking in anger. Azalea ached with loss and helplessness. She looked blankly at her screen and then closed her laptop. Too heartsick to cry, she curled up on her bed and clutched her pillow, sorrow overtaking her as she fell into fitful sleep.

Azalea stepped out of the shower the next morning. She hoped a Florida sunrise would ease the pain in her heart, the recriminations in her thoughts.

But to no avail. Her heart was heavy, and she realized for the thousandth time that she was trapped in a prison of her own making.

She dressed and began toweling her hair when she heard a knock on her front door. She stopped, listening closely, and heard it again—this time insistent.

She walked to the living room and saw Susana's car parked in front of her house. Throwing open the door, she exclaimed, "Suze! What are you doing here? Is everything okay?"

Susana strode into the house. "Nope," she said in a firm voice. "Everything is most definitely not okay." She took in Azalea's wet hair and bare feet. "Finish getting ready, *hermana*. We're getting out of here."

Azalea started to speak, but Susana held up a hand brooking no interruption. "*Apúrate, chica.*"

Azalea knew when to give in to her friend. She closed her mouth and returned to her bathroom, throwing her hair into a ponytail. She put on sandals and grabbed her purse. When she returned to the living room, Susana was pacing.

"Suze, what's wrong?"

"I'm kidnapping you, my friend," replied Susana. "We are getting out of this house, and we are not coming back until I get answers."

Azalea cocked her head, puzzled. "What are you talking about?"

"C'mon. We'll talk in the car."

For ten minutes, the two drove without speaking.

At last, Susana said, "Honey, I don't know what happened to you, but something is wrong. You try to act like everything is fine, but I know you, *'mana.*" She turned a concerned glance at her friend. "I know you."

It was true. She couldn't keep anything from Susana. For decades they'd been like sisters, knowing each other's deepest thoughts as well as their own.

"I broke things off with Esteban," she said in a subdued voice. She looked out her window, seeing nothing. "I can't be what he needs."

"I thought it might be something like that," Susana answered. "I want to hear everything, but for right now, I want you to sit back, close your eyes, and relax." She reached over and squeezed her friend's hand.

Azalea obeyed, but tears threatened.

Half an hour later, Susana pulled into the parking lot of a Mexican restaurant.

"C'mon, *hermana*," she said, patting Azalea's arm. "It's sangria time."

Azalea managed a wan smile. "A bit early, isn't it?"

Susana was out of the car but spoke loudly over her shoulder. "Nope."

The two walked into the restaurant and found a corner booth. Susana ordered a pitcher of sangria and they munched chips and salsa while they awaited their breakfast. After so many years of friendship, they were comfortable just sitting together without conversation, and Azalea waited for her friend to start. Once their food arrived, Susana set down her glass and looked hard at Azalea.

"It's like your light has just gone out and it's breaking my heart. Tell me what happened."

Azalea closed her eyes and offered a quick prayer of thanks for her food and her friend. Opening them, she saw Susana's concern. "I messed everything up. Like completely, irrevocably messed it up." She dabbed at her eyes with her napkin.

"I thought you were over the moon about this guy," prompted Susana. "What terrible thing could you possibly have done between the time we talked and the time you got home?

"It's Jeremy," Azalea answered flatly. "I never should have gone back to him and now it's destroyed any chance I had with Esteban. I know that—I've accepted it. I just have to find a way to move on." She shrugged, disconsolate. "I had my chance and I ruined it."

"*Mana*, you're not making any sense," said Susana. "What does that *pendejo* have to do with you and Esteban?"

"He won't let go, Suze."

Susana frowned. "I don't understand. What do you mean? Who cares what he wants? You've made it clear you're done with him."

"He took pictures of me when I was sleeping. *Nude pictures*. And he sent me one and told me that's where his heart is. And then he sent me flowers the other day and a note saying he's waiting for me to come back." She began to cry and covered her face with her napkin. "I've blocked his calls and I sent back the flowers, but how could I possibly expect Esteban to put up with that? Never knowing what Jeremy was gonna do or how he'd invade my life? You were right about him—it's all about keeping score." She shook her head. "No way. I'm not putting Esteban through that."

Susana looked at her friend, her gaze pointed. "Did you tell Esteban what happened?"

Azalea's face dropped. "Of course not."

"So you've just decided for him that it's too much to handle. Do you think maybe he might have an opinion?"

"I'm sure he would, but he deserves better. I'm not going to ask him to step into a mess like that." Azalea's lips quivered. "I don't deserve him," she whispered.

The waitress approached but Susana waved her off. "You know I love you, right?"

Azalea nodded.

"You're being an idiot." Susana locked eyes with her dearest friend until Azalea turned away. "Why would you turn your back on this? I don't understand you. We used to dream about amazing love—about incredible passion and connection—"

"And you got it!" interrupted Azalea, throwing her napkin on the table. "*You* did, Susana. You got Kique—the love of your life, the best man we know. What did I get? I got a man who cheated on me for most of our marriage. Then I got a man who won't let me go. I got *nothing*, Suze. *Nothing*." Her breath came in shallow gasps as the hurt poured out. "I am a complete failure at love. I'm not worth the trouble and I am not going to ask Esteban to love me.

"I can't do it, Susana." Azalea put her face in her hands and whispered so softly Susana almost missed it. "I can't face him rejecting me."

Susana reached across the table to stroke her friend's hair. "Oh, my sweet sister."

Azalea went to the washroom while Susana paid for their meal.

She looked in the mirror at her splotchy face and shook her head, disgusted by her weakness. *You have a great life,* she told herself. *Quit feeling sorry for yourself and move on.* As she walked back to the table, she saw Susana watching, love and concern all over her face, and Azalea nearly broke down again. She tried to smile when she got to the table, taking her purse and asking, "So? Did you get your answers? Can I go home now?"

Susana stood and put her arm around Azalea's shoulders. "Not yet. We have one more stop." She walked Azalea to the car, hugging her tightly before they got in.

Azalea was wrung out.

She'd worked hard to put Esteban out of her mind and to harden herself to Jeremy's advances. She was rebuilding her business, nearly from scratch, and she missed her sons. The daily toll was exhausting as she coupled it with nonstop recriminations over her choices in Barcelona. *If only,* she thought. *If only.*

And now her dearest friend was calling her out, making her face her choice to abandon the brief glimmer of hope she'd experienced.

Susana pulled into the parking lot at a local park. Picnic tables dotted the grass surrounding a large lake. Ducks waddled on the lawn or paddled in the water as children sprinkled breadcrumbs. The entire scene was peaceful and idyllic, completely at odds with Azalea's mood.

They walked to a large tree where a blanket was spread out. Kique stood and embraced his wife, then held out his arms to Azalea. He hugged her tightly, then kissed her cheek. "Thanks for coming," he said.

Azalea looked at Susana and said, "I didn't exactly have a choice." But she found she was grateful and the three of them sat down.

Kique opened a picnic basket and pulled out a thermos and cups. He served the women cups of strong coffee, adding cream and sugar to their mugs, then held his own up to toast them: "To lifelong friends who always speak truth." He sat back, pensive.

"My darling tactful wife texted me while you guys were at the restaurant," he said simply. "I'm not gonna call you an idiot." His smile was warm. "But I've known you as long as I've known Susana, and I am gonna tell you the truth."

Her stomach clenched. *What would he say?*

"Jeremy is a master manipulator. He doesn't deserve you—you already know that. But he also doesn't deserve your pain. He doesn't deserve your sacrifice. He may have had you for a little while. He may have levers he can pull to hurt you. But he doesn't deserve your future.

"Azalea, you know I love you like a sister. You're an incredible woman. You're smart, kind, and the most amazing friend." He smiled at his wife. "We know who you are and what you're worth.

"Do you?"

35

"Do you?"

Enrique's words echoed in her mind as she sat in her sunroom, watching the evening rainstorm. She'd spent the afternoon talking with him and Susana, recounting everything that happened in Barcelona. Where Susana was fiery and quick to speak her mind, Kique was calm and measured. It was nice to have a man's perspective, she realized. Susana wanted her to jump on a plane and reconnect with Esteban. But her husband had a different take, encouraging Azalea to forgive herself for her decisions, to stop beating herself up, and to do the self-reflection to understand who she truly was and what she wanted.

Between the two of them, Azalea felt loved, accepted, and encouraged. *Susana still thinks I'm an idiot,* she thought with a smile. *I probably am.*

It was easy to devolve into self-recrimination. She was a loving mother—but a failure as a wife. She was a talented businesswoman—but lost her premier client. She was interesting and attractive—but abandoned the man she might have had a future with.

But, but, but.

So who am I? she wondered.

Azalea fluffed a pillow behind her head and lay down on the love seat. The pounding rain was punctuated by lightning that lit up the sky. The thunder was rolling, almost a growl across the sky. She loved the storms, especially in the evenings. The air grew cooler, fresher, as the storm grew more intense. It felt like the thoughts inside her—relentless and powerful.

But for the first time since she got home, Azalea felt equal to them.

For every mistake she grieved over, she had successes to celebrate, she decided. She'd done well with her boys—they were self-sufficient and strong young men, now living their own lives. She had done her best work in Barcelona, work to be proud of. She could build on that success with new clients and make a good living. And even in the mess that was her love life, she'd started breaking through her fears and opening up to possibilities.

Who am I? she wondered again as a particularly bright streak of lightning crossed the sky. The light seemed to strike her heart at the same time.

I'm flawed, but I'm not broken.

Azalea sat up, startled as realization dawned: *I may be alone, but I'm not lonely.*

I am enough.

Azalea awoke with a stiff neck and a resolute spirit. She'd fallen asleep on the love seat but felt rested despite the cramped space. She stood and stretched, looking out at the sunrise, the sky dotted with cotton candy clouds. She was astonished at how good she felt. It was as if last night's storm outside mirrored her inner storm—and she was likewise awakening to fresh beauty, a daybreak of possibilities.

She padded into the kitchen to make coffee and consider her day. She thought briefly about attending church, but decided she wasn't ready to be around people—her newfound sense of well being was for her alone. She sipped her coffee and fought the urge to make a to-do list. It was enough to simply be.

After a while, she rose and sent a quick text to Susana and Kique.

You are the best friends in the world. Thank you for loving me and giving me the space to love myself.

Kique's answer came immediately. *You know your amiga is still asleep, right? =) We love you and know the best is yet to come. Don't go back to that dark place. Don't forget who you really are.*

She smiled. It was dawn on a Sunday and it would be hours before Susana answered. *I won't,* she wrote. *Thank you for reminding me. Kiss her for me!*

She spent the day puttering around the house, enjoying her newfound peace. She'd have to make some difficult decisions in the coming days, but refused to let them affect her Sunday glow. *Tomorrow,* she thought. *I'll tackle things tomorrow.*

Tomorrow came.

She awoke with a renewed sense of purpose. *I am enough,* she whispered as she opened her eyes. The day felt ripe with opportunity, and she felt strong and happy. She showered and got ready, dressing with care and putting on makeup as if she were going on a client meeting. After her coffee, she picked up her phone and called.

Jeremy answered after the first ring. "Azi! What a great way to start my morning. How are you?"

"I'm well, Jeremy," she said, her voice steady. "I'd like to see you. Do you have any time today? I can drive out to Orlando."

She heard the smile in his voice. "Let me rearrange a couple of meetings. How about lunch and then we see where we go from there?"

"Yes, that's perfect," she answered. They agreed to meet at noon, and she was just about to hang up when Jeremy spoke.

"I'm so glad you called, Azi. I can't wait to see you."

"Have a good morning, Jeremy."

She spent the next hour answering email and sending a proposal to a new client. Before she left, she looked at herself in the mirror. "Hello, Azalea," she murmured. "I remember you." She smiled, thinking about her refrain with her boys: "Go be your brilliant self."

Jeremy was already at the restaurant when she arrived. He waited outside the door and kissed her cheek before leading her inside.

Azalea was pleased to note how calm she felt and didn't flinch at his touch. They sat and Jeremy reached for her hand.

"Before we start, I want to tell you something. It turns out the kid in Barcelona really was just being used by the terrorists. They arrested the guy who put the gun and the list in his apartment. He's not getting out for a very long time."

Azalea nodded. "Thank you for letting me know."

"So what made you finally call?"

"How about we order first and then we can talk without interruption?" Azalea asked.

As if on cue, the waitress arrived and took their orders. As she walked away, Jeremy reclaimed her hand. "So?" he prompted.

Azalea looked long at him. He was tanned, handsome, and so sure of himself. She could imagine a life with him, a life that was pleasant and as exciting as his wealth could provide. There was no lack of physical passion between them. He was gentlemanly and attentive. She could make a life with him, she knew.

But it would be a life that drained the very essence of who she was. It was a life that served his needs, with little thought for her own. And there was an edge of cruelty to Jeremy that she saw in Barcelona. She didn't want to experience that ever again.

"I fell in love with you for all the wrong reasons," she began. "I've realized that I was more hurt than I knew from David's betrayal. After my divorce, I threw myself into my work and my kids, but I ignored my own needs."

The waitress returned with their meals and Azalea closed her eyes for a brief moment of thanks. When she opened her eyes, Jeremy was looking at her, his face somber. "I knew you were hurt, Azi. You didn't deserve what he did to you."

Azalea nodded. "No, I didn't. No one deserves that." She had a brief memory of her argument with Esteban. *Stay focused, Azalea.* She sipped her iced tea and continued. "When I met you, I didn't realize how lonely I was. You made me feel special and cared for and it filled something in me that was missing." Jeremy smiled and lifted her hand to his lips.

She pulled her hand away. "The problem is, I needed to feel those things for myself before I ever thought about a relationship."

"And you feel them now?" he asked.

"I do."

"So you're ready for a relationship." His smiled widened. "It's about time."

"No," she replied.

"What do you mean, no?"

"I mean I'm not ready for a relationship. I have a lot of work to do to strengthen myself—a lot of room to grow."

"We can grow together, Azi. You know we can. Think about those days in Barcelona." He reached again for her hand and his face hardened. "Think about those nights. You weren't so eager to leave me then."

"I think about them all the time, Jeremy." Her eyes were sad but determined. "I think about the two years I gave in to everything you wanted because I felt guilty that we weren't having sex. And in Barcelona I gave in to everything you wanted because we *were* having sex." She shook her head. "I've said this before and I need you to listen to me now: We are not good for each other."

"Azi—"

"No, Jeremy. *No*. We are too different and we want different things. You can't be what I need and I can't be what you need. And this endless dance is exhausting."

He pushed his plate away. "You're serious, aren't you?" he asked, an edge to his voice.

"I am." She frowned. "And I won't pretend that I'm not still furious over those photos."

He had the decency to look chagrined. "You were just so peaceful and so incredibly beautiful. I wanted to capture that moment forever."

Azalea gazed at him, steel in her eyes. "I'm pretty sure you could have found another way that didn't take advantage of me and violate my privacy."

"We were together," he protested.

Azalea held up her hand, forestalling more objections. "Delete them, Jeremy. Let's say goodbye with nothing ugly between us. I want to remember the good times and the love we shared without anything that detracts from what we had."

Jeremy sat back, wordless. *This may be the first time I've ever seen him so exposed*, she thought. A feeling of compassion washed over her. He was the manipulator Kique described, but Jeremy was also a broken soul.

Not my problem, she reminded herself.

Jeremy reached for her hand again, gently stroking it with his thumb. His eyes strayed to hers and she saw that she had finally gotten through to him. "You're serious, aren't you?" he repeated, this time seeming to relinquish his anger.

Her tone was firm. "I am."

He nodded, then released her and beckoned the waitress. After he paid the bill, he and Azalea walked to her car.

"I suppose I should thank you for doing this is person instead of dumping me on email," he said. Azalea said nothing, standing tall and sure before him. Abruptly, he clutched her hard to his chest, resting his cheek on the top of her head. At last he released her. "Goodbye, Azi."

She nodded, and Jeremy turned and walked away.

It's done and I am whole.

The days rolled by and Azalea's confidence grew. She lined up two new clients, hung out with Susana, Lauren, and Sara, and walked on her beach. She marveled at the contentment she felt and relished her newfound strength.

She received only one message from Jeremy: *It's done, I promise. Always, J*

She decided to believe him.

A month later, Azalea received a new text, this time from Esteban Junior.

Hola, Azalea! I hope it's OK for me to contact you. I don't know what happened with you and my father and it's not my business. But he has gone back to working nonstop and seems so unhappy. It's his birthday next week and I want to do something nice for him. Would you be willing to have a video call? Just to say hello? I think he would love it.

Azalea stared at the message, her heart skipping a beat. She watched the ellipsis that told her Esteban was writing more.

Please?

Azalea was torn. She longed to see Esteban—she missed him, even after their brief encounter. She'd finally achieved closure with Jeremy, and she was well on her way to peace.

Should I say yes? Self-doubt assailed her. She'd been so abrupt when she closed the door with him—surely he wouldn't want to talk to her. Junior was meddling because he loved his father and didn't know what had transpired.

But, but, but.

She'd abandoned her connection with Esteban because of Jeremy. With that problem resolved, was there any reason to say no? She admitted to herself: She longed to speak to him, even though it would be awkward and he might reject her.

Susana's words rang in her mind: *So you've just decided for him that it's too much to handle. Do you think maybe he might have an opinion?*

Azalea texted back: *Give me a bit to think about it, OK? I'll let you know by tomorrow. When is his birthday?*

Esteban's response was immediate. *Thank you, Bella! It's next Wednesday.*

After a run on the beach, a call with Susana, and a quick prayer, Azalea had her answer. She would call and wish him a happy birthday and gauge his reaction. If he were open, she'd happily continue the conversation. If not, it was one more thing in her life she could count as resolved. No more lingering questions about what could have been. It would be painful but not leave a gaping hole in her heart. Her epiphany during the storm had left her stronger than that. She messaged Junior.

OK, Esteban. I'll call. Thank you for asking me.

Now she just had to get through the next five days.

The time moved slowly, and Azalea's eagerness grew daily. Instead of the anxiety she expected, she felt excited and hopeful. When the day finally arrived, Azalea spent extra time on her hair and makeup, and selected a blouse she knew set off her coloring well. She arranged her desk lamp and laptop for the best video possible, and reread Esteban's last note a final time: *I will forever remember you fondly.*

Would that be enough?

Azalea pressed the button for the video call and Junior's face appeared in seconds. "*Hola*, Azalea!" he whispered. "*Momentito, por favor.*" He looked away from the screen and called out, "*Papá! Una llamada especial para ti.*"

She heard his father's deep voice coming closer. "*Quien es, mijo?*"

"*Mira, Papá. Es Azalea.*" Junior winked at her as he passed the phone to his father.

And there he was, just as she remembered him. His dark brown eyes widened as he saw her, his smile illuminating the screen.

And her heart.

"Azalea! What a surprise!"

"*Feliz cumpleaños*, Esteban."

"Ah, *muchas gracias*, Azalea. How are you?"

Azalea thought for a moment. How could she answer? It would take a very long conversation to adequately express how she truly was. "I'm well, Esteban," she managed. "Very well. And you?"

He waited as she had. "I'm fine," he responded at last. His eyes seemed to pierce her through the phone screen. "I'm very glad to see you."

It's all right, she thought. *It's all right.*

36

One year later....

The bride's off white gown, delicately embroidered with lavender and blue flowers, trailed softly behind her. Sprays of flowers festooned the chairs lined up on the beach, their colors matching her gown perfectly. She stood radiant, her long hair cascading down her back, her brow encircled with a wreath of fresh flowers. The ocean breeze lightly blew at her dress and hair, just enough to be picture perfect. Emily looked like a goddess as she gazed up at Tomás with bright eyes, hardly noticing as her bridesmaids arranged her train behind her, just so. She reached back absently to pass her bouquet to her maid of honor, never turning away from her groom who was likewise entranced.

Azalea wiped a tear and noticed David smiling at her. She smiled back, a tacit acknowledgement that even if their marriage had ended badly, they had done something beautiful together creating their boys.

Their young men, standing together.

Susana tapped her shoulder and Azalea glanced back at her best friend. "So beautiful, *'mana*," whispered Susana. Kique smiled his agreement. Wordlessly, Azalea nodded, tears threatening again to spill.

Esteban's arm rested lightly across her shoulders. He noticed her tears, reached into his pocket for a handkerchief, and offered it to her with a gentle smile. She took it gratefully and dabbed at her eyes. His own eyes, his beautiful brown eyes, gazed at her with deep emotion. "*Te amo, Bella,*" he whispered.

"*Te amo,*" she responded, squeezing his hand. They looked up again as the pastor began the ceremony.

The newlyweds left the reception hall for their honeymoon amidst cheers, hugs, and more tears. The guests left one by one until only Azalea and Esteban were left.

"I don't know whether to collapse or cry," she said with a wan smile. "I'm so happy and so emotional and…." She trailed off, unsure what she even meant.

Esteban gathered her in his arms, and she leaned her head on his shoulder. Slowly, he began to glide across the dance floor, humming into her hair. He took one of her hands and put his arm around her waist, spinning her slowly. She looked up at him with a smile.

For a long while, he continued to move around the floor, lithely turning, dipping, and swaying. Azalea had no problem matching his steps—they moved as one, even without music. At last, he released her waist and pirouetted her before pulling her close for a deep, passionate kiss.

They only broke at the sound of applause. Looking around, they saw the wedding planner smiling broadly. "Forget the bride and groom," she said. "You two are the most romantic couple here today." Azalea blushed and pulled away from him as Esteban took a courtly bow.

"*Muchas gracias,*" he said, his deep voice and Catalan accent making the simple comment exotic and almost theatrical. "It's hard not to be romantic with such a woman."

Azalea looked sideways at him, feeling awkward at the public praise but also reveling in it. *Will I ever get used to this?* she wondered.

They walked to her car and stood quietly. "I don't even know what to do. It's a very strange day." She shook her head, bewildered.

"Am I making too big a deal of this? I mean, people get married every day."

"Tomás and Emily aren't just 'people,' *querida*," he said gently. "He's your firstborn son." He looked around, then turned back to her. "It's still so early. Why don't we just go for a drive on the coast? Maybe stop somewhere for dinner?"

"I'd like that," she answered. "I'm not ready to go home." She looked at her watch and was surprised it was only four o'clock in the afternoon. She looked at Esteban in his suit and tie and back at her high heels.

"I have an idea," she said. "We might be a bit overdressed, but that's all right. There's a little town about an hour north of here called St. Augustine. It's the very first city established in the United States—and it was founded by Spain. There's an old fort there and some charming little restaurants. I think you'd love it."

"It sounds wonderful, *mi amor.*"

The couple drove up the coast, comfortable with silence. Occasionally he would reach across to stroke her cheek or slide his fingers through her hair. She would turn and find him gazing at her, love etched on his features. "What are you thinking about?" she asked.

"I'm thinking you are a beautiful, wonderful woman. I'm thinking that watching you with your children has been a revelation. I knew they were important to you, but it wasn't until now that I see the depth of your love—and how they adore you." He reached for her hand and kissed it lightly. "It makes me love you even more."

Tears gathered in her eyes. She glanced at him and then back at the road. "Thank you," she whispered.

At last, they arrived in St. Augustine. Esteban took her hand, and they walked toward the main avenue.

"I just love it here," she said, looking around. "It's like being back in Europe with the cobblestones and the old architecture." She pointed out the grassy area near a centuries' old chapel. "You should see this at Christmas with all the lights and the hot cocoa booths," she said. "A little different in the summer." The lawn was now covered with families picnicking and children running about in shorts and bare feet.

The late afternoon was warm, and Esteban removed his tie as they walked. "I guess we are a bit overdressed," he said, rolling up his tie and starting to put it in his pocket.

She held out her hand. "Let me put it in my purse," she offered. "It won't wrinkle as badly." He handed it to her and pulled her in for a quick kiss, his fingers lingering on her cheek.

"What was that for?" she laughed, glancing around as people walked by. *He's not Jeremy*, she reminded herself. *This isn't about control.*

"Just my way to say 'thank you,' I suppose," he replied. "Did I make you uncomfortable?"

She shook her head. "No—it's okay. I'm still not used to what the boys used to call 'PDAs.'" She smiled as she explained. "Public Displays of Affection."

"They don't seem to mind them now. They hug you a lot." He smiled. "And you hug them back."

"Hmm…that's true."

Esteban was thoughtful as they walked along the main thoroughfare. Families passed them on either side, children eating ice cream, couples holding hands. He looked at her. "I don't ever want you to feel uncomfortable with me being too affectionate," he said.

"No," she began, "It's just me—" She stopped abruptly, her face pensive. Memories flooded her, the speed and breadth of them almost overwhelming. In Barcelona, she'd been lonely, then fallen to Jeremy's advances while still resisting his overt affection. She'd been more than uncomfortable—she'd felt almost powerless. She hated the very thought.

But now? The truth sliced her, baring her heart.

It's not me. It's never been me. I love being affectionate with my boys, with my friends.

With Esteban.

The realization struck her like a Florida lightning storm and Azalea longed for nothing more than to stroll hand in hand, arm in arm with the man she loved. She wanted to kiss him in the middle of the street. The lightness she felt was liberating and glorious.

Esteban took a few steps away from her. "Perhaps we should walk farther apart. Would this help?" He stepped away and people walked between them. "Is this more comfortable?" he called in mock seriousness. "I could stay on the other side of the street if that's better." He began to move to the edge of the boulevard.

She laughed with abandon and shook her head at his teasing. *No.*

This *is what I want.* This *is who I am.*

Warmth radiated through her body as she walked toward him, threading her way between families on the busy walkway. She was filled with carefree joy.

With love.

"What am I going to do with you?" she laughed, taking his arm. He pulled away from her and dropped to a knee.

Azalea looked at him, perplexed. "Esteban—" she began.

"I know what I *want* you to do with me, *querida*," he said, his mirthful tone gone. People around them stopped walking and stared at the couple. It seemed the entire boulevard hushed as he took her hand. He spoke first in Spanish, his eyes gleaming and intent. "*Querida. Cásate conmigo.*"

At her quick intake of breath, he repeated himself in English. "I want you to marry me."

Yes. Oh, yes.

This is what I want, she thought, looking into his eyes and nodding with joy. Azalea barely heard the clapping as she reached for him, this man who understood, respected, and loved her.

No eres perfecto, pero eres perfecto para mi.
You aren't perfect, but you're perfect for me.
Love *is* for me.

ACKNOWLEDGEMENTS

This book would never have seen the light of day without a nudge from my good friend, Dr. Diane Osgood. When I got the first draft back from my editor, the brilliant Michelle Meade, I was ready to throw it in the trash bin and quit writing fiction forever. After she listened to me whine, Diane told me I had to keep writing because, "Cindy, people like you. But they *love* Azalea." And so I bossed up, read the editorial comments again, and realized that Michelle was absolutely right. About everything.

To Beverly, Jackie, Joann, Karena, Kathy, Lisa, and Margaret, my writing group friends who've become treasured sisters, thank you for our weekly Zoom calls and our glorious days at the lake. You are all fabulous writers and never fail to inspire me. I'm deeply grateful you encouraged me to write the next three books in the *Blooming* series. It turns out Sara, Susana, and Lauren want their own stories, and they're fortunate to have you as their advocates!

To my favorite beta reader Alison, thanks for never failing to ask, "Can't you add more sex scenes?" You kept me laughing and pushing myself as a storyteller.

To Louise, my deep appreciation for your effervescent *joie de vivre* and for your talent in uncovering the seed for the series title.

To Samantha Sanderson-Marshall, the designer of the gorgeous cover art, my deepest gratitude. You not only read the entire book, but you also genuinely understood and appreciated the characters. When you first described the design to me and explained how you were already thinking about the series and the boxed set long before *Bread Pudding* launched, I just about cried.

To Ted, my beloved singing, golfing, West Virginia banker who waited six long weeks just to hold my hand on the beach: Thank you for helping me breathe.

A very special thank you to kid number three who, during one of my darker times, wrote me: "You're an amazing woman. You're an amazing mom. You're an amazing author. You do everything you set your mind to. You're awesome." Alex, you have no idea how your words lifted my spirits and inspired me to push through.

And to all the professional women of a certain age who have longed to see someone like themselves in a love story, thank you for reading. I hope you'll continue to follow the series as Azalea, Sara, Susana, and Lauren learn that the most profound lessons bloom in the hearts of women who open themselves to friendship and to love.

Enjoy this preview of

Something Will Sing to Your Heart

Book Two
BLOOMING
The Series

Coming soon!

Sara walked into the tidy house she rented with her best friend Lauren. Just walking to the mailbox felt like melting in a sauna and she fanned her face to cool off. Even for a native Floridian, July in Daytona Beach could be horrid, she thought, feeling the sweat sliding down her back.

She lowered the air conditioning to 75 degrees and then flopped down on the sofa, looking through the mail, setting aside anything addressed to Lauren. She skimmed the bills and junk mail quickly, then stopped when she got to an envelope from Daytona Springs Middle School. She smiled and tore it open. It was a welcome letter from her new principal, thanking her for taking on the role in the mathematics department. After 15 years teaching kindergarten, Sara looked forward to the new challenge.

She set the letter aside and saw another. The return address was from a Natalie Allard, the handwriting crisp and all in capital letters: SARA MASTERSON. She opened it and began to read:

Dear Sara,

I have wanted to write to you for some time but was worried that I would interrupt your life. I guess I'm still worried, but I just couldn't wait any more.

After some research, I believe that you are my biological mother. I was born 23 years ago and placed for adoption with a wonderful family. Let me start by thanking you for giving me parents who have loved me and supported me my entire life! They weren't able to have their own children, so they've poured their lives into me and I'm very grateful.

The reason I finally decided to seek you out is a hard one. My mom Jocelyn is in remission from breast cancer. She's only 58 years old. Her mother died from breast cancer when she was 70, so it looks like it's hereditary. The obvious good news is that means I don't have their genes but it started me thinking about what genes I actually do have. Believe it or not, my parents encouraged me to find you.

I really hope this letter doesn't upset you and that you might be open to meeting me in person. If not, maybe just a phone call? Like I mentioned, I don't want to disrupt your life and I don't want you to feel guilty for the decision you made so long ago. I have a wonderful life and I'd just like to know more about you and where I came from.

Would you be open to it?

I look forward to hearing from you,

Natalie

Sara stared at the letter, her hands shaking. Emotions tore through her, faster than she could process. Shock and disbelief warred with guilt and sadness. Was it possible? Could this Natalie Allard be the infant her parents took from her so long ago?

Her daughter.

Carlos' daughter.

Tears pricked her eyes and her stomach clenched as she reread the letter again and again, until the tears dripped onto the stationery, smudging the ink and the neat handwriting.

He had neat handwriting. She remembered the notes he passed her in class, the drawings in the margins. Carlos had been an artist. *I wonder what he does now.* She thrust the question from her mind. Over two decades ago she locked all thoughts of Carlos and their baby into a mental strongbox and tucked it far, far away. So far it couldn't hurt her.

Am I ready to open the box?

Lauren flung open the front door with a groan. "Ah! Air conditioning!" She tossed her purse on the coffee table and sat heavily on the sofa. "It is so hot out there."

"Didn't you have your AC on in the car?" asked Sara.

"Damn thing went out on the way to work," snapped her friend. "I have the car for, what? A month before it goes out?"

Sara stared out the front window, the offending car the last thing on her mind.

"...so yeah, the warranty is good but it still means taking time off work to get it fixed—" her friend stopped abruptly. "Are you even listening to me? You're off in space."

Sara's eyes refocused, looking down at the letter. "So, we're best friends, right?"

Lauren sat up straighter, a look of confusion on her face. "Yeah... for like, almost twenty years." She frowned, then leaned forward. "Sara, what's wrong?" She glanced at the tattered letter in Sara's lap. "What's that?"

Sara looked long at Lauren, measuring her words. *I haven't told anyone about having a baby,* she thought. *Even my dearest friend.* "There's something I never told you." She paused. "I've never told anyone, actually.

"When I was in high school, I had a boyfriend."

Lauren gaped at her. "That's your big secret?" she asked.

"No, no...I—I got pregnant my junior year."

Lauren sat up straighter on the sofa and gazed at Sara. "Oh, damn. What did your parents say?"

"You know my parents so you can imagine. They were beyond furious. They pulled me out of school and made me do independent study during the pregnancy so no one would see me. Apart from taking me to the doctor every month, they just ignored my belly."

Sara watched as Lauren processed the revelation. Her friend's anger was barely held in check as she asked sarcastically, "I'm guessing Cecilia didn't throw a baby shower."

"It's not exactly the sort of thing you rent out the country club for," answered Sara. "As soon as she was born, they made me place her for adoption. We moved to Tampa and I never saw my boyfriend or the baby again." She looked up at Lauren and drew comfort from the compassion she saw on her friend's face.

"Damn," repeated Lauren. "You've been keeping that inside for all these years?"

"At first I was kinda numb," admitted Sara. "And then it got easier to just pretend it never happened." She frowned. "That's how things are managed in the Masterson family."

"So why are you telling me today?" prompted Lauren.

Sara lifted the note. "I got a letter from her. From my daughter."

Lauren's look was incredulous. "You're kidding."

Sara held out the tear-smudged letter. "Came today."

Lauren took it and began reading. When she finished, she looked up. "I don't even know where to start," she began, then shook her head fiercely. "No, that's not true—I know exactly where to start. But cussing out your parents probably isn't productive." She set the letter on the coffee table and held out her arms to Sara. "Are you okay? What can I do for you?"

The two women embraced for several moments before Sara pulled away. "I don't know how I feel," she confessed. "I've buried this for so long, I'm just kind of in shock. I feel like I *should* be happy, but I'm not. I'm not unhappy either, though. I'm glad she's had a good life and I'm curious to know about her." She sat back against the cushions and wiped her eyes with the back of her hand. "It brings up a whole lot of stuff besides having a baby. My parents have never been good, but this was them at their worst. Especially my mom."

Lauren pursed her lips in disgust. Sara hadn't told her friend about the baby, but she'd shared plenty about her mother. Cecilia Masterson was definitely not in the running for mother of the year.

"So what are you gonna do?"

"I don't know. I just don't know what's right."

Lauren shook her head. "I don't think there is a right or wrong here, Sara. I think you have to decide what's best for you. Do you want to meet this girl? Do you want to reopen that part of your life? Or do you want to push all this back into the past and just move on? You know I'm there for you no matter what you decide. You're my ride or die girl, remember?"

Sara grinned through her tears. "I know, and I love you for it." She closed her eyes to collect her thoughts, then almost whispered, "I need more time before I decide." She took a deep breath and this time her voice was strong. "I'm not 16 anymore and I don't have to be that scared little girl. I can make a decision without worrying about what my mom will do."

Need to know what happens next?

Sign up at www.cindyvillanueva.com or follow on
Instagram to receive preorder info for

Something Will Sing to Your Heart

Coming in Autumn 2024

Made in the USA
Columbia, SC
14 October 2024

44287799R10152